REVENGE OF THE WO

The wolf looked up at Anderso... with rage and hatred, and growle... owl. Anderson's instincts finall... and raced into the darkne...

For a long time h... rsuit behind him, making him wo... re too shocked at their leader's death t... rightened, or both. He glanced over his sh... and still saw no dark shapes following, then loo... forward just in time to see the tall figure that appeared just ahead to stop his flight.

Anderson slammed into the wolf-beast at full speed. The werewolf did not budge from its spot as Anderson was sent flying backward. In a panic, Anderson stood and fired in a circle until the clip of his gun was spent. He dropped the used clip and fumbled for the other. He strained in vain to see, to hear.

"If any of you can understand me—" Anderson was cut short as his gun was snatched away by an unseen hand.

The wolf that had destroyed his gun stepped forward. Anderson swallowed in a vain attempt to wet his dry throat. He heard a sound coming from the beast's throat that seemed like a growl at first, and then became more familiar.

"Tonight . . ." it said in a quick grunt, *"we feed."*

Books by Traci Briery

THE VAMPIRE MEMOIRS
THE VAMPIRE JOURNALS
THE WEREWOLF CHRONICLES
WOLFSONG

Published by Zebra Books

WOLFSONG

TRACI BRIERY

ZEBRA BOOKS
KENSINGTON PUBLISHING CORP.

ZEBRA BOOKS are published by

Kensington Publishing Corp.
850 Third Avenue
New York, NY 10022

Zebra and the Z logo Reg. U.S. Pat. & TM Off.

First Printing: April, 1996

Printed in the United States of America
10 9 8 7 6 5 4 3 2 1

For Julie, "Tamara," the real Lt. Becker, Joe Dante, John Landis, and as always, my mother, for the usual reasons.

Many Arigatos to Lt. Poe of the Huntington Beach Police Department, who provided me with information that I probably got wrong, anyway.

One

"How'm I doin'?" Loraine called over her shoulder while crawling on her knees. Silence followed save for the crunching of leaves and twigs as she moved about, searching for some lost item.

Behind her, Tamara Taylor crossed her arms and paced for a few seconds.

"How'm I doing?" Loraine asked more loudly.

"You're the only one who can tell me that," Tamara said softly. Loraine heard it so clearly that she did not realize that Tamara was being deliberately quiet. Loraine let out a quick, frustrated laugh before standing up and brushing the dirt and leaves from her pants.

"Couldn't you just tell me if I'm hotter or colder?" she joked. There was definite strain to her jocularity, however. "I've been looking for ten minutes! Why am I doing this, anyway?"

Tamara kept her arms folded while walking toward her reluctant pupil.

"You're still fighting it, then," she said quietly. "If you weren't, you would have found it in half a minute at most, and you'd know why."

"Besides having money in my pocket, why is finding a dime in the woods supposed to help me?" Loraine asked. "The guy we're after is a little easier to find than that."

"I'm helping you learn to protect yourself so that I don't have to help you find him," Tamara said sharply.

"This is supposed to help me protect myself?"

"Just find the dime."

"Fuck the dime! We need to—" Loraine was all but blown backward by the force and shock of Tamara's deafening roar. Loraine was embarrassed to find herself quivering, though Tamara's eyes were no longer yellow nor her teeth sharp as daggers.

"What . . . what . . ." Loraine stammered.

"I shouldn't have to explain any of this," Tamara said calmly. "If you were as willing to accept the wolf as you said you were, you'd know that doing something as 'stupid' as this could be a lifesaver. Think, girl! Why can't you find a dime in the woods? Yes, in time you could find it by crawling around on your knees. Anybody could. With luck, you probably could've found it in less than a minute, too. But you can't afford to use luck alone. You have *five* senses, not—"

"Yeah, I know—"

"Listen!" Tamara barked. "Yeah, you 'know' that, but keep using sight alone, anyway! Why? Because any human would. Because any human doesn't have good enough senses to use anything *but*. But you're *not* human—not completely anymore, and unless you accept that, you'll be stuck groping around when the lights go out. If you want to do it on your knees, fine, but use your other senses!"

"But how could I—how am I supposed to hear a dime?" Loraine asked. "No, really, I'm not dissing you. I just . . . I don't . . ."

"Close your eyes," Tamara said softly. Tamara was a singer; she could hit the sweetest notes or the raunchiest belches within the same measure. She could switch her speaking voice from a drill sergeant's holler to the gentle tones of a mother telling a bedtime story. Loraine owed her more than she could ever repay. She had given Loraine her first real break as her personal choreographer. She had given her confidence when the entire world seemed against her. Now she was teaching her how to survive.

"Close your eyes," Tamara said again. Loraine did so and took a deep breath. "Now tell me what you smell."

Loraine's nose crinkled as she sniffed. She cocked her head in confusion but kept her eyes shut. "I'm not sure what I'm supposed to be smelling," she said.

"Everything," Tamara said, shutting her own eyes and breathing deeply. "Stop using your human senses. They're too weak for this. You'll need the wolf to help you survive this."

"The trees . . ." Loraine said after some time. "I can smell the trees."

"Good," Tamara said. "What else?"

"I'm not sure what else."

"Oh, please don't tell me you can't smell the smog," Tamara said.

"Well—yeah, I guess, but—that's a given, right?"

"Don't use your human senses! Try to smell *me*. Can you smell my breath? My body?"

Loraine giggled. "What, am I supposed to start sniffing your butt now?"

"When am I exhaling?" Tamara asked, ignoring the joke. Loraine stifled her smile and concentrated.

"Now . . ." she said. "Now . . . now . . . now . . . Am I getting them?"

"Keep going," was the reply.

"Now . . . now . . . Wait a minute," Loraine said, opening her eyes. "Now I'm getting them."

"How?"

"I could smell it, and I could hear you breathing at the same time. And a . . . a really faint thumping somewhere. That couldn't have been your heartbeat, could it?"

"You tell me," Tamara said with a slight smile. "Can you hear it now? Listen for it especially."

Silence followed save that of the wind, which suddenly shot up in volume to Loraine. She gasped. The wind hadn't picked up in speed, but its sound had snapped into focus. Loraine turned away from Tamara and let her mouth hang open while she took in a whole new world of sound. All around her the wind whistled its song, accompanied by the soft, steady beat of Tamara's heart. Even her breathing kept up its own rhythmic accompaniment. Distant birds twittered away in counter harmony. They were far from the city, but a slight bend of the head let Loraine hear the steady bass of moving cars, industry and people. She spun around to face Tamara, her face flush with awe.

"Can you hear all that?" she said. "The wind and-and birds and our heartbeats? Can you hear all that?"

"When I think about it," Tamara said with a smile. "You could hear a fly rubbing its legs together in an empty room if you really thought about it."

"I want to try this again. Let me try it again."

"Try what?"

"The dime!" Loraine called, already turned away and

hunched over, all of her senses aiding in the search now. Tamara had made her turn around when she'd thrown the coin, so Loraine could not "cheat" and look where it had landed. It could have been anywhere within a thirty-foot radius. She moved away about twenty feet from Tamara and dropped to her hands and knees. She sniffed the ground and pricked her ears as if hoping to hear the wind whistling over a tiny piece of metal.

Until now the dirt had always smelled like just that: dirt. Until now she could never have distinguished between the dozens of different odors that make up "dirt." She could never have smelled the countless sticks, rocks, decaying plants and even insect droppings that flooded her nostrils. She crawled about in a zigzag pattern, oblivious to the soil caking onto her clothing and palms. It was Loraine, but not quite Loraine, who finally picked up a very faint but distinct scent of metal. To the left, it was weaker, as was straight ahead. Five feet to her right the scent was stronger, but never more than faint. The distant stench of car exhaust and industrial fumes was always much stronger. No wonder the wolf shunned the cities.

Tamara watched Loraine sniff at something before picking up a leaf and crying out in triumph. Loraine grabbed the shiny prize and leaped to her feet, cartwheeling all the way to her friend. With a dramatic gesture she took Tamara's hand and put the dime there, then bowed.

"Good," Tamara said, nodding.

Loraine was all smiles. " 'Good'?" she said, spreading her arms. "And . . . ?"

"Good," Tamara said. "You found it. That's good. Now—"

"But that's great! 'Good.' That's it? Look at how long it took me!"

"Yeah, I know. It took too long," Tamara said. Loraine tried to speak, but Tamara held up her hand. "Ah-ah—I have to be hypercritical. You know why. You gotta get outta town like right now, and I can't help you do it."

"Not even a bit?"

"Look, I'll loan you some money, but you need to find your own way outta here. I'm a celebrity, remember? Reporters follow me around no matter what I do, so you'd just get caught."

"And you'd get nailed for aiding and abetting," Loraine said. "I'm sorry. I wasn't thinking. I'm just scared, that's all."

"I don't blame you."

"But I can't leave," Loraine said. "You said that yourself just this morning. I need to stay here and find the mongrel who killed Roxanne."

"I know that's what I said," Tamara said. "But I've thought about it since then. It wouldn't be safe for you here."

"But that'll give the other guy a chance to get out of town, too," Loraine said. "No one but us even knows about him; the cops won't be looking for him at all. For all we know, he's been gone for days already."

"Do you think he is?"

"How would I know?"

"You were close enough to get his scent," Tamara said. "You can track him that way, for one."

"Yeah, right. Like I remember what he smells like."

"You *do* remember what he smells like," Tamara said. "At least, the—"

"—Wolf does, yeah, yeah."

"I'm serious, girl!" Tamara said. "Look: I can't make you do anything. If you want to stay, stay. But remember that there's a dragnet going on right now—for *you*. You were busted out of jail, so every cop in L.A. will be after you for at least a week. Then the numbers will go down. It doesn't matter to them that you didn't want to be busted out. Maybe some cop will make it his destiny to find you, but at least it'll be you against a few guys rather than the entire county."

"Or it could be the entire country if I get on *America's Most Wanted*," Loraine added as a joke, but neither of them laughed.

Two police officers and the occasional volunteer had been given "Press Duty," meaning to keep the press as far away from the crime scene as possible. The reason for the near mob of reporters and paparazzi was that the crime scene was in the police station itself. So far the Press Duty had been successful in allowing them no farther than the front desk.

Lt. Dan Hubbard pushed his way through the mob outside the station and gestured to a uniformed officer inside, who doubled his efforts to keep the reporters at bay. For now it was easy to ignore the flood of questions, as the lieutenant didn't yet know enough to whet anyone's journalistic appetite.

His detectives called him "Tin Man," because "the tinsmith forgot to give him a heart," as one detective had put it. Behind his back, of course. Few people knew anything about his private life. At work, he was nothing but business; sometimes he was all business while off work. Most knew that he was a confirmed bachelor, but no one tried to help him meet anyone. No one was brave enough to try. And most of all, no one was brave enough to make short jokes around him. He just made it to most men's shoulders and had apparently spent a lifetime overcompensating for his lack of stature by making as many people as possible feel smaller.

Hubbard had visited more major crime scenes than he would ever remember, but until now, none had been at the station itself. In many ways he seemed to enjoy the hubbub associated with the crime scene investigation. But instead of searching the closets of a hotel, the desk of a homeowner, or the swimming pool of a wealthy socialite, it was his own station that smelled of black fingerprint powder and chalk. In fact, he nearly scuffed up several chalk drawings on his way to see Det. Peter Thomas.

Hubbard knew that Thomas had arrived earlier to investigate. Thomas was by the door leading to the corridor of cells that was the sight of the real crime scene. He was scrutinizing some marks in the entryway.

"Good morning," Hubbard said to announce himself. No matter what sort of day it was or ended up being, Hubbard was a stickler for going through the motions of good manners. Thomas, however, was much better at following the flow of a mood. He looked at the lieutenant and nodded, then flipped back a few pages of his notebook and handed it to him.

"What's this?" Hubbard asked.

"The answer to your first question: how many casualties," Thomas said.

"Actually, that wasn't, but— Jeez, five dead, six in the hospital and three at home with injuries? Who did this?"

"Nobody knows," Thomas said, taking back his book

and flipping it shut. He motioned for the lieutenant to
follow him down the corridor. Hubbard was aware of
what happened that night, but had not seen the damage
until now. Halfway down the corridor lay a cell door. A
forensic team surrounded the door that lay, not in the
cell, but against the wall. Thomas gestured toward the
lock and hinges that had once held it in place. They had
been twisted so much in places that they hardly resembled their original shapes. Much earlier Thomas had
been tempted to feel them, as if not believing that they
were ever really steel. His training had been enough to
remind him not to touch any evidence. Not touching
anything may have been the hardest thing for all of the
police to remember. It was difficult enough to avoid
moving a weapon or piece of furniture prematurely, but
to be unable to pick up one's own chair or reposition
one's own desk was rattling more than a few nerves.

Hubbard peered over one woman's shoulder to better
examine the door. It was mostly intact, except for the
definite bend in many of the bars, as if several people
had grabbed hold and . . .

"What did they use to pry this off?" Hubbard asked.
"Any crowbar marks?"

The woman stood up, relieved to be fully erect once
more. She wiped her hands with a dusty handkerchief.

"We haven't found any tool marks at all, sir," she
said. "We can't even find fingerprints."

"No?"

"Well, these doors are touched by so many people all
day long. There's always somebody holding onto the
bars. There's too much overlap."

Her partner stood up now, displaying several notecards
and small plastic bags. "Here's what we do have," he

said. "There are no full prints, but we found several finger *marks* where the bars were distorted. And hair," he added, shaking one of the bags.

"How can there be no tool marks?" Hubbard asked. "Are you suggesting that somebody pulled the door off with their bare hands?"

"Nobody I talked to said anything about weapons, tools, or anything else that could have been used to pull off the door," Thomas said. Hubbard frowned and leaned over for a last look at the door. It did, for all intents, appear as though somebody had ripped it away bare-handed.

"Let's go," Hubbard said. He paused to gesture at the ident team. "Have this removed when you're finished."

"Yes, sir."

He and Thomas finished their trek out of the corridor and back into the shambles of the squadroom. It was only now that Hubbard noted a new detail: in various places on the walls, on furniture, and everywhere else were definite gouges or perhaps . . . slashes?

"What was this I heard about animals leading the attack?" he asked.

"Most of the people I talked to said that it was a pack of dogs," Thomas said with a sigh. "No people."

"You're telling me that a pack of dogs did all this?"

"Sir, I don't know what I can tell you," Thomas said. "Officer . . ." he added, flipping through his notebook, "Officer Martin said it best: 'like the gates of hell had opened up and all the demons spilled out into here.' "

"How many shots were fired?"

"That I couldn't say," Thomas said. "No one could give an exact count. We'll be digging shells out of the walls for weeks, I'd bet."

"So bullets were flying everywhere," Hubbard said, waiting for a nod from Thomas. "And not one of those . . . dogs was hurt?"

"None that we know of."

"Help me sort this out," the lieutenant said, rubbing the back of his head. "The suspect's name is . . . ?"

"Loraine . . . Loraine . . . oh, no last name," Thomas said after checking his notes. "Hollywood type. Brought in two days ago on a murder suspicion and . . . you'll love this. She escaped the first night, then *returned* the next morning."

"That's what it was," Hubbard said. "Then it's the same girl?"

"Looks like it," Thomas said. "An animal was involved with her disappearance, too, if you remember. Nice coincidence, huh? Then, at 9:33 P.M. last night, the station was attacked by the pack of animals."

"The dogs."

"I'm not too comfortable calling them 'dogs,' sir," Thomas said. "Not from what I've seen and heard. Whatever they were, they moved faster than anyone could see clearly, dodged gunfire, and ripped that door away just to break out this Loraine person. Believe me, we have everyone available out there now, and that's not many. We could use the county's help."

"That's not a problem," Hubbard said. "The more proactive we are, the faster we'll catch her."

Thomas privately cringed whenever he heard that word "proactive." The lieutenant used it as often as a child who'd learned the new word of the day. Or perhaps it was simply because he didn't particularly like the lieutenant, who had the imagination and the compassion of a brick wall. Thomas was more dedicated to the job than to his

superior and greatly missed his old boss, Lieutenant
Becker, who blustered and fumed over the slightest mis-
haps, but who would go to the mat for any one of his
detectives. This was before the department "retired" him.

Hubbard moved off to survey the area and talk to
other officers. Thomas then took a long-delayed break
from his investigation. He flipped through his notebook
without actually reading it. He knew he was not alone
in his feelings. Every cop in the city, county, state or
perhaps even the nation would be up in arms over the
deaths of so many of their own. Hubbard was angry,
too, but Thomas couldn't be sure if it was because of
grief or . . . embarrassment. It struck Thomas that that
would raise the lieutenant's hackles more than grief over
losing his men. He hoped he was wrong.

Thomas reflected briefly on his career in the Fugitive
section. Nothing was more rewarding to him than to
bring in a fleeing suspect. Like the lieutenant, he had
visited many crime scenes. He had seen one before at
a police station, when a suspect had managed to shoot
an apprehending officer and escape. That was many
years ago, and the details would be lost to the average
Joe, but Thomas would never forget a detail. There had
actually been very little damage—even the officer had
only been wounded—but Thomas remembered it as the
worst thing he'd ever seen. He'd been so proud when the
creep was finally caught. He knew that would be nothing
compared to the feeling of bringing in this Loraine . . .
and her little "dogs," too.

Loraine felt foolish wearing nothing other than a hat
and sunglasses to disguise herself, but Hollywood or not,

she knew no makeup wizards who could make her look like an old woman or even an old man. Tamara had left the woods alone. Loraine understood the necessity of this. Tamara had been more than generous, including her final $2,000 loan before leaving Loraine to her own survival. She wanted more than anything to stay in Los Angeles and find her roommate's killer, but avoiding the dragnet for now was her best chance for success. It may already have been too late. In half a day every airport and bus station in the county could be crawling with cops. There had to be some way "the wolf" could help her escape, but not even Tamara had offered any parting suggestions.

Loraine was a werewolf and had been for several months now. Before that time she had only been a poverty-stricken dancer. She had come by her new condition the "movie way," as she called it: being bitten by another werewolf. It had not been in Los Angeles, but in Wisconsin while visiting with her Uncle Bill and his second wife, Joanie on their llama ranch. It had been such a wonderfully relaxing vacation until a male llama was slaughtered. The next night poor judgment on Loraine's part had led not only to her own attack, but her uncle's death. So far her transformations had been unremembered except as murky dreams, and the wolf she became had apparently caused no human deaths.

Until now.

Or had it? Although Loraine was certain that another werewolf had killed her best friend, she had not learned how to remember the exact events. The wolf had been dominant then. She needed to learn how to merge with the wolf's thoughts and memories. That, Tamara had informed her, took the longest time to master. When it happened, though, she might learn the wolf's name. All of the wolves had their own names, Tamara had said, whose own wolf was named, appropriately enough, Song. Loraine had not even suspected that Tamara was a werewolf herself until that morning, when Tamara had tracked her down to a cheap hotel—something the police had failed to do.

She had to go back to Wisconsin. She had been trying to for some time but had been nearly penniless until finally finding work us Tamara's choreographer. That, and the full moon preoccupied her time. Now she had no choice but to leave, and going back to the scene of her attack might give her some new insight on the way out of her dilemma. At the very least, she could find the pack from which her attacker had been exiled. She had vague memories of speaking with a group of people under a full moon, and surmised they might have met with the wolf. If they were "her" pack, then they would have to help her. Right?

Two

Lieutenant Hubbard's office was located far from the carnage in the squadroom. Unfortunately, as head of the Fugitive section, all calls, from other stations to the press to concerned citizens, were directed to him. Officially, the comment so far was "no comment." The press was fed only basic information about Loraine and none about the circumstances of her escape. Nobody needed to start worrying about rabid dogs tearing up the streets.

He was still on the phone when Detective Thomas arrived carrying a large envelope and a folder. Thomas seated himself and waited silently for the lieutenant to finish up yet another media call. Hubbard hung up and immediately resumed his computer work.

"What do you have for me?" he asked without looking at Thomas. The detective leaned forward to toss the envelope onto the desk, and waited for the lieutenant to pull out the 8 X 10s inside.

"I got those from Tim," Thomas said. "He was working on Loraine's case after her arrest. That's her roommate."

"What's left of her, you mean," Hubbard muttered. "Why are you showing me this?"

"Does that look like something that she'd do?"

"That who would do?"

"Loraine," Thomas said. "Does that look like something she could do—hell, that *any*one could do?"

"I suppose," Hubbard said, slipping the photographs inside and pushing the envelope to Thomas. "Maybe. I don't know. I learned long ago that anyone is capable of just about anything. How her roommate died doesn't matter. Loraine's an escaped murder suspect. Our job is to bring her back and let Tim and the others handle the evidence."

Thomas was astute enough to open the folder at this point and flip to the second page. "Most everyone she knows is in L.A.," he said. "She was born in New York but wouldn't name any family members there. Tim found letters from someone named Joanie in Wisconsin. I think we should send word to police in Wisconsin, but New York? Unless she has names in her little black book, I don't know what to tell them."

"Wait until we have more information," Hubbard said. "It's a waste of time otherwise."

"And let us not forget Tamara Taylor and Loraine's actor boyfriend," Thomas said.

"I know," Hubbard groaned. "I don't wanna hear another question about her. I hate celebrity cases."

"This *is* Hollywood."

"Yeahyeahyeah," Hubbard said quickly. It was moments like that that reminded Thomas of the lieutenant's East Coast upbringing. Or perhaps that had come later, as every now and then he detected slight Southern inflections in the lieutenant's speech. Thomas had never cared to ask exactly where his boss hailed from.

"Anyway, I only get answering machines," Thomas said. "Or in Tamara's case, her agent or publicist or whoever the hell it is."

"Keep trying," Hubbard said. "She's bound to contact somebody."

"Hmmm," Thomas said, scratching his chin.

"What?"

Thomas didn't react at first, and then felt the lieutenant's gaze on him. He waved it off, however.

"Uhhh, nothing," he said. "Sorry. For a minute I was thinking of calling the pound."

Hubbard's expression was blank. "To ask about the animals that assisted her escape?"

Thomas continued. "Maybe she got some animals from the pound and trained them. A pack of dogs could sure have done this to a person." He tapped the envelope containing the photos of Roxanne.

"An interesting theory," Hubbard said. "Pass that on to Detective Curry. That's up to him to pursue. We're just bringing her in."

"Yeah, I know," Thomas said, rising from his seat. "I'll let you know when the other photos come in. They managed to get some freeze frames in Surveillance."

"Good," Hubbard said. "I'll need to see them right away."

"I know, sir. No problem."

Loraine lost count of how many times she had the urge to call her apartment and remind her roommate that she'd be leaving town for a while. Each time she was forced to relive the painful knowledge that no one was there to answer the phone. No one alive, that is. Her former roommate was staying at the morgue now, literally torn to shreds by an inhuman beast. The worst part of the memory of Roxanne's remains was that Loraine could not turn away from them. She could hide her eyes all she wished, but her thoughts would never be shut out. The shredded mass of flesh that had been her best friend was burned into her mind's eye forever.

How long ago had it happened? It made her sick to remember that it had barely been two days since she had gone hunting for a renegade werewolf and had awakened to find an apartment full of policemen, paramedics, her boyfriend Michael, and a corpse. She wanted to call Michael as well, but fought that urge. He knew nothing of her "condition" and could never be expected to believe her story. She also didn't have time to explain anything to him. It was time to get out of Los Angeles. If she could do that and avoid the local dragnet for at least a little while, maybe she could formulate a plan. Right now all she could think of was going back to Wisconsin and finding the pack. If they really were "closer than family," as they had told her, then they would have to help her.

Loraine had no car—unthinkable to most Angelenos—and had to wait at a bus stop. Two Mexican women who talked together waited with her. She slouched into the corner and pulled her hat down. Her heart skipped a beat or two whenever a police car came near. Only one actually passed her street, but too many of them were turning corners or taking cross streets. It was very little paranoia on her part that convinced her that every one of them was looking for her. One didn't break out of jail without some consequences, even if it had not been her idea to do so.

The bus that finally arrived would not be going near a terminal. Cursing herself for that waste of time, Loraine tracked down a phone booth and dug out the number of a taxi service. She used the name Roxanne

Taylor and waited in as much shadow as the approaching afternoon would allow. The sidewalks were becoming busier, creating a cursed advantage: more people to blend into, and more people who might recognize her.

In twenty minutes a cab arrived. Loraine crept inside and announced her destination in a deeper voice than her usual soprano. As an afterthought, she realized that a limousine might have been wiser, with its darkened windows and omnipresence on L.A. streets. Now she could only pull down her hat, slump into the seat and pray for no policemen. She did spot more black and whites on the way to the bus terminal, but so far her driver hadn't given them cause to pull him over.

Thirty minutes and thirty dollars later, she was making her way to the bus station's ticket booth when she spotted several uniformed police in the distance. Two were standing idly while another was pinning up notices on a kiosk. Loraine didn't dare cast a second glance, but pulled her coat tighter around herself and scurried into the restroom. If anyone else had been in there, they might have seen little more than a blur before feeling the rush of air in its wake, finishing with the slam of a stall door.

Inside, Loraine set down her bag and rubbed her temples in a vain attempt to calm herself. A dozen questions, and not one plan, cascaded and collided in her mind: *Now what? Did they see me? Are any lady cops in here? I didn't look! Where else to go?*

She barely managed to stop any tears and gathered the strength the stand. She took her bag in shaky hands and opened the stall door to a slit, then hesitated before flushing the toilet. If anyone else was there, they would have no reason to wonder what her business in there had been. This proved unnecessary, as no one else was in the bathroom, after all. Still, she could not help tiptoeing up to the sink. It took most of her courage to remove her sunglasses, and the rest of it to remove her hat. It would not have surprised her at that moment if every stall door had suddenly burst open to reveal armed policewomen on permanent PMS. In reality, she was still alone.

Loraine leaned forward to examine her face. She slipped the sunglasses on and off to see how much they really helped. They were a start, but any suspicious cop could order them removed. Makeup? She had none with her. A stray thought made her think of transforming herself and rushing past them, which led to the thought of transforming and pretending to be somebody's seeing-eye dog. These brought only brief smiles in the end, before they were replaced by quiet despair. She even thought of fighting her way out. After all, their bullets wouldn't kill her unless they were silver.

Loraine buried her face in her hands and fought off tears again. As before, nothing worse than a sniffle escaped; then a flash of hope lit up her face. A full transformation was unthinkable, but could something less be pulled off? Once, to help convince Roxanne of her story, she had transformed her hand into a wolf's paw, but that wasn't the sort of change she needed. Never had she wanted or needed Tamara more than now, but Loraine had to try it alone. Making certain once again that she was alone, Loraine returned her attention to the mirror and concentrated.

For too long, nothing happened, until her face suddenly felt as though it had been given a rough shove. Her nose and mouth shot out into a snout; her ears were still sliding back along her skull before she could stop it. In a few seconds her face was back to normal. With shaky hands Loraine slapped water onto her face and worked at taking slow, deep breaths. It was more than a few moments before she found the courage to try again. As before, her face stretched out into a full snout, but she pulled it back more slowly this time. It helped to use her hands to sculpt her face into something definitely human, but different. With a tremendous amount of concentration, she managed to flatten the snout into a normal face, but with a longer nose and smaller chin. An unexpected, but welcome, effect was that her eyes became green instead of the usual blue. It still didn't seem enough, difficult as it was to maintain even this appearance. She racked her brain for even the smallest memory of other changes during the transformation. Her palms were sweating from the effort of holding this form, but it had to work. She was accomplishing what glasses and a hat could not. Then she remembered: the brown fur that blanketed her skin just before consciousness faded away. Her normal hair was darker, so with a last burst of effort, she "dyed" her hair from dark brown to a reddish brown.

Loraine let out a loud sigh of relief, only to discover that some of her teeth were longer and sharper than usual. No amount of effort was sufficient to flatten them without compromising her disguise, so Loraine made a mental note to keep her mouth shut as much as possible.

After patting her face a few times as if checking its stability, Loraine gathered her things and made for the door. She reached it just as it burst open. Loraine jumped back a step, also startling the woman who had entered.

Feeling her face again, Loraine muttered an apology and pushed past the woman.

She slipped on her sunglasses and wiped her hands on her pants. The police were still in the terminal. Several stood right by the entrance to the buses. She reached the ticket counter, only to learn that the farthest destination that day was San Jose. She purchased a ticket reluctantly and used her best casual walk to stroll about. *Come on, girl,* she thought. *You've been scared before; you're a dancer. Pretend it's just another audition!*

These thoughts helped, except that losing this "audition" would mean much more than simply going home jobless. She kept her cool even when passing a kiosk and seeing her face had been plastered up there along with the rest of its rogues' gallery. Again she touched her face with quivering hands, and felt her nose shift, but not enough that she couldn't reposition it.

Loraine picked a seat that faced away from the cops, but quickly grew restless and wandered over to examine the magazine rack. She bought two gossip rags and sat down to bury her face in them. Soon enough she was feeling the strain. Not only her hands, but her face broke out into a nasty sweat. Her features would not keep their new shapes any longer. Even her hair was fading back to its original darker color, but if anyone noticed, she didn't care. Loraine made a beeline for the restroom, where she splashed her face with cold water. The shock made her features snap back to their original shapes. Loraine winced in pain, as the effect was much like cracking her neck and being stung by a rubber band at the same time.

There was a small cracked bench off in a corner that became her shelter for the next hour. Only a half hour remained before she could board the bus. Loraine had reread the latest self-help article for the fourth time, when a new "friend" entered the restroom: a female cop. Up went the magazine before Loraine's face. She dared to peek and see if the cop entered a stall, but she busied herself at the sink instead. Loraine tried not to watch, but stared as the woman washed her hands and arms, and then her heart leaped when the cop pulled out her gun. Instead of aiming it at Loraine, the cop simply made a quick check of it before reholstering it. Up went the magazine again, but this time Loraine used it to hide her other hand, which was frantically pushing and prodding her malleable features. She pulled down on the nose, pushed in her chin, and imagined herself as a near-redhead.

"How ya doin'?" a voice interrupted her thoughts. Down went the magazine to reveal the lady cop now approaching Loraine. She met the woman with wide eyes instead of a greeting. Finally the cop stopped and rested her hand casually on her pistol.

"Did you hear me?" she said.

"What?" Loraine said, stifling the urge to poke at her face. She had no way of knowing if her disguise was in effect. "Hear you what?"

"I just asked how you were doing, that's all," the cop said.

"Oh," Loraine said. "Fine. Just . . . waiting, you know."

"Yeah, these buses take forever, don't they?"

"Yeah," Loraine said with a forced laugh. "It's a long wait."

"Where you headed?"

"Uh, Wis—San Fran—San Jose, I think."

"You think?" the cop said with a smile, taking a step closer. "Better double-check your ticket."

"Huh? Oh, yeah," Loraine said. "No, it's San Jose."

"Hm, good town," she said. "I got a brother there. You have relatives there, too?"

"Uh . . . uh, no. They're in—all over, really."

"Ahhh," the cop said, leaning over to snag a paper towel. She moved a little closer. "Is that light good enough to read?"

"To . . . Oh, yeah," Loraine said. "Yeah, it's fine. I can see well in bad light, I guess. It's warmer in here, too." This time she did feel her face. Her cheek was quivering.

"Well, you enjoy your trip, then," the cop said, rolling up her towel to slam dunk it into the waste can. "Maybe you can say hi to my brother. He works at the police station there."

"Imagine that," Loraine muttered to herself. Her "friend" apparently heard nothing, and sauntered outside, leaving Loraine alone to breathe a loud sigh. She relaxed her features, noting that it was even more difficult to maintain them while speaking. It might have been the dim light alone which had prevented any suspicion from the cop.

At long last she made the trek across the station to the boarding gate. As before, several cops loitered at the entrance. Her "friend" from the restroom stood with them. As she neared, the lady cop held out her hand. Loraine slowed to a stop.

"Hello again," the cop said. "Your bus is finally ready, huh?"

"Yeah," Loraine whispered.

"Where were you headed again?"

"San Jose."

"Oh, yeah," the cop said. "Well, listen; we need to make just a quick security check to ensure everyone's safety. Do you have a minute?"

"Uh . . . uh, yeah," Loraine said. She felt her cheek twitch, and sucked in her breath. Instead of checking her bags, the cop produced a color photograph of a very familiar face: Loraine's.

"Would you happen to know or have seen this woman at any time that you can recall?" the cop asked.

Loraine stared at the photograph as if really trying to remember, but in truth, she was doing everything possible to prevent herself from resembling it.

"Ma'am?"

"No," Loraine said. "Sorry, I don't."

"Are you certain of that?" the cop asked. "Take as long a look as you need."

Loraine deliberately turned her gaze away. She shook her head. "I still wouldn't remember it," she murmured.

"All right, but thank you for looking, ma'am," she said. "Also, could I ask you to remove your sunglasses?"

"Is my bus leaving?"

"Not just yet, ma'am," she said. "Would you please remove your glasses?"

Loraine tightened her lower lip and removed them slowly. The cop alternately studied the photograph and Loraine.

"Do you still think I know her?" Loraine offered.

"Actually, there seemed to be a small resemblance," the cop said, lowering the photo. "Is that your natural hair color?"

"Heh . . . yeah."

"Why the smile?"

"Oh, 's'nothing," Loraine said, remembering to shut her mouth again. "People just ask that a lot, that's all."

"Oh," the cop said, nodding. "And do you wear contacts or any other corrective lenses?"

"No, nothing like that," Loraine said.

Silence followed while another cop approached and whispered something to the policewoman. She nodded as he spoke, then lowered the photo.

"We're sorry for the delay, ma'am," she said. "Thank you for your cooperation. Enjoy your trip."

"Oh—that's okay," Loraine said. "Hope you catch whoever you're looking for."

"Ma'am?"

"Or whatever you're looking for, I meant," she added. She gave them all a quick wave before turning to enter the boarding area. She never turned around to make certain, but Loraine felt somebody's gaze on her as she walked. It would not have surprised her to learn it had been the lady cop's.

She boarded the bus and found a seat at the very back. That way she wasn't right next to a window and could finally relax her features. It was a strange sensation to feel her body altering its shape, no matter how small the change. Still, it was much like having that one good stretch in the morning, when the joints snap themselves back into place and the blood jump-starts from its bedtime pace. Loraine relaxed her entire body and released a sigh of near contentment. She wished again that Tamara were there so she could see how Loraine measured up so far.

Three

"Now this is great," Hubbard said, throwing down the photos. "You can see all the men just fine, but those dogs are just a blur. How fast were they going?"

"Like I said, everyone we talked to said they just shot right through—sshhhhoooo," Thomas said, letting his hand "take off" like an airplane. "Like demons coming out of hell."

"That's not appropriate, Thomas," Hubbard said.

Thomas considered a response, then folded his arms and sighed loudly. "I thought the pictures would be helpful, too," he said. He gathered the photos and prepared to return them to their folder, but paused to scrutinize one. It took Hubbard a while to notice this.

"Something wrong?" he asked. Thomas snapped out of it and finished putting the photos away.

"Uhhh, nothing, I guess," he said. "It just looked like some of them were on two legs, but they're so blurry . . ."

"Send them to the lab," Hubbard said. "They might be able to clear up some of it. Every little bit helps."

"Yeah, I guess I'll do that," Thomas murmured, letting his finger run along the folder.

* * *

Loraine tried to call her Aunt Joanie collect from San Jose, but a machine answered. The operator cut off the call, and Loraine slammed down the receiver. A bus wouldn't be leaving for Wisconsin for another day, so she bought a ticket for Idaho instead. It was late at night; she had four, possibly five hours of sleep available before needing to return to the station. She made her way to a motel across the street and almost checked in as "Phyllis Taylor," but decided that it was too close to her real name. She wrote in "Clara Taylor" instead and got her key.

The motel was too cheap even for cable television. She tossed her sack on the bed and peeked out the window. Satisfied that a SWAT team had not followed her, Loraine double-locked the door and turned on the bathwater. While stripping, she clicked on the TV, channel-surfing until she found a local newscast. She was down to her underwear by the time they finished their story on the President's latest press conference, then heard:

"In Los Angeles, police continue their hunt for murder suspect Phyllis Turner, also known as Loraine Turner, who escaped from a Los Angeles jail Tuesday night. There are unconfirmed reports that the breakout was orchestrated by accomplices using large dogs to attack a station full of police officers. At least five officers have been confirmed as dead, but police are withholding the total number of casualties."

Loraine's mugshot appeared on the bluescreen behind the anchorman. Her heart shot into her throat and she didn't realize that she'd stopped breathing until she became lightheaded. Meanwhile, the scene switched to various reporters swarming around a police lieutenant who waved them all off with several "No comments" throughout. The anchorman then returned to sum up the story.

"Singer Tamara Taylor has also found herself in the news again, not because of her upcoming tour, but because Loraine Turner had been working for her as a dancer and choreographer. Taylor's only comments have come through her publicist:

'We have stated before, and will state again, that Tamara Taylor has spoken with the police, and she has said all that she has to say at this time.' "

"Oh, man," Loraine sighed, slumping onto the edge of the bed. "Tam, I'm sorry you've been dragged into this."

The anchorman finished the report by urging everyone to call the police if they saw her, and not to attempt to confront her directly, for she was expected to be "armed and dangerous."

"Or fanged," she added before clicking off the TV. For a long time the bathwater made the only noise in the room, until Loraine shut her eyes and began to growl. It began quietly and then grew in intensity, until she threw up her arms and yelled. A crunching sound made her stop, not to mention the fear of disturbing anyone with her cries. She looked at her hand to see that the TV remote was now in two pieces. She dropped it and jumped back as if it carried some disease, then crept along the walls, flinching at every outside noise.

Now it was time to curse as she found the bathtub overflowing. There were only two towels and two washcloths available to soak up the water, leaving no towels for herself. The whole floor was slippery, but she survived the descent into the tub. Loraine had always found baths to be more relaxing than showers, but not now.

She spent most of her time frozen in place, imagining every unknown sound as the police, FBI and Army getting ready to break down the door. But no one, not even a maid, knocked that night. It wouldn't have mattered if anyone had disturbed her; insomnia was her bedfellow that night.

Loraine had not altered her features when she first checked in, but hoped for the best and made her subtle changes before entering the lobby. A different clerk was there, but she maintained the new facade in case he was a news fan. He hardly glanced at her as she checked out and left the motel, just in time for her facial tic to make another appearance. She relaxed the disguise while approaching the bus station, and "fixed her face" just before entering. She had figured out by this time that police officers were always somewhere in a bus station, and didn't need to take any chances.

The bus trip allowed her some time to relax and enjoy the scenery. Still, she could never let her guard completely drop. Being a fugitive was probably a snap in the old days, when radio was the world's television. Somehow, "Be on the lookout for a young woman with dark brown hair" was not quite as effective as being the featured story on *America's Most Wanted*. She would have found this amusing if it didn't frighten her so much. The irony of her situation wasn't lost on her, either. Television had become quite an effective tool for bringing in felons on the lam, and she applauded that. Now she wished that the damn box had never been invented.

Halfway to her destination, Loraine remembered that she needed to do more than just escape the law—much more. Tamara would have been appalled to see her pupil wasting her time looking at the mountains, when there were plenty of lessons to be learned. Or perhaps she would have been proud to know that Loraine had taught herself a new trick. No, Tamara was not one who was easily satisfied. The only praise Loraine would get would come after she had proven her innocence.

She needed to find and talk to the only material witness to her roommate's murder: the wolf Loraine had been "asleep," but the wolf had seen everything. But how to contact it? Or her, as Tamara had pointed out. Loraine shut her eyes and attempted something that Roxanne had tried to teach her. She didn't remember what it was called—something about imagery—but it wasn't exactly meditation. She pictured herself sitting in front of a tree in a deserted park. Now she imagined a boulder some twenty feet away, and stared at it in her mind. Roxanne had stressed that it was important to relax the mind completely and not daydream, but to allow the subconscious itself to decide what would come out from behind the rock. Loraine had a disorganized mind, though, and the scenes kept shifting around. Most were not pleasant, either: arguing with her boyfriend, the murder scene, Roxanne's body, being arrested, the moment of her attack, and even her mother's very unwelcome visit in the hospital.

A bump jolted Loraine from her thoughts. A glance at her watch revealed that it was more than her thoughts that had been jolted; she had been asleep for an hour. Her dreams had been uneasy, yet not one of them involved a conversation with her "other half." *Stupid, mangy dog,* she thought. *I'd still be in L.A. if not for you. I wouldn't be wanted for fuckin' murder!*

"You're *not* human, and unless you accept that, you'll be stuck groping around when the lights go out. You need the wolf to survive." Tamara had said that, and Loraine heard the words as clearly as if Tamara were sitting beside her. Except that no one was beside her. There were other passengers scattered about, but none had done more than glance at her when she'd first gotten on.

Another feeling came over her. A familiar, yet unwelcome feeling that she was being watched. It had been so long since she'd felt this way. Or had it been that long? How many days had it been since Roxanne's murder? Loraine was not interested in counting the days, or remembering the details. Not that shredded body again. She swallowed and concentrated on that familiar feeling instead. Loraine had never quite determined where it came from. At first she had wondered if it had come from the other wolf—the one who had first attacked her—and then had decided that it very well could be the wolf within her.

Hello? she thought. *If that's you in there, please talk to me. I know you're in there; you can't deny THAT.*

Nothing. Even the "watched" feeling faded away.

Is that you trying to talk to me? she thought. *Please say it is. I have to talk to you. Look: I'm sorry if I keep fighting this, but you understand, don't you?*

There was no sound save the rumbling of the bus.

Goddamn you, quit hiding from me! That was you making me remember what Tamara said, wasn't it? Well? If I need you, you need me, too! Didja think of that?

Loraine looked from one passenger to the other, as if expecting them to have heard her mental shouting match.

No one turned around or made any other move toward her, and neither did her alter ego.

"Stupid dog," she muttered just quietly enough to be muffled by the bus's engines. She sighed loudly and folded her arms, slumping back into the seat to brood.

"I need you to call the sheriff's office."

Hubbard's voice came from right behind Detective Thomas, whose feet all but flew off of his desk. A small stack of papers followed, and Thomas stooped over to collect the papers and himself. Rather than help, Hubbard waited for the detective to finish piling up the pages.

"The sheriff?" Thomas said. "What's happened?"

"They picked up a woman answering Loraine's description," Hubbard explained. "They need her prints."

"Again?" Thomas said. "We sent those when this first started." He shook his head and grabbed the phone, glancing back at the lieutenant. "Um, yeah, I'll take care of it."

Hubbard listened a few moments to Thomas muttering to himself while waiting for an answer. In this case, he was verbalizing a list of people who might have received the fingerprints.

The lieutenant's eye was caught by a stack of handwritten letters on the desk. One of them was addressed to Loraine's old name of Phyllis, so he picked it up as Thomas finished his call.

"They have 'em," he said. "We'll know soon enough if that's our girl. That's an unmailed letter to one of Loraine's friends or relatives; I'm not sure which one yet."

"Mm-hm," Hubbard said, pulling out the letter inside. *It's funny that I was there so short a time ago, but I miss you already. Sometimes I wonder if I should keep being a dancer, or screw it all and raise llamas with you.* He paused in his reading. "Llamas?" he said.

Thomas shrugged. "Don't look at me," he said.

Hubbard continued reading. *Ha ha! But seriously, I hope I can visit you again soon. Very soon. I still feel terrible leaving you like that after Uncle Bill died*—"Oh, well, this 'Joanie' must be her aunt, then," Hubbard concluded.

"Or cousin."

Some things have been happening here that make me want to go back there. You know I'd help with—"Etc, etc . . ." Hubbard said, and shook the letter. "Does she say what 'things' were happening?"

"No," Thomas said. "That's the only letter from Loraine that we have. She kept the replies, though—the ones that Tim collected. Oh, we have contacted Wisconsin. They'll be talking to 'Mrs. Joanie Turner' and get back to us. I'm still sorting through her replies. If it turns out that the sheriff got our girl, then great, but if not—" he took the letter from Hubbard, then held it up—"I'll bet this is exactly where she's trying to go."

"Yeah, well, let's hope that they have her," Hubbard said. He frowned at the sight of a particularly unkempt object on the desk, and pointed at it. "What *is* that?" he said.

Thomas followed the finger to the remains of a tiny book. He picked it up gently; to do otherwise would surely have disintegrated it entirely.

"This?" he asked, and dared to open it. Loose pages,

partially covered with faded to fresh names and numbers, tried to break free of their former binding.

"Her address book," he announced. "The people who haven't been lost to a sudden draft have been contacted."

"What?" Hubbard said. "People lost in a draft?"

"I meant—" Thomas began, then reconsidered explaining his joke. "We've gotten through most of the names. Some have even called back, but they were busts."

"Ah," the lieutenant said. "Anyway, if you don't hear from the sheriff in ten minutes, call them." Then he turned and left abruptly, leaving Thomas to pick up the tiny pages that had drifted to the floor.

The local media was having a field day with the latest womanhunt. Hubbard might not have minded their involvement but for the strange circumstances of the breakout. The police across the county had strict orders not to discuss the "wild animals," either from rumor or memory, because the media had already learned about and were using that angle. The media's help in tracking down their fugitive was welcome, as long as it wasn't accompanied by headlines like "Jailhouse Rocked by Hounddogs." That had been Detective Thomas's joke, not Hubbard's. Even Thomas had muttered it not to get big belly laughs, but to help diffuse the anger that everyone was feeling about the massacre at the station. The only exception might have been Hubbard. Thomas wasn't certain if the lieutenant had felt anything about the men who were killed and injured.

* * *

Joanie Turner was just opening a can of vegetable soup when her phone rang. She carried the can with her to the wall phone and answered mechanically. An even more mechanical operator announced a collect call from a Loraine.

"Loraine?" Joanie said. "I'm sorry, I don't know a—"

"Joanie-it's-me-Phyllis!" Loraine yelled as quickly as she could.

"Ma'am, will you accept the ch—"

"I didn't hear that," Joanie said. "Who is it again?"

"Phyllis!" she cried.

"Oh, my goodness," Joanie said. "I'm sorry, dear, I forgot about—"

"Ma'am, I need to know if you'll accept the charges—"

"Well, of course I will!" Joanie said. "I wouldn't be talking to her if—"

"Thank you," the operator said, and clicked off.

"Honestly, she wasn't even going to let me finish," Joanie said. "I've never liked op—"

"Joanie, thank God you're home!" Loraine said. "I'm at a bus station right now, and I wish I could have warned you, but— Could I stay at your place again? For a little bit, anyway."

"Well . . . I don't see why not," Joanie said. "You're always welcome here. But why do you seem so excited? Is something going on, honey?"

"You might say that, yeah," Loraine said. "Haven't you been watching the news?"

"Well, no, I've been busy most of the day lately, and never watched much TV, anyway," she said.

"Maybe it's best that you don't, then," Loraine said. "I do feel bad about giving such short notice, but I've been taking the bus until I get there. I just need a place to stay for a while."

"Something's wrong, then," Joanie said. "What is it, honey?"

"This must be costing you a fortune," Loraine said.

"Don't change the subject."

"Couldn't I tell you when I get there?" Loraine said.

"Well, yes, but—oh, damn, it's my other line. Could you hold on while I get rid of whoever it is?"

"Sure." Loraine had wanted to say no, but didn't have an excuse if questioned. Joanie had already given permission for her to visit, so there was little point in prolonging their conversation. Loraine couldn't completely discount the fact that the authorities could very well have tracked her there and were listening in.

"Hello?" Joanie said to the other caller.

"Is this the residence of Mrs. Joanie Turner?" a man's voice asked.

"Yes, it is," she said. "But I have someone on long distance on the other line—"

"It'll just be a moment, ma'am," the man said. "I'm Detective Bunche from the Dunlevy Police. We were contacted by the Los Angeles Police regarding the escape of a Phyllis Turner from a police station in Hollywood. Have you been keeping correspondence with a woman of that same name?"

"Well, yes," she said. "She's my niece. By marriage."

"I see," Bunche said. "And has she corresponded with you or attempted to contact you in the last few days?"

Joanie's mouth opened, but nothing inside moved. She caught herself staring at tomorrow's vet appointment on the wall calendar.

"Ma'am?"

"Wha— Oh," she said, just catching the phone before it slipped from her shoulder. "I'm sorry. No. She hasn't called or written for . . . well, a long time, anyway. At least a few weeks. Is she in trouble with the police? Did you say she escaped from jail?"

"We just need to locate her, ma'am," he said. "I'd like to give you my number in case she does contact you. Would you please write this down?"

Joanie did drop the phone this time while reaching for the pen and paper. She apologized twice, and then wrote down the detective's name and number. He thanked her for her time and disconnected. Joanie quickly switched to the other line.

"Hello?" she said. "Hello, are you there?"

She heard nothing save a low hum and a little static. Joanie clicked the receiver and called out some more, but there was still no answer. She made one last attempt to reconnect with her niece, then slowly hung up the phone.

Phyllis was obviously in bigger trouble than anyone was telling her. It was then that Joanie realized how much trouble she herself must have been in for lying to a police officer. And when Phyllis arrived, would she lie again, or would she point out her niece's hiding place when the cops stormed the ranch?

If only someone had warned her long ago about the dangers of llama ranching.

Four

Tamara watched the sky from her hotel balcony. She tried to remember how long it had been since she'd really seen the stars without the obscuring lights of a big city. She knew that it had been many years since she'd seen the Milky Way. Then she thought of Loraine, and how Loraine was probably getting a much clearer view of the stars than she, if it mattered to her. Loraine had more important things on her mind, such as survival. Still, there was just a touch of envy in Tamara. Loraine was escaping, even if temporarily, into the heart of the wolves' lands. If she found the pack, perhaps they would convince her to stay with them this time. Loraine might very well find the happiness that had always eluded her.

No, Tamara thought. Loraine was more of a city girl than even Tamara. And she wasn't likely to rest before Roxanne's murder was avenged. She hadn't known Loraine's friend that well, except as one of those who had auditioned for the tour. But she did know that Loraine had told no one but Roxanne about her "other self," and that told Tamara all she needed to know. There was no reason, no point to her murder. It made Tamara want to track down and slaughter the real killer herself, but that would have been unfair to her missing friend.

Tamara had considered listening in on her manager's

phone conversation, but opted to suppress the wolf's superior hearing. Soon enough, though, she heard the screen door being scooted open, followed by Paul's slow footsteps.

"That was the *Times* again," Paul sighed, sitting opposite her.

"No interview," she muttered, her eyes still focused on the stars.

"Yeah, I know," he said. "But I set one up for Saturday."

"What??" she said, standing abruptly. "I'm not—!"

"Tam, if they ask about Loraine, then just ignore them," he said. "I made it clear to them that you'll only discuss the tour. Bringing attention back to the tour is the best way to deal with this. We can't afford any more delays."

"Your compassion is noted."

"Thank you," he said. "It's my job. Seriously, you know I liked her, too, and she was a hell of a choreographer—"

"Is."

"*Is* a hell of a choreographer," he corrected. "You have to get past this before it ruins you. This is the last thing your career needs. You're hot, honey, and you have to keep the heat going yourself to get through this."

"Man, who writes your scripts, Paul?"

"Hah?"

"Never mind," she said. "I know what I have to do. I don't need the lecture."

"You pay me to lecture you," he said. "And we're not the only ones who could lose on this. Remember the—"

"The dancers, the band, the fans, the record company,

the President," she said. "I know, I know. I just hate it, that's all."

"I know you do," he said quietly. "And I know you're really gonna hate tomorrow."

"Which is . . . ?" she said. "I can barely remember my name, let alone what day it is."

Paul allowed himself a slight smile. "Tomorrow we look for her replacement," he said. "We need a choreographer. It's just the business, Tam."

"I know," she whispered. Nothing else was said. Paul, having said his piece, knew better than to loiter outside while she brooded. He knew that she understood even if she didn't agree. He rose from his seat and wandered back inside the living room, only pausing long enough to wish her a good night. Tamara waved in response and returned her attention to the stars. It was only a first quarter moon, but "Song" wanted to call to it.

Not now, Tamara thought to her other self. *He's right, after all; it's just the business. We'll try to find a place for her if*—when *she comes back, but if we can't, she'll still make it. If she can survive what's coming, just surviving life in the city will be a snap.*

It probably was a bit safer by now to take a plane the rest of the way to Wisconsin, now that Loraine was out of Los Angeles. Still, national television made it likely that she could be spotted on a full flight, and then there would be nowhere to run. Traveling by bus was slower—and more expensive—than she cared for, but at least there were fewer chances of being spotted. Loraine could alter her features for a few minutes at best, not an entire two or three hour flight.

She wondered why it could take so long to get to
Wisconsin before vaguely remembering her own long
journey, by car, from New York to California so many
years ago. Had she really been just seventeen when she'd
fled from home, and worse, made the trip alone? It had
been six years ago, but even then it was a safer trip than
now. It seemed as though the crime rate had been mul-
tiplying exponentially from year to year. Not long ago
she might have been afraid of fighting an assailant for
fear of being killed. She might still be afraid to fight
back—but this time for fear of killing the attacker.

She smiled a little for the first time after realizing
that most of these thoughts were Roxanne's fault. Roxanne could quote current Rape and Other Violent Crimes
Against Women statistics for just about every major city.
She had known exactly how much women earned compared to men for practically every occupation, and how
many female Congresspersons (never Congress*men*) and
top corporate executives there were at any given time.
Loraine had once joked that her friend had been a full-
time feminist and part-time dancer.

Roxanne's other "hobby," health, led to frequent
quotes of nutritional statistics on fat, cholesterol, caf-
feine, nicotine, drugs, alcohol, sugar, and anything else
that a normal human would even consider consuming.
Her food bills had always been higher than Loraine's
due to the specialty stores that she'd frequented. Roxanne's food had always been quite safe around Loraine,
who single-handedly supported the fast-food industry in
her neighborhood.

Fortunately Roxanne had never preached—only reminded. Loraine had actually been trying to limit her
meat consumption, but things had changed. The wolf

needed meat and made certain that Loraine knew this. She always craved meat now, especially as the full moon approached, but it was still controllable. Now she tried to remember what Tamara had eaten whenever they'd gone out. Meat? Salads? Some combination of everything? People rarely remembered their own meals, let alone other's; Loraine was no exception. There was still much else to think about. She needed to look for the wolf again. Tamara had once told her that the wolf had its own name, but what? If she knew it, it might help her make contact. But then, she could not learn the name without making contact first. She was in no mood to appreciate the irony. To an extent, contact had been made, but on the wolf's terms. Why couldn't it be on hers?

That bizarre imagery meditation was worth another try. The worst that could happen was that she'd fall asleep again. Loraine took a few breaths and cleared her mind, and then imagined herself sitting under a tree in a park. She pictured a boulder this time, "placed" it in front of her, and waited.

After several minutes of waiting, Loraine was surprised to "hear" a sound from behind the rock. She almost lost the image of the park completely, but kept it together in the end. The most difficult part of this meditation was not to allow her imagination to take over. Roxanne had stressed the importance of letting the subconscious think for itself and form its own images.

A few moments later she "heard" another sound, which resembled a grunt, and then "saw" something hobbling its way from behind the boulder. Each step was accompanied by that grunt-like sound, until she "saw" the distinct form of an animal dragging itself into view

with two crippled front legs. She was not surprised to
see a wolf emerge from behind the boulder, but did not
expect to see it in such pain.

It dragged itself into full view now, and let out a few
quick breaths. Loraine looked directly at it, but it would
not meet her gaze. *This is . . . too weird,* she thought,
and was quite tempted to end this. But she had never
made it this far trying to contact her other self. *Now
what?* she wondered. Then she remembered that Roxanne had put it quite simply: talk to whatever you see,
no matter what it is.

Um . . . she thought to the beast. *Hello?*

The wolf stayed where it was, still not meeting her
gaze, still not moving.

Can you . . . talk? she thought. *Or something?*

Wrfffff, it thought, and nothing else. Loraine imagined
herself standing up now and approaching the beast very
slowly. She crouched down as she neared it, and then
held out her hand.

Hello? she thought again, and reached out to its muzzle. The wolf snapped at her hand, causing her to cry
out and fall backward onto her rear. Imaginary or not,
she "felt" the pain of landing. It was almost enough to
bring her out of the meditation, but she had to keep
going. She was so close.

She brushed off the dirt from herself, then sat cross-
legged and stared at the beast. It had resumed ignoring
her and was licking one of its front paws. After a long
time of this, Loraine looked down and poked at the grass
a moment.

I guess I don't blame you, she thought. *I remember
Roxanne telling me about this . . . whatever it is. She
said that no matter what came out, it could still talk.*

How delightful, the wolf thought. The shock almost sent Loraine onto her back again. She regained her composure and met the wolf's gaze; it had finally decided to return the favor.

Holy shit, she thought. *God, I don't even know what to say now. But then, I'm dreaming, I guess, so—*

You are not dreaming, the wolf thought. *You control me no more than I control you.*

But I was here first.

Were you?

Well, yeah, of course I was, Loraine thought. The wolf winced and inched its way backward a painful step or two. Loraine felt a chill shoot down her spine.

You're in pain, she thought. *But why? What happened to you?*

A fool could see 'what happened,' it thought.

Hey—!

During the moon, I am stronger than you and can defend myself, it continued. *But it should not be this way. You hate me. You break my limbs and tear at my flesh and—*

What are you talking about? Loraine thought. *Break your legs? Until now I haven't been able to . . . to even see you, let alone talk to you!*

And why should I 'talk' to you now? it thought. *You want me dead.*

I just want to be normal, she thought. *I don't want you dead. Is it a crime to want to be normal?*

And what do you imagine will happen to me, the wolf thought, *should you become 'normal' again?*

I don't know, Loraine thought. *You can go wherever you want to. Am I supposed to enjoy being a werewolf?*

The wolf shut its eyes and moaned in pain. Loraine felt a lump come to her throat, but forced it away.

So you're dying because I want to be human, she thought. *Is that what you're telling me?*

I will not die, the wolf thought. *Your hatred of me breaks my limbs, and burns my bowels and tears at my flesh, but it will not kill me. I have always been a part of you—always, but until now, I did not have a way to emerge.*

You make it sound like I've always been a werewolf.

Perhaps—it stopped to grunt in pain—*you have. Some have the wolf in them, as you do, yet it never emerges. It never does, but only suffers, as I do. You hate me, and as long as you do, I WILL HATE YOU.*

Loraine felt a wave of anger coming from the wolf. She felt her stomach churn and twist as long as the anger was directed at her. Finally it stopped, and her stomach settled.

So now you're going to attack me? she thought.

I do not have the strength to, it thought. *At least, not until the moon next appears.*

You mean . . . the full moon, Loraine thought.

It is the only moon that matters, the wolf thought. *I am whole and strong then, and can make you suffer, if I wish. I did not wish to before, but you have begun this war yourself.*

Wait a minute, wait a minute, Loraine thought. *This is . . . This is like nothing that's ever happened to me before. You're right. This isn't a dream at all. I'm really talking to you. The wolf. I'm just . . .*

The wolf lifted a shaky head to lock gazes with her. Loraine felt her eyes misting up, which confused her. How could she be tearing up during an hallucination, or whatever this was? Still, she wiped away the coming tears.

I'm just scared, she thought. *I'm afraid of you. I can admit that. I'm afraid that you're going to kill somebody. Maybe you already have!*

I have not.

Then . . . you didn't kill Roxanne?

I did not, the wolf thought. *Your feelings were . . . are strong for that two-legger. Your anger would have been too great.*

'Two-legger'?

Your fear of me is your own doing, Loraine, the wolf thought. It surprised her that the wolf would know her name, yet she still didn't know the wolf's. It disturbed her to "hear" the wolf use her name. Perhaps "two-legger" would have been preferable after all.

You need me, it continued. Loraine had heard that plenty of times already.

But do you need me? she countered. The wolf's ears pricked. A long silence followed. It was during this time that Loraine realized that she had not imagined other sounds in her park.

Perhaps, it thought finally. *But without you I would be free to run with the others. With the pack. It is you who made me leave them.*

Me? she thought. *I didn't do anything! I don't even remember 'running with the others.' That was you doing the talking.*

I am not yet strong enough to resist completely your pull to the two-leggers' world, the wolf thought. *But do not think that will be forever. It seems that you, too, wish to find the others, as do I, but for different reasons. We shall see whose will survives then.*

Loraine wanted to respond, but could only watch the wolf slowly, very slowly, push and drag itself onto four shaky legs. It shut its eyes and sighed. Loraine rolled up onto one knee, but the wolf shook its head. She watched as it slowly and painfully turned around, grunting with every step.

You can walk, Loraine thought. *Sort of. Does this mean you're getting better?*

The wolf did not answer, but continued its slow journey back to the boulder. Loraine sat up onto both knees.

You're leaving, aren't you? she thought. *Are you leaving? Don't leave, wolf.*

The wolf paused to glance over its shoulder, then continued its return to her subconscious. Loraine struggled to her feet, but found it very difficult to keep her balance. It reminded her of trying to run or fly during a dream. Eventually she was reduced to crawling after the wolf in a mockery of its natural four-legged stance.

Wolf! she thought, but the beast was already halfway behind the boulder. *Goddamn you, you can't—! Oh, jeez. I'm sorry! You're right; all I ever do is yell at you and— Please don't leave, wolf. I need you. I really do!*

Loraine reached out for the tip of the wolf's tail, but could not quite reach it. She gave up just as the last of the animal disappeared behind the rock. Only then was Loraine able to stand up and walk around it. She saw nothing there.

Shit, she thought, slapping her forehead. *It hates me. It wants me dead, or enslaved or whatever. And I forgot to ask its name!*

Loraine needed a moment to realize that the inside of the bus was not part of her hallucination. She shielded her face from the brightness of the sun and glanced at her fellow passengers. No one looked at her, easing her fears that she might have been speaking out loud during her "talk" with the wolf. Or perhaps she had been, and the others were simply ignoring the crazy lady who talked to herself. Next time she would make certain to be alone.

Five

Lieutenant Hubbard had a court appointment that morning, leaving Detective Thomas free to join in the dragnet by car. The sheriff had confirmed that their suspect had *not* been Loraine, and had to release the very shaken young woman to the real world. No real leads had surfaced as to Loraine's whereabouts. The only reason the media had any interest in her was due to her connection to Tamara Taylor, and that was bound to die out soon enough. The dragnet wouldn't last beyond another few days, even though every cop in the county would have given up their badge for just one crack at the alleged cop-killing "dog lady."

Despite this, Thomas was in good spirits. He had managed to arrange a meeting with Tamara Taylor. "A very, very short meeting," her manager Paul had put it. So far she had been quite adept at avoiding the press, but was kind enough to cooperate with the police—to a point.

He pulled into the studio parking lot and radioed his position, then checked his hair and clothes in the mirror. Really, his wife was the big fan, of course, but it never hurt to look presentable. Inside, the receptionist flashed him a slightly irritated look after seeing that yet another cop had come to visit Tamara. Thomas said nothing to ease her apparent discomfort. That was her own problem.

A heavy door opened, revealing Tamara, followed by a man Thomas believed to be her manager. She forced a smile and shook his hand. Thomas's smile didn't need to be forced. He followed her and the other man into the bowels of the studio. She led the way to a small, soundproofed room and sank onto a well-padded couch. Thomas sat opposite while the other man remained standing.

"Ms. Taylor, I wanted to thank you for taking the time to speak with me," Thomas said. "But may I ask who's joining us for this talk?"

"Hm? Oh, that's Mr. Cardenas, my attorney," she said. "My manager insisted on it."

"Your attorney?" Thomas said. "I doubt if you'll need one. I only have a few questions—"

"—About Loraine and whether or not I know anything about her disappearance?" she finished. Mr. Cardenas patted her shoulder and shook his head slightly. Tamara smiled. "Actually, he's here so I can make him nervous. I tend to say what's on my mind, anyway."

"I can see that," Thomas said, pulling out his notebook and clearing his throat. "As you know, Loraine escaped from jail a day and a half ago. I apologize if you've been asked the same questions already, and that some of them may seem a little strange, but you were her employer, correct?"

"Correct."

"Has she made any attempt to contact you since her escape?"

"No." Tamara was not one who lied easily. The truth

was that Loraine had *not* tried to contact her. She had contacted Loraine.

"Did she have pets?"

"Pets? Not that I know of," she said. "Why?"

"We have reason to believe that she had accomplices who were not entirely . . . human. Witnesses to the escape confirm that a group of animals, or maybe people dressed as animals, assisted her escape."

"What kind of animals are we talking about here?" Tamara asked.

"If you'll just answer my questions, ma'am."

"But I did," she said. "You asked if she had pets, and I said I didn't know."

"Do you know if her roommate had any pets?" Thomas said, ignoring her snappy tone.

"I doubt it," she said. "Besides, they lived in an apartment. They probably weren't even allowed to have any."

Thomas scribbled more notes onto his pad, then asked: "Did she ever discuss her family with you?"

"Not really," she said. "Mostly we talked shop. About work, I mean. All I know is she came from New York 'cuz she hated her mom or something. I didn't need to know anything else."

"Did she ever speak to you about someone named Joanie?" he asked.

"Joanie? Sounds kinda familiar," she said. "Maybe. I guess."

"She corresponded with someone named Joanie, and she lives in Wisconsin," he said. "Does that help?"

"Not really," she said. "Wouldn't it be a better idea to look for her in L.A.?"

"We are, ma'am," Thomas said, suppressing a smile. "We're just looking into every possibility."

"Oh," she said. "Well, sorry I couldn't help you better. She hasn't contacted me. I'm not surprised, I suppose. Too many people recognize me. Hanging with me wouldn't be a good idea, then, would it?"

Thomas closed up his notepad and tucked it away in his coat. "No, I suppose it wouldn't," he said. "Thank you for your time, ma'am. But . . . I did have one more—well, two more questions for you."

"They have to be quick."

"I understand," he said. "The first is, if Loraine did contact you, would you try to convince her to turn herself back in?"

"She doesn't have to answer that," Mr. Cardenas said. Thomas cocked an eyebrow as Tamara took a long look at her attorney, then met the detective's gaze.

"I doubt it," she said.

"Then . . ." Thomas said, glancing at the attorney, "if she asked for help, would you give it?"

"I think so," she said, prompting Mr. Cardenas to throw up his arms in defeat.

"I see," Thomas said. "Are you aware that that would be against the law?"

"It seems something like that would be, but I know she didn't kill her friend," Tamara said.

"I understand how you feel, ma'am, but she did escape from lawful confinement," he explained. "The murder charge will be determined in court. We just want her back so she can have a fair trial."

"That's the idea, I guess," she said. "Was that both of your questions? I wasn't counting."

"No, the other one can wait," Thomas said. "It wasn't an official request. I'd just be taking up your time. Thank you, ma'am."

"You keep calling me 'ma'am,' and I won't let you leave," she said.

"Excuse me?"

"Last chance for your second question," she said.

"It's not important," he said, clasping his hands together. "It was just something for my wife. She's kind of a fan, and—"

"Oh, your *wife's* a fan," Tamara said.

"No, really, she is," Thomas insisted. "I'm not just saying that because—I know that she'd just kill me if she found out that I talked to you and . . . didn't get a memento or something. She'd be happy if you just signed a napkin for her. That was my second question."

"I see," she said. "Wait right here."

She was off the couch and at the door before Thomas could pull out his notepad for her to use. He hardly had time to reflect on just how quickly she had left the room. No doubt she kept herself in better shape than most.

In only a few moments Tamara was back, carrying a photograph. She snatched a pen from Thomas's breast pocket.

"What's your name?" she asked. "And I don't mean 'Officer Whatever.' "

"Detective," he corrected. "Oh, wait, this really is for my wife. Meg. That's her name. I really appreciate this, ma—Ms. Taylor. She's been bugging me for tickets to your concert, but . . . not until the house loan is paid, I keep telling her."

Tamara finished her scribbling and handed both the photo and the pen back to the detective. He tucked the photo under his arm and shook her hand vigorously.

"Thank you, Ms. Taylor," he said. "She's gonna love this. Really."

"Tamara," she corrected.

"Tamara," he repeated. He flashed the photo her way while thanking her again, then left the building. Back in the car, he reported his departure on the radio, then realized that he hadn't read her message. The photo was a standard "glam shot" like any celebrity's, but he decided that she was more attractive without all the makeup and flattering lights.

To the sexiest cop who ever interrogated me, it read. *Love, Luck, and Lollipops, Tamara Taylor.*

His wife would have to wait some time before seeing it.

Loraine was certain she had seen a movie long ago about a man on the run, "wanted for a crime he didn't commit," as she was, that had something to do with Mount Rushmore. It had been a last-minute decision to stop by the monument and play tourist on her way to Wisconsin. For the moment she had forgotten the date and even what day it was while nibbling at junk food grabbed from the snack bar.

She was so exhausted she couldn't fall asleep, and so terrified she felt no fear. She wanted to shrivel up and die as well as fight to the end for her life. It briefly amused her to consider phoning her mother in New York—collect, of course—and saying, "Hi, Mom. You know how you always thought that only lowlifes were *dancers?* Well, now I'm wanted for murder and a jail break. Bye!"

She still did not forgive her mother for showing up at her hospital bed before Uncle Bill's funeral after she was attacked. It didn't matter that Bill was her brother

and Loraine was her daughter; Loraine had convinced
herself long ago that her mother cared about only one
person: herself. Their arguments were legend among the
Turner family, yet Loraine could not even turn to her
siblings for comfort. They were all much older than she,
and had outgrown rebelling against authority in order to
join its ranks. Her memories of family life consisted of
arguments with her mother and fights among her siblings. Father was never part of Loraine's picture, although he had been for the others. Her mother's
becoming pregnant with Loraine must have been the final straw, as Loraine's father left shortly before she was
even born. Perhaps it was then that her mother decided
to bury herself in cigarettes and booze. Or perhaps it
had been much earlier.

Loraine crushed her soft drink cup and slammed it
into a trash can. She had fled that life before she'd even
turned eighteen, to escape those problems and to seek
her fame in kinder places, like Los Angeles. Now, years
later, it seemed she had not stopped being a runaway.

This is different, she thought. *I can't stay there while
every cop around is after me. Even Tamara said that. At
least in Wisconsin I can see Joanie again and see if the
pack will help me. But what if they help the wolf instead?*

Loraine moved into a more secluded spot and shut
her eyes. It wasn't difficult to be alone, as evening was
approaching fast, and the monument, while a tourist at-
traction, was hardly Disneyland. Loraine visualized herself in the park again, complete with the usual boulder.
She lost track of how long she waited, but nothing appeared.

Wolf? she thought. *Wolf, please come out.* Nothing
moved. *I just want to ask you something. It'll just take*

a second, I swear. Not even a slight grunt came from the boulder. Loraine sighed in her "dream" as well as in real life.

Maybe you can hear me, anyway, she thought. *You are in my head, after all. I just wanted to know: if I—I mean when we find the pack again, could I talk to them? Could I do the talking and not you? Just at first if that's okay. If you want to talk later, okay, but I just want to ask them some things. Okay? Wolf? Can't you at least answer that?*

Loraine strained to "hear" even the slightest sound from behind the boulder, or to see something show itself, but there was nothing. Then she felt something—not something physical, but a subtle feeling crept its way into her. It was cold and warm at the same time, an uncertain, jumbled feeling. It was unclear if it had come from the wolf or her own unsettled thoughts. Loraine tried to be an optimist about it, but there was no way to interpret it as a sign of acceptance or rejection. Still, she ended her "visit" with a sense that the wolf would not always be so undecided. Whether the final answer would be "yes" or "no" was what brought the sweat to her brow on this cool evening.

The sun had set by the time Loraine arrived in the Dunlevy bus station in Wisconsin. Just before stepping off the bus, however, she felt it wise to alter herself. For all she knew, every cop in the country was after her. Fortunately the local police allowed her through the station unmolested. It wasn't until she reached a distant phone booth that she realized an odd thing: remembering to alter her appearance seemed more like an instinct than a conscious thought. She smiled to herself, wondering if the wolf had "made contact" again.

Joanie had been expecting her call. She sounded quite concerned, which didn't surprise Loraine. Joanie promised to arrive shortly, leaving Loraine with the task of finding a secluded spot. Shielding herself with a magazine helped.

By the time Joanie arrived at the station, the only encounter Loraine had had was with a panhandler. Loraine spotted Joanie and discarded the magazine, remembering to relax her features to their usual state, but almost forgetting her tote bag in her haste to greet her aunt. Joanie looked quite pleased but worried, especially at the sight of the police. She pulled Loraine closer.

"My car is right outside," she murmured. "Do you have everything?"

"Yeah, let's go," Loraine said.

Joanie grabbed Loraine's single bag and eyed the police as they left. One might have thought, viewing her, that Joanie had been the escapee and not her niece. Outside, she hustled her niece into the car and tossed the tote bag onto the rear seat. Loraine had never ridden with her aunt before, so she wasn't certain if Joanie always drove so quickly.

"Were those police talking to you?" Joanie asked after they'd left the station behind. Loraine turned on the radio before answering.

"Nope," she said. "Except 'hello' or something."

"Why were they there, then?" Joanie asked.

"Cops are always at bus stations," Loraine said. "You know, like at airports, too. Haven't you ever been to a bus station?"

"Yes, I have," Joanie said. "I guess I forgot, hon."

The radio began its slew of commercials, so Loraine surfed through the stations until something resembling hard rock came up. Joanie, unknown to her, had been looking into the rearview mirror about every three seconds as if afraid of being followed.

"Are we going to the ranch?" Loraine asked after some time.

"Yes, of course, hon," Joanie said. "You don't have to stay at a hotel."

"I was asking for a different reason," Loraine said. "In fact, you should drop me off somewhere. I'm not really here to see you."

"Really?"

"Ah, I guess that didn't come out right," Loraine said. "What I meant was there's another reason I came here. I should've just taken a taxi."

"Do you remember when you called from Idaho?" Joanie asked, glancing into her mirror again. "When another call came in, and I didn't get back to you?"

"Yeah."

"That was a policeman," Joanie said. "He wanted to know if you'd been in contact with me recently."

Loraine said nothing. Joanie also said nothing. Loraine reached for the radio dial again, then reconsidered.

"I guess we're going to the cops, then," she muttered.

"No," Joanie said quickly. "I said we're going to the ranch, and we are."

"I'm sorry I haven't told you anything about this," Loraine said. "I've just been so scared. Really, you should drop me off somewhere. Right here, if you can."

"We're on the freeway, hon."

"You know what I mean," Loraine said. "Please,

Joanie. Let me off. They'll arrest you for helping me. All I've done since coming here is screw up your life. Pull off there."

"You have not screwed up my life," she insisted. "Just keep low."

"But Uncle Bill died because of me, and now—"

"I don't want to hear any more talk like that," Joanie snapped. "Now just stay low like I told you to. You can tell me what happened on the way or when we get to the ranch—that's your choice—but enough blaming yourself about Bill."

"I'm sorry," Loraine whispered, slumping down into the seat until her head just barely reached the window. Joanie clicked off the radio. The music had been helping Loraine relax, but she knew better than to object.

"Like I said," Joanie continued, "the police called while we were talking. I told them we hadn't spoken."

"Ah, jeez, you lied to them?"

"I guess I did," Joanie said quietly. "But it's been done, so . . . The least I can do is offer you a place to sleep and eat for a day or so. Even so, why would you come here of all places? Or are you just trying to get as far away as possible?"

"That's part of it," Loraine said. "The other part is that there are some people here that I need to see. Are you really going to try to hide me from the cops?"

"I wish you wouldn't put it that way," Joanie said with a sigh. "It would help if you told me more. Whatever happened isn't exactly the top story here."

"Thank God," Loraine said. "I'm not as famous as I thought," she added, forcing a laugh. The sigh that followed was not forced. "They think I killed Roxanne. She was my roommate and best friend."

"My God!"

"I don't think I did, though," she said. "I mean—no, of course I didn't kill her. She was my best friend. Practically my *only* friend, so why would I kill her?"

"You mean that you escaped the police while being arrested?"

"Something like that," she said. "But not because of me. There were some other people who broke me out, thinking they were doing me a favor. But they weren't. I know that they live around here, so they're the ones I need to meet."

"Who are these people you're talking about?"

"I'm afraid that's the part I can't tell you about," Loraine said. "I'm sorry, Joanie. Really. It just wouldn't be a good idea for you to know. I appreciate any help you've given me so far—especially this—but I won't be able to stay very long. Maybe a day at best. After that I have to find them and make them help me clear my name." She added under her breath, "If I can."

Silence settled between them. Joanie never abandoned her habit of looking out the mirror every few seconds. Loraine turned toward the car door eventually, still slumped as low as possible into her seat, and spent the rest of the trip afraid to even peek out the window for fear of who might see her.

Six

Officially, the countywide dragnet was over due to lack of funds and manpower. Unofficially, the search would never end until Loraine was found in one condition or another. Detective Thomas spent his breakfast staring at the blurry photographs taken of the breakout. The photo lab people had done their best to enhance and clarify the images, which had not amounted to much. He was still stuck with fuzzy shots of fuzzy creatures, at least one of which might have been running on two feet.

Phone taps had long ago been placed on Michael, Linda, and Tamara. Linda was Roxanne's girlfriend, or "widow," as she had described herself to one officer. So far no one seemed to have had any contact with Loraine, and the taps were due to be pulled. Too many concerned citizens had called in with tips, all of which had been dead ends. Thomas had never been so frustrated by any case. There weren't even any fingerprints to check. Yet there seemed to be clues everywhere; why couldn't he put any of them together?

He felt silly pursuing his "trained animal" angle—he had even called every animal shelter and zoo in the county—but there seemed few other explanations. "Like someone was cutting me with a hot knife," said one officer who had needed twenty stitches in his chest. A call to Missing Persons added more to the stress count: Officer Devon Wyman had still not reappeared since being attacked the day before Loraine's escape, and Thomas couldn't shake the feeling that Loraine had something to do with it.

As usual half of his breakfast was tossed as he headed out. As usual it was cold, anyway. He'd had a suspicion about someone since the day before, and it was time to act on it. Getting permission from Hubbard would be harder than arm-wrestling a bear, but since the lieutenant was elsewhere just then, Thomas would have to suffer the consequences later. He was certain the results would be worth it, though.

Loraine had fallen asleep right away in her old guest room, but she had troubled dreams. She was almost used to them by now. She had already been trying to contact the wolf while asleep, on those rare occasions when she knew she was dreaming, with no results. Visualizing the boulder in the park seemed the only way to find the beast so far.

She was greeted with the heavenly smells of Joanie's home cooking that morning. She was even given a choice of eggs and bacon, leftover quiche, or wheat pancakes. She asked for a little of all three. It was only after she'd sat down that Loraine noticed something about Joanie.

"Have you lost weight?" she asked.

"Oh, I don't know," Joanie said. "I haven't weighed myself in ages. Maybe I have, though. Now that I think of it, some of my clothes have been going on a little easier. Maybe it's the Mourning Diet at work."

"The 'Morning Diet'?" Loraine said, who prided herself on having tried every diet known and unknown. "Never heard of it."

"And may you never have to, dear," Joanie said with a bittersweet smile as she set down her own breakfast. "I suppose I just haven't been eating as much since Bill died. It's just me to cook for now."

"Oh," Loraine said quietly. "The 'Mourning Diet.' I see what you mean now. I'm sorry."

"It's just a little joke, hon," Joanie said, patting her hand. "It's nice to be able to cook for somebody else again. And . . . I realize you can't stay long, but it's nice to see you again."

"I just don't want you to be in any more trouble than you probably are," Loraine said. "For helping me, I mean."

"I believed you when you said you didn't kill your friend," Joanie said. "I just wonder if you know who did, then?"

"I've got a good idea," Loraine said, taking the last bites of her first decent meal in too long. Joanie was too polite to chide her for eating so quickly.

"Well," Joanie said, poking daintily at her own food. "If there's anything I can do—"

Loraine tried to speak, and only managed some loud mumblings through the food in her mouth. She waved her hands frantically while swallowing as much as she could. Some of it didn't quite make it, sending Loraine for her drink. Joanie waited patiently for her niece to calm down.

"Don't worry about me," Loraine croaked out finally.

"I know you will, anyway, but try not to. The less you know, the better."

Joanie did try to squeeze some more information from her niece in spite of her admonition, but Loraine insisted on secrecy. Perhaps sometime soon she would share all with her aunt, but until then, Loraine would try to protect her the only way she knew how.

True to her word, Loraine gathered her things after breakfast and hugged her aunt good-bye. She stepped out into the daylight, then shrank back when she spotted a distant figure coming up the long driveway. Loraine ducked into the doorway and stared at her aunt.

"Who's that coming?" she asked. "Is it a cop?"

"What?" Joanie said, peeking outside. "Oh, no, that's just Roger."

"He shouldn't see me."

"Why not? He'd be delighted to see you again," Joanie said. "Or . . . maybe not?"

"To be honest," Loraine said softly, "I kind of miss him. But do you think he's the kind of person who'd turn me in?"

Joanie almost answered, then peered around the corner as Roger's truck pulled ever closer to the house. She held Loraine by the shoulders and began guiding her away from the door.

"I don't know," she said. "I really don't."

Loraine nodded and let Joanie lead her to the back door. She promised to distract Roger long enough to allow Loraine to make a break for the rear gate. Roger was already making his way up the front steps when

Joanie appeared in the doorway. He tipped his hat as he approached.

"Morning, ma'am," he said. Joanie took him by the arm and ushered him inside.

"Just the man I needed," she said with a smile. "Would you happen to have any idea how to set my VCR to tape something every day?"

"Uhh, I suppose," he said. "I thought you hardly watched TV."

"Well . . ." she said, "there's this one cooking show I caught the other day, and—"

"Yeah, that makes sense," Roger said, patting her hand.

Outside, Loraine spotted the rear gate. It appeared to be about a hundred feet farther away than she remembered. She had no choice now but to trust Joanie to keep Roger busy. No one else was present but some stray llamas who chewed away contentedly at the moss and lichen. Allowing a glance or two back, Loraine kept low and crept toward the gate, her back hairs raised in readiness for anything.

She neglected to prepare her ears for the assault that sent her to the ground in a tight ball. The closest llamas were no longer grazing contentedly, but shrieking and wailing at nothing more than her very presence. Loraine kept her hands clamped over her ears and found the strength to raise her head and lock gazes with the closest, and loudest, beast of the lot. Rather than run like the others, fear locked it into place as it screamed at this strange and new enemy.

Loraine was quickly becoming its enemy. A rage was building fast, and not because of the horrible shrieking. Her rage was equal to a hunger that grew as quickly.

She stood up slowly, pulling her hands away from her ears to let the full volume assault her senses. Her fingers stretched, as did her fingernails, until a set of ten small knives stood ready to open this miserable beast.

Another noise from inside the house startled her. She did not look back, but shot past the beast at full speed. Two figures ran from the house, determined to calm down the livestock. The llama finally broke free of its terror and ran from the two to join its companions. Joanie and Roger watched the animals in amazement. Suddenly none of them seemed the slightest bit agitated anymore, when the whole herd had been screaming their throats raw seconds earlier.

Roger scanned the area, and caught sight of a blur that moved far too quickly for any animal that he knew. It seemed to be running on two legs, likely making it a human being, but then, a human being could not have cleared the twelve feet of gate with one running jump.

"What the hell was that?" he asked himself more than Joanie.

"Say again?"

He pointed to the now empty distance. "Did you see that?" he asked. "Something was running away from the ranch. Probably what spooked them. You didn't see it?"

"Well, describe it," she said. Roger took one long, last look at the gate, then turned away.

"Ahh, hell," he said, waving it off. "I couldn't tell you anything. We'd better check out the animals. Forget I said anything."

"If you say so," Joanie said, staring off into the distance and whispering a brief prayer for her prodigal niece.

* * *

Detective Thomas sipped at his lukewarm coffee and set it back on the dashboard. He had been parked across the street from a small performing arts center for a few hours now. Fortunately Hubbard had not attempted to contact him at all that morning, as there was little to justify his actions so far.

His stomach grumbled in protest at skipping yet another meal, so Thomas stepped out and headed for a fast-food stand. It was still within sight of the arts center, allowing him the opportunity to stretch his legs. Not for long, though; he was halfway through a burger when several people emerged from the building. Some were dressed in leotards and suits—dancers, no doubt—but one woman was escorted to a car by a phalanx of men. Thomas left the remains of his lunch behind and hurried back to the car, being careful not to look too rushed.

His unmarked car was parked across from and behind Tamara and her entourage. He was occupied getting his car started and into gear, or he might have noticed Tamara's apparent glance his way just before being ushered into the back seat of her own car.

Thomas waited until the car was just within eyesight before pulling out into a U-turn. He was careful to keep one or two cars in between his and Tamara's. Still, it was a chore keeping up with their convoluted path. He surmised that none of them were locals, or they might not have been driving as though lost. On the other hand, he'd seen far worse driving from so-called "experienced" Angelenos.

Twice he actually lost the vehicle—briefly—until it pulled into a restaurant parking lot. He waited for the others to reach the entrance before getting out himself. He paused outside the front for a few minutes to allow for seating, and then headed inside. His timing was good; the group had been seated. At a glance he saw that Tamara had her back to him—even better. Thomas took a seat at the bar and ordered a diet soda. A mirror lined the wall, allowing him a partial view of the table. He noticed some movement, then glanced back to see Tamara rising and heading off for some other part of the restaurant. From his vantage point he would be able to see her returning to the table.

After a moment, someone passed behind him and nudged him, mumbling, "Excuse me." He murmured a reply, then saw in the mirror that it was Tamara, who had somehow circled the entire restaurant without his seeing it. He looked down and waited for her to move on, then heard more voices just behind him.

"Excuse me, I'm so sorry, I know you're eating, but aren't you Tamara Taylor?"

"Yes, I am."

"Oh! Oh, this is just wonderful. I just love . . ."

The conversation was directly behind him and continued in this vein for a minute or so as Tamara indulged the young woman's request for an autograph. Thomas was suddenly lightheaded and realized that he'd been holding his breath. He resumed breathing normally and hiding his face with the menu. Finally the female fan was appeased, and Tamara headed back to the table without further incident.

The return to the arts center was even more confusing than before. The driver seemed to be making up his own laws of the road as he went along. At the arts center, street parking had disappeared, so Thomas began circling the block when a dispatcher broke in.

"One-twenty-three, report ten-twenty, over."

Thomas snatched up his radio. "This is one-twenty-three, on Gower and Vine, over."

"You have a ten-nineteen from Lieutenant Hubbard, over."

"I'm not surprised, over."

"Shall I repeat his exact words, one-twenty-three?"

"Negative. ETA in fifteen minutes, over."

Hubbard ran his fingers along his thinning hair and sighed. He held a file in his hand and seemed undecided as to what to do with it. He appeared quite calm, but for all Thomas knew, underneath Hubbard could have been a full blast furnace. Not knowing frightened him more than any temper tantrum could have. Lieutenant Becker had been famous for his tirades, but at least Thomas had always known where he stood. Not so with this new chief.

"May I ask what you were hoping to accomplish out there?" Hubbard asked finally.

"Just trying to get a lead, sir," Thomas said.

"And without a partner?" the lieutenant continued. "Why were you out there alone?"

"No one else was available, sir," Thomas said, his voice fading as he spoke. He cleared his throat. "You know what we have on this. Plenty of clues and not a single lead from any of them. Except Taylor. When we last spoke, I just—I don't think she told the truth about not having made contact with Loraine. And she admitted that she'd help her."

"And that was enough to waste half the day?" Hubbard said. "What kind of evidence is that? Look at this," he said, finally tossing down his file. "You know these are just a few of the cases. Some have escaped from lawful confinement, just like our little starlet Loraine. All of them have been gone longer than she has."

"Sir, that girl is a cop-killer."

"No one reported that she harmed any officers," Hubbard said. "I understand that for most of the people here, bringing her back is personal. Police officers were killed or injured during her escape, but you can't let your gut feelings and hunches decide everything you do."

"I'm just frustrated, sir."

"I appreciate that," Hubbard said. "We all are. But you know how the press has been about this story. We can't afford to do anything that's not standard operating procedure."

"Considering how bizarre this case is to begin with, you sure we should be by the book?" Thomas asked.

"We should always be by the book," Hubbard said. "That'll be all."

Thomas had more to say, but reconsidered. It was probably best that the lieutenant not know the details of his encounter with Tamara. He turned to leave the office, then heard Hubbard speaking quietly.

"Detective," he said.

"Yessir."

"Consider yourself reprimanded."

Thomas paused a moment. "I see," he said, then left the office. He remembered a longtime detective who had been "reprimanded" for various reasons very shortly after Hubbard had arrived. Within two months that detective had been suspended. Soon enough Thomas's "reprimand" would be in his file, and he knew where that could lead. Still, it was not in his nature to cower in a corner and genuflect to the Powers That Be. He would do the best job he could even if it got him fired.

Thomas wanted to operate under standard operating procedures himself, but not every case was cracked that way, and this was one case that seemed to defy any such procedures. The lieutenant had spoken, however, which meant that Thomas would have to be even more careful about making his own S.O.P.s.

Seven

Loraine never in a moment held the illusion that she was the outdoor type. She preferred the concrete confines of a city over wide-open spaces any day. To her, the smog-colored sunsets of Los Angeles were much prettier than anything this clean air could come up with. Yet, like it or not, a part of her had been awakened that wanted nothing more than to be lost in this wilderness forever.

If she had remained at Joanie's instead of bolting in panic, she might have packed a few amenities for her trip. As it was, Loraine had fled with nothing more than a breakfast in her belly and her tote bag. It was nightfall now. Her bag held a flashlight in desperate need of new batteries, yet she kept it packed away. The others might not appreciate light flitting around their eyes.

Who "the others" were was not entirely clear to her in this form. Loraine had never met them as herself, only as her alter ego. She sniffed at the air a few times and cocked her head to listen for . . . what, she didn't know. This place was much colder than California, even at this supposedly warm time of the year. Her bag held only two other sets of clothing besides what she wore, although Joanie had made certain that they were clean again. She counted over $1,600 left from what Tamara had given her. If she continued spending it at this rate, it might be gone in a week. It was small consolation that the ones she sought most likely had no use for money.

She sat alone at the edge of the woods and fought the growing despair that moistened her eyes. She was cold, hungry, and thirsty and missed everything that she had taken for granted: running water, electricity, and most of all, television. It had been more of a parent to her than her real mother. It taught her how to read and write, share, sing, and even how to laugh. Sometimes it had been her only friend. She used to watch daytime talk shows, not out of boredom, but for amusement. Most had been funnier than any sitcom, but the humor escaped her as she realized that her present situation would have been perfect for any one of them. "Are you a werewolf wanted for a crime you didn't commit? Call Ricki now!" At another time she might have laughed at this, but not now. It only served to drive her deeper into her sorrow.

Loraine forced herself to push aside the anguish, anger and fear as best she could, shut her eyes, and imagine the park again. As in real life, night had come to her park, and she sat by her imaginary tree and watched the boulder for movement. It was very difficult for her to picture the place at night. As a child she had always been terrified of the dark, and she still feared it considerably. Yet the wolf flourished in darkness. If she could contact it again, it might feel more welcome in such an environment.

She "heard" nothing from behind the rock. No grunts, whimpering, or even a bark. Without a sound the wolf emerged from behind, standing tall and without a sign of pain. Loraine felt her face flush, but whether from fear or from joy, she was uncertain.

The wolf moved to a few feet in front of the rock and watched her. It could not show expression like a human, but from the sparkle in its eyes, Loraine sensed that it was pleased with her meeting choice this time.

Hello, wolf, she thought. *Or do you have another name? A . . . two-legger friend of mine says that you do.*

She is not a two-legger, thought the wolf.

Oh, she thought. *Yeah, I guess she isn't, really. She's like you. Or me. She's like us.*

The wolf's lips curled very briefly in what could have been a smile. *What do you want with me?* it thought.

You probably know what I'm trying to do, Loraine thought.

I do not know, it thought. *I only know that I seek the others. I care not for your plans.*

But that's what I'm doing, too, she thought. *I'm seeking 'the others.' You see? We want the same thing. Maybe we don't have to be—*

We do not seek the same thing, the wolf thought. *I will find them, and they will not speak to you.*

And why not? she thought. *They were human, too, once. Or is a two-legger beneath them now?*

I would not presume to question the others, the wolf thought. *My goal is to join them and learn their ways for all time. I do not think you would have a place with them.*

Well, I will if I have to, Loraine thought, now standing from her spot under the tree. She was surprised to see that she barely stood higher than the wolf, who was larger than she thought a wolf could be. *Am I really this big when I change?* she thought to herself.

That will be up to them—allowing you to speak, the wolf thought. _Is this all you wished to say to me? That you seek the pack?_

_No,_ she thought. _No . . . well, that's part of it. Look, I can see that we both want the same thing, but for different reasons. If they really won't talk to me, do you think you could talk to them for me? Let them know what we need?_

What you need, the wolf thought. _Not I._

Then it doesn't even matter to you that my friend was killed by one of us? Loraine thought. _You have no desire to punish him? To make him pay for slaughtering an innocent person? He ripped her to pieces!_

The others severed their bond with him, the wolf thought. _You do not understand how great a punishment that is for our kind. We—_

Yeah, yeah, Tamara told me all about that, too, Loraine thought. _And she chose to leave her pack, so it's not like we're gonna die if we don't run around with a bunch of dogs for the rest of—_

Dogs?

Why won't you help me, wolf? Loraine thought. _Think about it! Maybe being exiled is a great punishment for our kind but that means he's still free! He's probably still in L.A., ripping up as many people as he wants, and who could stop him? Nobody can shoot him unless they have silver bullets, and who has any of those? Not your typical cop, I know that!_

What does this have to do with me? the wolf thought.

So even that doesn't bother you? Loraine thought. _That he's free to keep killing more people? More best friends? More . . . Roxannes?_

The wolf was silent for a long time. It pulled its gaze

away to look about as if hoping for the others to arrive and take it away. But the two of them were alone. Loraine could feel it getting ready to leave, and concentrated on the wolf, trying to make it stay. So far it seemed to be working.

The pack . . . did what it thought best, the wolf thought finally. *I am but a cub to them. I would not presume to question their ways.*

I can't do this without you, wolf, she thought. *I need your help—your skills, to track him down and punish him. I know I was wrong to fight you the way I did. To hurt you. And . . . I was hoping you could tell me your name. So you won't be such a stranger to me.*

Again the lips curled briefly into the pseudo-smile. *Perhaps I will not be a stranger some day,* the wolf thought. *But until then . . .* It disappeared behind the rock before finishing its words.

The wolf kept its nose low to the ground as it prowled through the darkness. Even in the thick of the woods, it was difficult to steer clear of the two-leggers' dwellings. The place she sought would need to be far from any two-leggers. Her search would be long and tiring, but the bond would guide her. It was weak, and she strayed often, but the bond never left her. It would always be there unless the others broke it. This fate she would fight to avoid at any cost, even if it meant destroying the two-legger within her. She might be destroyed herself as well, but it would be worth the risk.

No welcome sounds or scents filled the air. Crickets chirped, wings fluttered, but the pack song was nowhere, nor even the pounding of their feet as they hunted their prey. She wondered if they had yet returned from the south.

A faint rustling of bushes caused her ears to prick. There was no wind to speak of that night, so she lowered her head and searched for a scent. It was difficult without a wind, but the ground revealed faint traces of a small animal's path. Her ears flattened as she crept up to the bushes. Another faint rustle sounded just to the side; a small shadow moved behind a bush. The wolf saw well enough without the moon's light and followed the shadow to a spot between the bushes. With barely a grunt she sprang forward, surprising a raccoon, which only had time to squeal before dying.

She ripped and tore at the creature, pulling off and swallowing whole limbs, and gulped down the animal in barely five bites. Licking her lips, she backed away from the bushes into the clearing and turned around, then yelped. Ten dark shapes surrounded her, and ten pairs of different colored eyes seemed to float within the darkness. They made no sound—*had* made no sound—in their approach. She listened for their heartbeats, their breathing, but could hear only her own working at twice their normal paces.

Clumsy, one of them said. She cocked her head and was able to breathe again. One of the shapes moved closer—the one that had spoken. She still could not make out any features.

You were clumsy, cub, it said again. *We have been following you all this time.*

Follow——? she said. *But I sought you all the while. I-I felt for the bond, for your scents, but the bond was weak and there were no scents. Wait. Please don't say that——*

It has not been severed, the voice said. It was a female's voice. She could also see the other wolf better, and realized that it was probably the Alpha that she had met before. *You are of the pack, if you still wish it,* the Alpha continued.

I am glad, she said. *Yes, yes, I wish to be of the pack. I sought you because of this. And yet—yet—*

You must conquer your other self, the Alpha said. *Then the bond will be much stronger.*

She wishes me to speak with you on her behalf, she said. *She does not think that—*

Her wishes mean nothing to us, the Alpha said. *In time, they will mean nothing to you. Run with us.*

In an instant the air was filled with the dark forms of the wolves who rushed by, and even over, her. Their speed caused a wind that whistled through the trees and bushes. Night birds screeched and fluttered away in fear, and she realized they would speak to her, but on their terms only. She followed their wake and struggled mightily to keep pace with them. She never quite caught up completely, and almost lost them several times, but used the bond to steer her as best she could.

It was an hour at full speed before the others slowed enough for her to begin to catch up. It had been too long since she had felt the earth under her feet and the breeze licking at her face. She panted loudly as she ran, but from excitement, not fatigue. It filled her with such joy that the pack would let her run with them. She finally saw the Alpha slowing to a walk. Her excitement got the best of her, and she leaped forward, hoping to engage the Alpha in play. The Alpha spun around, spread her front legs, and let loose a growl that could have stopped her in midair. It almost did. Her legs flailed in an effort to slow herself down. She missed the Alpha and landed on her rump, then scrambled to her feet and shook off the dirt, spraying some in their faces. The Alpha snapped at her. Her eyes widened into miniature plates, and then she hung her head.

Forgive me, she said. *I only thought— I just wanted to—*

The Alpha stepped forward and circled her slowly. She dared raise her head just enough to see a twinkle in the Alpha's eyes.

It will take time to master our ways, cub. But are you here to run with us, or to follow the wishes of the two-legger?

She now locked gazes with the Alpha. Clearly she was the oldest female of the pack. Something had happened to her mate—the real Alpha—but now was hardly the time to inquire. That time might never come.

Do you ever? she asked the Alpha. The Alpha seemed puzzled. *Do you ever . . . let the two-legger emerge?*

Not for many years, the Alpha said. *And it will be this way forever, as it can be for you.*

Her attention was caught by the others, who stood around them both in a circle. One of them, a male, seemed very familiar to her.

You, she said to him. The male's ears pricked. *I remember you. You are with the pack because of me. I was . . . in a cage . . .*

You speak the truth, the male said. *You brought me over. But I do not blame you for this. My place is here, with the others. If I had been in a cage, I, too, would have lashed, as you had.*

Another two-legger . . . shot me with a loud thing, she said.

A gun, he said. *My partner meant to stop you with it because I was being bitten.*

Forgive me for—

Cub! The Alpha's bark startled her. In an instant her attention was back on the old female. *The two-legger confuses you,* the Alpha said. *You must learn to make her sleep before you can truly learn all our ways.*

She . . . she wants me to find the one who brought me out, she said.

That one is no longer spoken of, the Alpha said. *He does not exist.*

But he killed her friend, she said. *Because of him, the two-leggers think she killed her friend, and she wishes my—perhaps even your help at finding him again.*

The Alpha made a sound that, to a two-legger, would seem like just a bark, but she knew it as laughter.

Her wishes mean nothing to us, the Alpha said. *And that one is not to be spoken of again. He disgraced himself with his cowardice. This is all that need be said. Let the two-leggers hunt her. She will be gone, forever asleep within you while you run with us for all time. For now, your thoughts are addled, cub. No doubt your two-legger wishes to seek the exile and kill him, if she is able. They seem to exist for no other reason but to kill each other. We freed you from the cage because the exile had failed so miserably. Now you are free to join us.*

I . . . I wish to join you, Lady, she said, her head low. *But the two-legger . . . She is so angry that he can still hunt, even if alone.*

Run with us, the Alpha said. She heard the words, then looked up to see nothing but a blur of motion quickly disappearing into the darkness. Panic motivated her to follow more than the bond this time. The gap was widening quickly, until she heard a voice not from the others but within her own mind.

Follow them! it cried. Her legs moved at twice their speed now; the pack was actually growing nearer. As before, the pace was nonstop for an hour. The ground was growing steeper and rockier, but she never slowed for a moment. She followed the pack's path between the trees and over rocks and ledges, until the top of a steep hill came into view. The moon was as high and as bright as it would be at this phase, which was hardly enough to illuminate the eyes staring at her from above.

Only a few members of the pack watched her finish the climb to the top, where she joined them in their circle. The elder members looked up at the stars and let their voices come out in a chord like she had never heard before. One by one the others joined in, until all but the cub had united in the pack's song. She expected the song to be about the moon or the sky or hunting, but it was a song of mourning for the Alpha's former mate. So strong was the emotion of the song that she finally joined in, fighting tears forming for a wolf she had never known. But she felt his loss as keenly as any of the others.

Eight

Two males circled each other. One was older, but smaller than the cub that challenged him. None of the pack made a sound, not even the newest member who watched the ritual in awe. So, too, did the former policeman among them, who had never seen the contest to become the Alpha. By now the new female had learned the wolves became stronger with age; the older wolf would have that advantage if the younger were not so large. No one knew which would win: strength and experience or size and speed.

She wondered if the entire challenge would consist of mere growls and snaps, until the younger wolf made the first attack. He leaped straight for the elder's throat, who rolled forward at the last instant. The two beasts tumbled over each other until the younger managed to pull free first and snap at his opponent before baring his teeth. The elder shook away the dirt but made no noisy displays of courage. He simply circled the younger wolf slowly, never flinching once from his gaze. The younger turned to follow every step, until the elder stopped, and waited.

With a grunt the younger leaped again, counting on its mass to knock the elder senseless, but again at the last instant the elder's front paws became claws. He stepped aside on almost human legs and grabbed the huge beast by the neck. The younger wolf yelped as its own momentum was used to fling him far up and away, many feet from the pack. He somersaulted over bushes, only to be stopped by a very solid tree in its path.

All of them heard the snap of bones. The elder wolf remained as before, as the pseudo two-legger, and listened. For a long time no sound but the song of crickets was heard, so the elder turned toward the female Alpha, transforming back to its "normal" form with every step. The pack surrounded them in a circle to acknowledge the victory and to show acceptance of their new leader. The cub hung back, however. She could not help searching the darkness for some movement from the challenger. Strangely enough she felt disappointed at how brief the battle had been. Surely they had been more evenly matched than that.

Finally, with her head low, she joined the others, who soon began their song to welcome and honor the new Alpha. She eventually joined in, but with less joy in her voice than the others. Then she was startled by a new voice behind her, and turned to see the younger wolf, beaten but still very much alive. It was true, then, she remembered, that they did not die from normal wounds. Just as she had healed quickly from the two-leggers' bullets, so had he from shattered bones.

It was still night when Loraine woke up. She lay in a fetal position against a very large tree. She surmised that it might be near morning, as it was not very difficult to see. Looking up at the stars, she saw that a full moon hung low in the sky. Her heartbeat quickened, for she remembered that it had been weeks away from a full moon the last time she and the wolf had "spoken."

It was not until she dragged herself back onto her feet that she noticed something strange: silence. It was night, yet not a cricket, bird, or anything else made a sound. The woods were also different than she remembered. She was surrounded by trees and bushes as before, yet somehow they seemed much simpler than the real thing. They were almost . . . abstract versions.

A sound from behind startled her; Loraine whirled about and almost fell over a large rock. The dark eyes of a wolf glared at her, but she was afraid for only a moment.

Wolf? she thought, straightening up. *That's you, isn't it?*

It gave only a grunt as a reply. Loraine took it as a positive response and stepped away from the boulder. She stopped and looked back at it, then at the wolf, and pointed at it.

Wait a minute. She stopped and looked all around herself once more, her gaze finally resting on the wolf. *I didn't call you,* she thought. *Or is this a dream? It doesn't seem like a dream.*

They will not help you, the wolf thought.

What? Who won't?

The others, the wolf thought.

The pack won't help me? Loraine thought, still in amazement over what the wolf had accomplished. It had imagined its own version of her mental park and summoned *her.* This feat also disturbed her, but the wolf would never know that if she could guard her feelings well enough.

And why should they? was the wolf's reply.

Because they got me into this mess, that's why!
Loraine thought. *Shit. Are you sure I can't talk to them?
Tell them they have to talk to me!*

They would rather that you sleep, the wolf thought.
What?

You must find the exiled one on your own.

On OUR own, you mean, she thought. *Where I go,
you go, remember?*

The silences in between their "speech" were never
more eerie than now.

Can you feel it also? it thought finally.

Feel what?

The pull, it thought. *They still want me to run with
them. Can you not hear their call? Their song?*

Loraine shook her head, baffled, until her head turned
toward a new sound. It was very faint, very distant, but
a chorus of howls could be heard drifting in from the
woods. Loraine listened for a long time before turning
her attention back to the wolf. It did not return her attention, but kept its own focused on where the pack was.

Stop it, Loraine thought. *You're doing that yourself.
These are your woods; you can put whatever you want
in them, so that's just you and not them.*

The wolf shut its eyes and began humming very softly.
It was already standing, and now began swaying back
and forth to some hidden rhythm. It never hummed
loudly enough to truly sing with the others, but its body
swayed even more to its own beat. To Loraine, it was
just noise.

After a moment Loraine realized that the wolf was
not going to sing, but was dancing to the others' music.
She watched wide-eyed as it ran to and fro in a primi-
tive, but quite elegant, dance. And for a moment—just

a moment—she felt very much what the wolf felt. She felt the joy and longing of the beast; then the feeling was gone, replaced by her own anger. Without thinking, Loraine dropped to her hands and knees, kept her head low and growled. The wolf seemed not to hear at first, then stopped its dance mid-step to stare at her in bewilderment. Only then, looking at the beast, did Loraine realize what she was doing. Her hands shook as she rose to two feet once more. She and the wolf watched each other a long time. Silence had replaced the wolfsong.

I'm sorry, Loraine thought. *Yes, I can feel it. But we can't join them. Maybe not ever.*

What?

Maybe we can come to some compromise, Loraine thought, *but I couldn't bear spending the rest of my life running with a pack of animals. They're not even going to help us find 'the exiled one,' whoever the hell that is. Can't you even get a name from them? A picture?*

A picture?

Dumb question, Loraine thought. *How about a name? Where he might be now and how to track him down?*

I will run with them, the wolf thought. *They will teach me these things. Perhaps.*

I said I don't want to run with them, Loraine thought.

But I do, the beast thought. *And if your only thought is to 'track him down,' this I will learn. The exiled one knows our ways better than I. I have no wish to face him unprepared.*

Well, I don't want to, either, Loraine thought. *Which means that I don't have much choice but to trust you. But how long are we supposed to 'run with them'?* An uneasy silence followed. Loraine wished for some sound—any sound, even the pack's howling—to break it.

I do not know, the wolf thought at last.

Detective Curry made it a point of showing the final coroner reports on Roxanne to Detective Thomas. The two had worked in the same department for years, but had never been partners. Still, they had struck up a fast friendship that easily withstood their respective department changes. Both men had always been quite open to "crossing over" cases more than many other detectives, who adhered to a "you do your job, I'll do mine" philosophy.

Thomas was on the phone as Curry dropped the coroner's folder into the "In" tray. Thomas flipped through it without missing a beat in his conversation. He winced at the photographs within, but made no sound to indicate to his listener that he was reeling from disgust. After a moment, though, he was forced to shut the folder until he could wrap up his conversation.

He slammed down the receiver and held his stomach. "Jeez, Tim, I haven't had lunch yet," he said.

"Well, then, there's nothing in there you can toss out," Curry said, taking back his photos. "I thought you'd be interested in knowing what we're dealing with."

"Good point," Thomas said. "What the hell *are* we dealing with?"

Curry flipped open his folder and turned to the coroner's description. "Well, someone who can cause multiple lacerations, massive loss of blood, major organ damage, etc. etc. . . ."

"And the coroner thinks our little runaway did that?"

"He doesn't know what to think," Curry said. "He found this girl's blood and our little runaway's mixed in her blood. Loraine had her friend's skin and hair under her nails, but the doc thinks her friend's wounds were too wide and deep to have been caused by some girl's fingernails. They're more like slash marks."

"I thought a weapon was never recovered," Thomas said. "Does he think she used a knife?"

Curry shook his head. "Wounds are too big and uneven," he said.

"So she used a dull knife."

"You know what I think . . ." Curry began.

"Yeah, that animals did it," Thomas finished. "The same ones that broke her out of here and trashed half the station to do it. But what are we thinking about here? Does that mean that Loraine trained a pack of vicious animals to rip apart her roommate, and not only that, but took a few swipes at her herself? This is getting sicker and sicker."

"Isn't it, though?" Curry said. "And it's all yours until she's back in the slammer."

Thomas did not reply. Curry could see he was already deep in thought, although he had one last question for his friend. Curry's voice finally managed to pull Thomas from his sea of thought. He straightened up in his chair.

"Sorry?" he said. "Did you say something?"

"I asked if Officer Wyman is still missing," Curry said. Thomas nodded vaguely. "Not back since his attack?" Curry asked. Thomas shook his head, his attention still on the photos. He looked over at the desk beside his, whose splintered corner was yet to be sanded down since the breakout.

"You okay?" Curry asked. Thomas looked up and forced a smile, then shook his head.

"Ahh, just stuff," he mumbled. "Sorry, Tim. You need to get going, I know. So do I," he said, rising to pull on his coat. He and Curry headed for the exit, when Thomas caught a glimpse of the mail clerk dumping a manila envelope into his box. It was not an interoffice envelope, but a plain one marked "Detective Thomas—Personal." His curiosity was piqued in spite of his haste to leave. Curry stood by while he fumbled with the opening.

"Expecting something?" he asked.

"With my luck it's a love letter from Hubbard," Thomas grumbled, then pulled out another 8 X 10 glossy of Tamara Taylor.

"What the—?" Curry said from behind him. " 'To the sexiest cop who ever followed me. Love, luck and lollipops . . . Tamara Taylor'? Hell, I'm in the wrong department!" he said, giving his friend a swat on the back. "All the glamour is with the fugitives!"

To Curry's surprise, Thomas crumpled up the photo and packed it down into the trash. Curry threw up his arms. "Hell, you could've given it to *me* if you didn't want it!"

"Fine, take it," Thomas muttered as he pushed through the squadroom. "It's just some sloppy work catching up with me."

Detective Thomas had only about two minutes before Lieutenant Hubbard went home. Both men had had very long and unproductive days. Detective Curry had let

Thomas borrow Loraine's file again. He tossed it onto the lieutenant's desk.

"You ought to look at these," he said.

"No time right now," Hubbard said. "What's it say?"

"Only that it's just as inconclusive as any of our evidence," Thomas said. "But could you do me a favor and take this home tonight? Just take a few minutes to look it over. It tends to support what I've been saying about Loraine using animals."

"I can take it home, but I can't promise to look at it," Hubbard said. "By the way, does Homicide know you have this?"

"Them?" Thomas said. "I just took it from their files. They won't miss it."

"Excuse me?"

"It's a joke, sir," Thomas said, his voice low. "Yes, Curry gave it to me. But if you do get a chance, I was wondering if you could . . . ?"

"Could what?" the lieutenant asked while buttoning up his coat.

Thomas shrugged. "I dunno," he said. "Maybe just . . . keep an open mind about what it's in there?"

"In what way?"

"Any way, I suppose," Thomas said. "Never mind. 'Night, lieutenant," he said, knowing that Hubbard's mind was about as "open" as a bank on a holiday. The lieutenant raised an eyebrow, then shrugged to himself after Thomas left. He would never understand how that detective thought, nor did he think it wise to try.

It was a few days later when Thomas got a call at 2:12 A.M. from his friend Curry. Meg Thomas was blessed with the ability to fall right back to sleep any time her husband's work interfered with their bedtime. Thomas fumbled with the phone while his wife drifted back into dreamland.

After a brief conversation, Thomas hung up and fumbled about in the darkness to get dressed. In the kitchen he left a note for Meg, filled his traveler's mug full of coffee and made his way to the door. Just then he remembered something and turned back to tiptoe into the bedroom. His wife was no doubt already in a deep sleep. He could not see in the darkness, but guessed her cheek's location correctly as he kissed her gently. She groaned quietly, then was silent. This was a woman who had slept through California's big earthquake, later admitting that she had dreamed of being on a cruise ship during a storm. He'd often teased her about her deep sleeps, but in reality he envied her ability to shut out the troubles of the world so completely, if only for eight hours at a time.

A normally quiet park in Culver City was crowded with parked cars—some black and whites but most unmarked. Because of the hour there were almost no bystanders. Thomas arrived as the body was being put into a zippered gray bag before removal. Curry waved him over quickly.

"Hold up a second," he said to the men from the morgue, and unzipped the bag enough for Thomas to peer inside.

"Jesus," Thomas muttered, looking away. Curry's face was implacable. The inside of the bag was already red with the man's congealing blood. Curry opened the bag all the way to the legs and directed Thomas to look again. He pointed his flashlight at the torso.

"Please tell me that's not what it looks like," Thomas said.

"You mean like something took a few bites out of him?" Curry said, reclosing the bag and nodding to the morgue attendants, who hauled the body away. "Looks like it to me. We'll see if the medics think so, too."

"But did this happen before or after he died?" Thomas said. "That's what I wanna know."

"And you will," Curry said. "Looks like he's been dead five, six hours. So . . ." he continued, thrusting his hands into his pockets and heading for his car, "think this matches your girl's m.o.?"

"Maybe," Thomas said. "I'm beginning to wonder if she's even involved in this anymore."

"Really?"

"It's just too weird," Thomas said. "It's too sick. Besides, he looked like a big boy; Loraine is just a petite little thing. Unless she was using a very nasty knife, I don't see how this can be her work?"

"So you're saying I'm supposed to keep looking for a wild animal?" Curry asked. "We've talked to animal control at times, but . . . hell, I've even called the zoo."

"So have I," Thomas said. "That's what we're inclined to think, I guess. That some wild animal did this, like the pack of dogs or whatever the hell they were that roared through the station. I can believe that a rabid dog would try to kill or even eat a man. But those slash marks . . . I dunno. I've had dogs before, and they just don't slash at things, not even when playing. They bite. You know how dogs are."

"I'm a cat person myself," Curry said. "Now cats *do* . . . Wait a minute."

"What?"

"A cat?" Curry said, his voice drifting off. "A *big* cat. What do you think about a mountain lion?"

"A lion," Thomas said. "Here in L.A? The zoos would've told us if something got loose."

"There are wild mountain lions, too," Curry said. "Hey, this is no worse than your pack of dogs. Have you ever seen a mountain lion? They're *big,* and they may not live around here, but . . . hell, maybe one got lost or something. And ever see a cat fight? They bite, they slash, they do whatever they can to win! The least I could do is call out someone from the zoo."

Curry slid into the driver's seat and rolled down the window before shutting the door. Thomas leaned onto the window as they spoke. Curry's excitement suddenly waned; he sighed loudly and looked at his friend. "I have not been getting enough sleep," Curry said. "Now I'm coming up with the stupidest theories in the history of police work. Meanwhile, back in the real world, I'll pass on the autopsy after I've looked at it."

"Thanks," Thomas said, rubbing his stubble. "And don't feel bad about your cat idea. At this point, I say go for it. Call in your animal specialist. And if you still wonder if you're crazy, just ask yourself if you can honestly look at what's happened here and say you're one hundred percent sure that a human being did this?"

Curry started his car's engine and let it idle. "I wish I could," he sighed. "God knows I wish I could."

Nine

A quiet dragnet was resumed, this time with an unusual alliance of law enforcement and animal control agencies leading the way. The dragnet was intended to be kept out of the media, especially considering its tendency toward the hyperbole. The truth was that nobody was clear as to the exact nature of the killer, human or animal. It took some prodding on Detective Thomas's part before his friend Curry would admit to his hypothesis about the large cat. No zoos or animal control agencies confirmed any disappearances of a large cat. The coroner did confirm that the slashing marks shed doubt on their belief that a large dog or coyote was the cause of the latest victim's demise.

With just as little to go on as before, Thomas decided to pay another visit to Loraine's actor boyfriend, Michael Ryder. He made an appointment to see him on the set of his soap opera, *As We Live*. Thomas believed that, like most celebrities, Michael had changed his name and chosen the flashier "Ryder" over whatever he'd been born with. It wasn't important enough to him to ask, or he might have learned that it actually was Michael's real name.

Michael hid his nervousness well around the detective. Thomas had been very vague over the phone—"just to ask some questions" was just neutral enough to sound ominous—and for that reason it was quite unusual that Michael would agree to meet him in his dressing room. To his relief, the questions were mostly of a follow-up nature. He had still not been contacted by Loraine since the breakout, nor did he expect to be. Then the detective asked about her trip to Wisconsin.

"Wisconsin?" Michael said. "She was there a few months ago. But how would you—? Oh, I guess you got that from her when you— Uh, what did you need to know about Wisconsin?"

"Certain information has indicated that there was an incident there," Thomas said. "Apparently she was hospitalized for an animal attack?"

"Yes, she was," Michael said. "She didn't know what it was, though."

"Were you with her at this time?"

"No," Michael said. He leaned forward, now finding it difficult making eye contact with the detective. "See," he began, "we were kind of broken up at the time. She wanted to start living together, and—" he shrugged, then looked up and let out a nervous laugh. "Well, I guess that's not important. Funny thing is that it was supposed to be a vacation for her. She was visiting some relatives, and then gets attacked by some wild animal. Her uncle was killed by the same animal, I think. Unless . . . Were you able to find out what it was? I'm just guessing that you checked the hospital records or something."

"They were inconclusive," Thomas said. "I wish I could tell you more myself. But one more question, if you could."

"Sure."

"Did you notice any changes in her behavior after the

attack?" Thomas asked, and waited. Michael seemed confused by the question, then rubbed his chin in thought.

"I guess there was," Michael said quietly, and straightened up. "She was more . . . more determined when she got back. She was determined about a lot of things after coming back, like her work, and the dancing. Even our relationship. I guess in the end that hasn't worked out, but as for her work, well . . . You must know that she was Tamara Taylor's choreographer."

"Yes, we did."

"But then, it makes sense that she changed," Michael said. "She almost died there. It must have made her see things differently. It was like she had some new spark because of what she'd been through. I was glad for her when she got that new job. Very glad. And then Roxanne was—" He stopped now, his lips tightening from the memory of what he'd found that morning. Roxanne's body, ripped into a bloody mass, and Loraine's naked body, covered in her friend's blood. Thomas waited patiently for him to compose himself.

"Sorry," Michael said. "Every time I think I've forgotten what they both looked like . . ." He let out a long sigh. "If it helps, I don't think she did it. In fact, I know she didn't. She and Roxanne were best friends. They were like sisters. I just wish . . ."

". . . Wish what?" Thomas said after a long pause.

"Nothing, I guess," Michael said. "I just wish that she'd been able to tell me more about what happened in Wisconsin. Even after. She was more determined about things, but more secretive, too, like something else was going on that she didn't want me to know about. That didn't make any sense, did it?" he added with a nervous laugh.

"Some," Thomas said. "More secretive, huh? But you have no idea what that secret was?"

"I don't even know if there was any secret at all," Michael said. "Maybe it was just that time of the month or something. I pretty much learned to stay far away during that time. But seriously, if there really was something more going on, and she wouldn't tell me, I can think of only one other person that she would tell, and that's Roxanne. I don't think they kept secrets from each other. Except . . . she's dead."

"Yes, she is," Thomas said, closing up his notebook. He thanked Michael for his time and rose to leave, when Michael called to him.

"Detective," he said, "if you do find Loraine again, will she be okay?"

Thomas turned just enough to meet Michael's gaze. "We always do our best to make sure of that, sir," he said, and then left the studio without looking back.

"We need federal help," Thomas said, tossing a folder onto Lieutenant Hubbard's desk. The lieutenant picked it up without opening it.

"Good afternoon to you, too," he said.

"Sorry," Thomas said. "Hello, sir. I just wanted to say that if you compare those two reports, I think you'll agree we could have a pattern going here."

"Two reports?" Hubbard said, flipping it open. "There's one on the jogger already?"

"Oh, not him," Thomas said. "One of those is the report on Roxanne. The other is from the coroner in

Wisconsin. Loraine's uncle was killed by a man or animal using the same m.o. as both Roxanne and Jogger Doe."

" 'Jogger Doe'?" Hubbard said. "Is that what they're calling him?"

"Until we get an ID," Thomas said. "Better than John Doe, isn't it?" The lieutenant's expression was unchanged. Thomas's smile faded quickly, and he leaned forward to point to spots in the reports.

"Anyway," he said, "as I've been saying, this confirms my feeling that whatever happened in Wisconsin is connected to what's happening here. I'd say we could use federal help, then. Maybe they're already out there in Wisconsin."

"I think we would've been informed," Hubbard said. "You're forgetting that Loraine was in Wisconsin, where there was a violent death. Now there's been two violent deaths since her return. Granted, we still can't determine if it was man or beast that did the killing, but your job is just to bring her in."

"So no federal help," Thomas said.

"I didn't say that," Hubbard said. "I'd like to find out what they know myself, if anything."

"You realize that Loraine was attacked by a wild animal while supposedly on vacation," Thomas said. "I wish I could explain why, but I'm just not convinced that she's still in L.A."

"And where do you believe her to be?" Hubbard asked.

Thomas rubbed his chin. "I wouldn't be surprised if she was on her way back to Wisconsin," he said.

"So you don't believe she was responsible for . . . 'Jogger Doe's' death?" Hubbard said, handing the reports

back to Thomas. "Local police already contacted
Loraine's aunt in Wisconsin without result. But, yes, I
will contact federal authorities and see if they have any
information. You do understand that, if there really is a
connection, they could end up taking ownership of this
case."

"Oh, *please* don't let that happen, sir," Thomas said.

"I doubt if I could stop it," Hubbard said. "But whatever happens, we're going to cooperate with them,
right?"

"Oh, yeah, I don't mind cooperating," Thomas said.
"I just don't take well to the ones who start giving orders. I think you know what I mean."

"I suppose," the lieutenant said. "Is there anything
else?"

"Not at this time, no," Thomas said. He picked up his
reports and made to leave, but hesitated. For a moment,
Thomas was tempted to ask the lieutenant's opinion on
the nature of the killings. What did he think about the
killer? Did he believe him or her to be human or beast?
The answer could at least reveal something of the lieutenant's capacity for imagination. It would help to know
what other possibilities lay before him.

"Thomas?" Hubbard's voice broke in.

"Hm?"

"You said there was nothing else?"

"Oh," Thomas said. "Oh, sorry, sir. No, there's nothing else." He "saluted" the lieutenant with his report,
then left the office. He was still tempted to get Hubbard's opinion on this case, but that would need to wait
for another time.

* * *

Most of all Loraine missed the music. She was tired of the wolves' songs filtering in to her subconscious every night. She enjoyed the sounds of nature as much as anyone, but a chorus of wolf howls was getting tedious. She was also tired of waking up in strange places, all but naked, and not just during full moons as before. She had no choice for now but to let the wolf emerge every night if it was to learn the ways of the pack.

Ten

Federal Agent Anderson had spent half the day with Detectives Thomas and Curry, poring over the details of their respective cases. His partner, Agent Davis, was no doubt undergoing a similar ordeal with the Wisconsin police. In all, many phone calls and faxes had been exchanged. No one had had a decent meal all day by the time Anderson was comparing the photos of Loraine's supposed victims for the umpteenth time. The most recent photos, those of the half-eaten jogger, were enough to make the stoutest of examiners queasy. Anderson tucked them back into an envelope.

"I'm about ready to pass out," he announced. "Who wants a burger?"

"The possibility," Anderson said, tiny bits of ground meat clinging tenuously to his chin, "of something other than a human being responsible has been investigated, I hope."

Detective Thomas dipped several fries into ketchup while nodding. Detective Curry had been unable to join them for lunch. "Attempts have been made," he said. "I can't say it's been easy convincing the lieutenant that we really could be dealing with something 'other than human.' "

"Even after looking at your evidence?"

Thomas shrugged. "You've looked at it yourself," he said. "You've seen how contradictory it is. We don't think a person could kill someone else that way, but Loraine was covered with her roommate's blood and had other samples under her fingernails. They had to have been fighting."

"Yeah, I suppose it looks like that," Anderson said, finishing off his drink until only a loud sucking noise came from his straw. Thomas used to do that as a child, to his parents' great irritation, but only rarely came across an adult with the same habit. "What about Loraine herself?" Anderson continued. "Did she have any scratches or other wounds when she was apprehended?"

"Yes, some," Thomas said. "She had one particularly big scratch on her abdomen. It looked like she was going to need stitches. But this is where it gets weird." He paused to dip more fries, long since cold. "That scratch was gone when she arrived at the station. I didn't see that personally, but it's in her report. *And,* if her roommate had supposedly caused that wound during the fight, there was no evidence of this under her nails or on her body at all."

"You'd almost think more than one person was involved," Anderson said.

"Her boyfriend was at the scene," Thomas said. "In fact, he discovered the crime and called us. Tim checked out his alibi, and it was tight for just about every hour of the day. He works on a soap and wasn't even off work until. . . . oh, I don't remember, but it was pretty late. Then he was with some friends all night."

"Well, not necessarily her boyfriend," Anderson said. "Just . . . anyone, if there really was someone else there. Someone who probably did wound Loraine when her roommate couldn't."

Thomas let out a sigh. "All I can say is that you're getting at why we've asked for your help. I've never seen a case like this and with this kind of evidence, if it can even be called evidence. I have one lead, and it's barely even a lead."

"You think she's trying to get to Wisconsin?" Anderson said.

Thomas nodded.

"Why?"

Thomas clenched his teeth behind his lips. He disliked having to explain himself. Still, this agent seemed to be working toward something and not just blurting out questions as the lieutenant did. Thomas forced a smile.

"Loraine had been corresponding with a relative in Wisconsin," he said. "After looking into her background and family history, not to mention the contents of some letters, I had a hunch that this was the person she felt close to. Or could trust. It was only later I learned about the way her uncle died."

"What do you think killed those people?" Anderson asked.

"Don't you mean *who?*"

"Who, then," Anderson said. "Or what. I want your opinion, not whatever the coroner has said, or the experts, or the lieutenant. Just thinking of how all those people died, what do you think did it? If a person, what kind of person and how? If an animal . . . what kind of animal?"

Thomas held a French fry near his mouth, then set it back onto the plate. "I have an idea," he said finally. "But it's not the right answer, of course."

"Any ideas you have could be useful," Anderson said.

"Not this one," Thomas said. "I wish I could say for sure what kind of person or animal has been doing this. Maybe it really is a mountain lion on the loose, like Curry thinks. All I know is that whatever it is, it's big, strong and very fast. Could even be something on two legs, but I doubt that. Trouble is, no zoo or shelter knows of any missing animals."

"And that's what you think the 'wrong answer' is?" Anderson asked. "That a big strong animal has been killing people? What about your off-the-record theory? If you have one."

"I'd only have something like that if this were a different kind of world," Thomas said, eyeing the agent curiously. "But since it isn't, that's what we're stuck with. And what are you getting at, anyway?"

"I'm just curious," Anderson said. "Whenever I work with somebody new, I like to find out how they think. This may be our only opportunity to find that out, before the dirty work starts. So what if this were a 'different world'?"

Thomas stared at the agent for a moment, then looked away to finish off the last of his fat-laden meal. His wife would've popped him over the head with his own gun if she knew how he'd been eating lately. He'd promised to watch his diet, but in truth the only time he ate healthy meals was on those rare occasions when he ate at home. He took a moment to think of a prayer to save his hardening arteries, then returned his attention to the federal agent.

"If this were a different world," he said, "I'd say that a big, fast, strong and two-legged . . . thing has been ripping up people with very sharp claws and teeth. Something faster and stronger than any man. But just what connection it has to Loraine, I have no idea."

"And what kind of image does that bring to mind?" Anderson asked.

Thomas looked past him as he shook his head. "I wish I knew," he said. "One thing's for sure: no matter what's out there, man or animal, it's a monster. A cannibalistic monster."

"I want to tell you something," Anderson said, finishing off the last of his own meal. "When I was five, my family moved to Canada, just north of Idaho. We lived there for six years. My mother didn't find out until later, but even at the age of five I loved to go exploring the woods by myself. I think the only reason it took her so long to find out was that I never got lost, and that I was never really gone long enough to get them worried. I've always been pretty good with directions. I can't remember the last time I've missed a turn, an exit, or been lost in a strange town. And believe me, my job requires that I visit a *lot* of strange towns.

"Anyway, as I got older I started going out at night, after they'd gone to bed. This happened when I was about ten. There was a full moon. I was out wandering around, when I heard voices nearby, so I snuck over to check them out. Just some guys out on a camping trip, I figured. But as I got closer, the voices got louder. Somebody was in pain, and the others were shouting to him, 'What's wrong? Whatchoo doing?' Things like that.

I was still on my way there, when the shouts became screams. And I mean *screams*. These horrible cries of pain and terror. I heard animal noises—growls and snarls—and then the sounds of things being torn.

"I guess any normal kid would've had sense to get out of there. But I kept going. I finally made it to where I could see what was happening, and through the firelight . . ." Anderson stopped for a moment and sipped at Thomas's untouched water. "Through the firelight," he continued, "I saw something . . . big. It was on two legs, but I knew in a second that it wasn't a man or even a bear. It was thinner than a bear, and it was picking up those men and tossing them around like the wind blowing leaves. I looked to one side and saw the . . . remains of one of them. The others I didn't need to see. My senses finally woke up, and I took off like a jack-rabbit. But just before I took off, I saw what looked like a tail on that thing. And I only say that because I don't know of any two-legged animals that size that have tails."

"Is any of this for real?" Thomas asked.

"I'm not done yet," Anderson said. "I never did look back while I ran. I was afraid that if I did, I'd see it right behind me, snapping at my heels. But I did hear it. The screams of those men died as they did, but just after that there was a long, loud howl. It just filled the whole forest. It came from every direction, but believe me, I kept up my beeline to back home.

"My parents were up when I got back. I wasn't surprised. By that time they knew that I'd been exploring the woods all those years, but until then, not that I'd been going out at night. I remember having to lie on my side that night, my butt was so sore. But it didn't matter. I counted my blessings that night that I'd gotten just a spanking compared to what could've happened to me.

"The next morning, the bodies were found," Anderson continued. "What was left of them, anyway. They never found the killer, not that I knew of."

"Maybe it was Bigfoot," Thomas said. "You *were* in the woods."

"In time, as I relaxed my thoughts, more details came into play," Anderson said, ignoring the detective. "I was questioned that morning, but couldn't tell them very much. Everything was dark and happened too quickly— but later, I remembered something." Anderson paused to take another sip from Thomas's water glass. "The thing was wearing clothes. Or remains of clothes. Tatters hanging from its arms and legs. Maybe even a belt. But it was wearing clothes."

"Maybe pieces of the campers' clothes got stuck on it as it was killing them," Thomas said.

"Maybe," Anderson said, sucking up the last of the water. "Do you consider yourself to be open-minded?"

"I try to be," Thomas said. "I guess you have to be in this kind of work. But I'll stop at considering that your mystery monster was one of the campers, if that's what you're getting at. We have to look at the facts."

"Really?" the agent said. "That's too bad. I only meant to suggest that we don't know everything about the criminal mind, or the world itself, for that matter. I don't remember the exact quote, but it's said that if you eliminate the impossible, all that's left, however bizarre, has to be the truth. I probably got it wrong, but I've found that it really has worked that way at times. Think of it this way: those people were not killed by a human being. Those campers were not killed by a human being. What exactly did kill them may just be what's 'bizarre.' "

Their server brought the bill, which Anderson insisted on paying. Thomas watched in silence as his new partner signed off on his account. Thomas's line of work had required federal assistance many times before, but until now he had never worked with such an unusual agent as Anderson. He had probably never worked with such an unusual person, period. Thomas really did consider himself to be open-minded, but Anderson could very well lead them too far off the path if he let him. On the other hand, he wrestled with the nagging feeling that he himself could push them away from the truth, whatever it might be, should he continue looking only for the "bizarre."

Loraine didn't bother with birdsong, gentle breezes or other frills at the park. She needed all of her concentration this time. The wolf took longer than usual to appear behind the rock. Loraine tried to sense its thoughts, but detected only a weariness that matched her own.

I'm sure this is all very inconvenient for you, Loraine thought, *but I have to know something. We need to move forward now and not just hang around here.*

And if we are not ready? the wolf thought.

It doesn't matter if we are, Loraine thought. *Before you—before we get too comfortable here, we have to move on. And to start, I need to know—* Loraine thought, and then shut her eyes and sighed.

I need to know what happened the night Roxanne

died, she finished. *From the time you first woke up to when she died.*

The wolf looked at her, then away and lay down, resting its head on its front paws.

Please, wolf, Loraine thought. *I have to know.*

They tell me that I may lead them in bringing down the deer tonight, the wolf thought. *If not tonight, then the next time we find one.*

Please, wolf.

It is difficult to hunt, the wolf thought. *The elders say that there used to be many prey, but no longer.*

Look, if this is a bad time for you—

That night, the wolf thought, lifting its head, *I woke amongst the two-leggers.*

That night she had an inkling of what her other self had been seeking. Find the other and make him leave somehow. To a point, she was willing to help, as he had tried to mate with her against her wishes. Another part of her wanted to be free of this place, away from these noisy, smelly two-leggers, and out where the moon could shine unhidden.

It was a dark, smelly place. Many two-leggers passed by and did not see her. Watching them so quietly from the shadows made her mouth water. All the screaming and running they did whenever they knew of her presence made them less appetizing; they seemed much more palatable now that they weren't assaulting her ears. She shook off this temptation. This was a bad place to hunt; their numbers alone sufficed to make her the hunted and not the hunter, should she move against them.

The hair on her back began to stand. Something very unlike the two-leggers was near. Had it always been near? This place assaulted her senses so that she felt unable to use them. She turned and raced deeper into the darkness, dodging or leaping over the metal obstacles set out by the two-leggers. It was a narrow place, this dark tunnel. It ran between two tall concrete caves and abruptly turned, causing her to slide before regaining her footing.

She did not need her senses to tell her she was being followed, and closely. He had found her before she'd even begun the hunt. If her other self wanted revenge, it would not come easily. He was larger and more experienced. No two-legger could stand against her, yet to him she was merely a cub. Running was not her only plan, though. Even her great endurance would fail before his, but she needed to find a place without two-leggers before this happened.

She barely lifted her tail in time to avoid the snap of his jaws as he grew nearer. It was too late to find a suitable battleground. She fell to stop herself, sending him into and over her. Both tumbled as one before pulling free of their painful tangle. The male was on his feet first—the female followed in half a second—but it was all the male needed to leap again.

But instead of the sting of its teeth or claws tearing into her flesh, she felt the male's thoughts smashing into her own. At first she understood nothing through the mental assault, only a jumble of raw feelings, until words slowly took shape.

Stop! was the first word she comprehended. *—By the others! Sent by the others for you!*

"RrrrR?"

No speak, the male said. *Think. Yeeesss,* he thought as she fought to calm herself and respond in like manner. *No speak. Think. Think your word to me.*

It was impossible to ignore the male as long as its muzzle pressed into hers. He had managed to push her between metal obstacles. She might have been able to knock them aside and run, but his hold on her mind was far stronger than she would have believed.

Leave me, were the first thoughts she managed to send to him.

No, he said. *They made me come here—to bring you back. Bring you back with me, to join the others.*

You frighten her, she said. *My other self, she—*

Thought you could destroy me? he said. *Your world is not hers. Come with me. I awoke you, and now you belong to me.*

Belong to you?

As those you awaken will belong to you, the male said. *The time was not right for me to awaken anyone, but it was done and—they made me come to bring you back, and then to teach you.*

You tried to mate with me, she said. *You tried this in the desert, yes?*

Yes, he said, stepping forward. *It . . . puzzles me why you resisted. You belong to me.* She could only step back half of his distance, allowing him to come very close. She could feel his thoughts, and they were unwelcome to her. Bracing herself, she stiffened and bared her teeth, sending flashes of anger at him. In return she sensed only amusement from him, sending her into a rage. She clamped onto his neck and bit hard, wincing at his shriek of pain, but it did make him step back.

She let go and leapt up and over him the moment he

had stepped back far enough. Now it was his turn to send rage. She had a headstart that she knew would be overtaken very soon. She had no choice but to escape this darkened passageway and out into the bright lights and noise where the two-leggers walked. Screams from the two-leggers and their metal carriages stung her ears, but fear of the male's wrath pushed her on. Even if he were not as young as she, he had lived with the others and knew the wolf's ways better than she. But she . . .

But she knew this place. Or her other self did. There had to be a safe place for her somewhere, and her other self would know it. It was so difficult to concentrate. She could feel the male at her heels, when a picture appeared in her mind. Her other self felt safe in the place she saw, or as safe as possible in this stone and metal jungle. She made an abrupt turn that sent the male plowing into some two-leggers. She did not need to look back to know what was causing the screams of pain behind her. Even when giving chase, this male never hesitated to hone his slaughtering skills.

She reached a concrete cave that was known to her other self. Perhaps this was wise, after all. She could hide in this place and hope it was strong enough to keep him away until sunrise. But if not . . .

She found an opening and raced uphill, followed closely by the male. Panic pushed her up faster; she had not been quick enough to keep him outside. Now this cave could quickly become her tomb. At the top of the jagged hill was another foolish two-legger, who did not scream but was wise enough to turn and run. He reached an opening and ran inside, shutting a door with a loud bang. Soon enough she ran out of room in the passageway and had no choice but to turn and face the male.

He slowed down but continued his approach, his ears pressed down and his eyes gleaming red.

Fool! he said. *You will come with me! This is not our place!*

You have no wish to obey the others, she said. *I can sense it. Leave me and find another mate!*

Wrong, he said. *What they wish, I wish, as you shall, too. How can you resist their call? Can you feel them calling you now? You cannot survive this place alone!*

Stop there! she said, pressing her ears flat and baring her teeth. *You . . . She remembers . . .*

You listen too much to the two-legger, he said. *Come with me. I will teach you our ways.*

I have no wish to be your mate, she said, lifting her head to show him her teeth.

Come with me!

With a howl, she leapt at him, but he stood his ground and pushed her back. She skidded across the floor and hit a wall with a booming thud. Behind him, an opening appeared, followed by the face of a female two-legger. With a snarl he whirled around to deal with this new threat and smashed into the two-legger.

The two-legger was known to her other self. She struggled back onto all fours and raced through the opening, leaping onto the male's back just in time to knock him away from the two-legger. Now things seemed even more familiar. Yes, this was the place that had come to her mind when seeking a safe place.

Loraine sighed at the wolf. *It's my fault,* she thought. *I was supposed to help you get away, and I led you right to my apartment. Right to Roxanne.*

It seems a common belief of two-leggers that their caves are safe, the wolf thought. *I learned from you what I expected to learn. A safe place to run.*

She tried to prepare herself for the male's next attack. To her surprise he seemed to be growing taller and larger. Soon he was standing on his hind legs, his front paws now stretched out into claws. She could do this, also, but not quickly enough to stop him from gripping her neck from behind and tossing her up and over him. The two-legger no doubt had been trying to escape, but she heard screams as she smashed painfully into a wall, blocking the two-legger's path.

The male allowed her just enough time to assume her half-shape and stand on her hind legs. Unfortunately, the male stood nearly a foot taller, with a reach to match. This shape was not as comfortable for her, either. She lost her balance while avoiding his lunge. Her head was down now, so she could only guess that the sounds she heard meant the two-legger was trying to attack the male. She looked up in time to see the two-legger's limp form sailing past like a leaf in the wind.

Her sudden rage surprised her, and perhaps the male as well, for her charge sent both of them tumbling over several obstacles in the cave. Some were soft, some were hard wood or metal, and some shattered, leaving small, clear pieces imbedded in their flesh. They took turns slashing and biting at one another, tossing whatever objects were close by. In spite of her fury, she always found herself trying to stay between the male and the two-legger, as if daring him to go through her. He was enraged himself, but not so much that his eyes did not show a glint of hunger whenever his gaze fell on the two-legger. Somehow she remembered that this particular two-legger was special to her other self, and the male's attentions infuriated her.

A moment of silence as the two wolves circled each other was shattered by a cry of terror—perhaps having been held in for too long—from the two-legger. Her concentration was broken; she glanced over her shoulder, allowing the male to snatch up a large object and smash it over her head. She felt and heard bones break, and then true darkness came.

The blackness did not lift until I awoke in the metal cage, the wolf thought. *When the two-leggers shot me with their pellets.*

Then . . . Loraine thought, *then he knocked you out before Roxanne died.*

Yes. But I do not doubt that he killed her. I do wonder why he did not eat her, though.

How could you say that? Loraine thought.

He looked at her with hunger in his eyes, the wolf replied. *She was never more than food to him. I meant no disrespect; only because of that does it seem strange that he did not feed on her.*

Jeez, I don't know, Loraine thought. *Maybe the cops came right after that. You guys were throwing furniture at each other. Somebody must've called. Or maybe . . .*

Maybe?

Maybe he was trying to frame us, Loraine thought. *I know it sounds corny, but it's possible.*

I do not know what 'corny' is, but he was quite enraged, the wolf thought. *If those were truly his inten-*

tions, he showed his cowardice by such actions. The pack was wise to exile him.

Yeah, but they made our job harder, too, Loraine thought. *Wolf?* she continued. *If I heard you right, it sounds like you were trying to protect Roxanne.*

I recognized her as a protected two-legger, the wolf thought. *Even while asleep, your thoughts . . . influence my actions, just as mine will do yours. Two-leggers who are protected are difficult to harm.*

Because of some kind of mental block?

Yes.

So it made you protect her?

No, the wolf thought. *Nothing, 'made' me do that.*

Then why— Loraine began, and then stopped. She didn't need to ask her question. In spite of her months of inner rage and hatred, of trying to "kill" the wolf, the beast actually cared for her. Perhaps it even cared about Loraine's loved ones. A chill shot down her spine even in this imagined place as she considered her past actions and thoughts. She owed a great deal to this beast. Perhaps it was time for her to end the struggle.

Wolf, she began, *Tamara says that you all have names. Her wolf's name is Song. Do you have one?*

Yes.

What is it? Loraine thought. *That is . . . Would you please tell me?*

The wolf raised its head to look her square in the eyes. *Jan,* it thought.

Jan? Loraine thought. *That's your name? Jan?*

Yes, the wolf thought. *Does this displease you?*

No, Loraine thought quickly. *Of course not. I guess it just wasn't what I expected. It's better than Wolf, though.*

Sorry about calling you that all the time, but you wouldn't tell me your name until now.

I suppose the best way to explain why not is that you had not earned it, Jan thought. *But even that's not why. Using your words is . . . difficult for me.*

You don't have to explain . . . Jan, Loraine thought. *Yeah, I guess the more I say it, the more it fits you. I can't explain why.* She laughed to herself. *See? Using my own words is 'difficult' for me, too.*

Loraine imagined Jan smiled at her—in her own way—before returning to her own world.

Eleven

Detective Thomas arrived at work to see his desk commandeered by Agent Anderson. He had never thought of himself as a particularly territorial man, but it was a strain to hold his composure. The federal agent had settled himself in quite well, and had spread a large map across Thomas's desk. He seemed to be unaware of Thomas's presence, even after the detective set down his coffee and began stripping off his coat.

Thomas studied the agent's map as he draped his coat over the chair. Only then did Anderson acknowledge his presence.

"Oh, hello," he said quickly, then glanced at his watch. "Or good morning, that is."

"How long have you been here?" Thomas asked.

"Uhhhh, since—I don't know, five-thirty, I suppose," Anderson said, then held out a cautionary hand. "Believe me, I am *not* a morning person. I must still be on Washington time."

"Oh," Thomas said, and studied the map again. "Did you know that you have a large map on my desk?"

"Yes," Anderson said, grabbing the edges to turn it toward Thomas. "As you can see, it covers North America," he said, then pointed to the part of Canada just north of Idaho. "This is where I lived as a boy, and where the incident I described took place. This is the part of Wisconsin where Loraine was attacked, and her uncle was killed. Did you know he owned a llama ranch?"

Thomas nodded.

"Ever see one?" Anderson asked. "Up close, I mean. They're like a cross between a camel and a goat."

"I know what llamas look like," Thomas said.

"Then you *have* seen one."

"No, I—" Thomas sputtered, then calmed himself. "Enough about llamas! What is it you're getting at?"

"Sorry," Anderson said. "Where was I? Oh, so, here was the attack in Wisconsin, and finally we have the attacks in Los Angeles. Notice anything?"

"If you're trying to show me a trail—"

"Maybe," Anderson said. "These locations do form a somewhat curved line, but a pattern could be there. And it's going south, not north."

"But you're including something that happened 25, 35 years ago," Thomas said, thrusting a finger at Canada. "Loraine wasn't even born yet!"

"I'm not saying that she killed those campers in Canada," Anderson said. "My point is that I don't think we're dealing with one individual."

"A whole family of killers?" Thomas said. Anderson leaned back and scratched at his teeth with his fingernails. He seemed to be examining what had come off, and then spoke.

"Not exactly," he said, pulling out a folder from under the debris of paperwork. Inside was a photograph, which he handed to Thomas. "I had Agent Davis Fed-Ex this. Have you seen it yet?" Thomas shook his head. "That's a photo of the fence surrounding Bill Turner's llama ranch the morning after one of his llamas was killed. Note that that's a chain link fence."

"With a big hole in it," Thomas said.

"Yes, but does it look like it was cut to you?" Anderson asked. "This photo was taken from inside the ranch. See how the hole is uneven, as opposed to a straight line or circle that somebody might have cut? Also, it looks like a lot of the wire is thinner at the cut points, like it had been stretched open and not cut. Doesn't all this seem to you that the killer was literally ripping the fence apart?"

"Well . . ."

"When I got this, I called Davis and asked what the locals thought," Anderson continued. "The best they could come up with was a bear, but no one knew of any bears big or strong enough to do this to so much metal. Some believed that somebody had cut his way in. Only some. Turner had it repaired that day, but the next night the intruder came back, killed him and wounded Loraine."

Thomas set down the photo and ran his fingers through his hair. He checked his fingers to make sure that no stray hairs remained on them. This habit annoyed his wife, who always assured him his hair was just fine, but wouldn't be if he kept pulling at it. As if to prove this, his hairline was receding little by little each year, perpetuating his need to check for more damage.

"I'm not saying a damned thing," Thomas said quietly. "You can say what you think all you want, but I'm not in that position. Not with this boss."

"I'm not sure I follow you."

"Nobody can look at this case and think that anything other than a . . . nonhuman is responsible," Thomas said. "Except the lieutenant. I'm not about to go to him and say that—"

Anderson waited, but Thomas only shrugged and shook his head. "And say what?" Anderson asked.

Thomas shook his head again. "Uh-uh," he said. "Forget it. If I stay on this 'nonhuman' angle much longer, he'll have my ass. Trust me, the man is a robot."

"Then he should be very open to this sort of thing," Anderson said, folding up his map and tucking it under his arm. "After all, he's nonhuman himself."

"I didn't mean it that way," Thomas said. "He can't see anything beyond the 'real world.' Am I making any sense?"

"Oh, yes," Anderson said. "And frankly I'm surprised he made lieutenant with that kind of outlook. Excuse me, I'll be right back."

Anderson left the desk and passed through the rest of the office. Thomas realized that he had not yet checked his phone messages, and he fished around for a notepad while the tape rewound. He had scribbled out three of them when his pencil lead broke, and not entirely by accident. A sudden nausea had caused him to mash down on the point, but snapping a pencil was the least of his concerns. He rushed from his seat and around the corner, stopping just within sight of Hubbard's office. As his gut feeling had warned, there stood Agent Anderson with map unfolded and pointer stabbing away at select spots. Even from here Thomas recognized the lieutenant's baffled expression. There were just certain things that some people would never comprehend.

The moon had almost arrived. Although the pack rarely left their forms, even when the moon did not rise, the full moon brought them their greatest joys. It brought the three nights when their inner selves were completely "asleep," with no hope of fighting their way free, unless the wolf deliberately sought contact. The pack never did. They were free to be themselves with no boundaries, no limits, and no regrets.

Until now Jan had never been awake but during those three nights, when her inner self lost to its power and let her free. The others in the pack had conquered their inner selves for all time, but even the oldest of them felt a struggle, even if only slight, during other moons and especially daylight. They accepted this, knowing the struggle was scarcely worth their attentions. Eventually Jan's inner self would succumb, and she could run with them forever.

The pack taught her their Eve of the Moon song, one of their most joyful . . . so full of hope. She had also learned that their best hunting was during the moon, which gladdened her.

After that night's repast Jan wandered away from the others, but never completely out of sight or scent. She hoped to listen to the forest itself, to smell it, to feel it. She had seen some of the elders all but fade from view before her eyes, their bond with the woods was so great. Someday she hoped to join them.

Something cold pushed at her from behind. She jumped forward and yelped, then heard chuckling in her mind.

You jump well, a male said, and she turned. He was known to her. She had brought him to the pack herself not very long ago. Not directly to the pack—he had been alone before they found him first, and let him run with them. Now once again he sought out his "creator." Jan found herself craning her neck to look up at him. No doubt he had been a large two-legger before crossing over.

The others call me Bluefur, he said. This was no surprise to her. His coat was gray, but reflected blue, especially when the moon was bright enough, as tonight. Tomorrow it was sure to be glowing. There was some other reason he made her think of blue, but that would need to wait until later.

I did not mean to frighten you, he continued. *I thought you felt my approach. I only wanted to smell you.*

Smell me? she said. *You . . . wanted to smell me?*

You have a nice smell, he said, and tried to stand behind her again. She made certain their muzzles faced each other. *I have no wish to harm you,* he said. *I only wish—*

I know what you wish, she said. *But tonight I . . . thought I would only contemplate. It eases my troubles.*

You are troubled?

Jan lowered her head in a small nod, then flashed a sad smile with her eyes. *It should pass,* she said. *Perhaps tomorrow.*

Tomorrow then, he said. *The moon will be here then. We do more than just hunt on those nights.*

I know, she said, and let him approach her closely enough to lick her muzzle. Then he left her side to rejoin the others. Jan resumed her efforts at communing with the woods.

Because it was not yet the moon, her inner self could still make itself felt, if not heard. Or perhaps it was not her inner self at all, but Jan's thoughts that made her look back.

Bluefur! she called. He looked back, as did the others. Jan almost turned away in embarrassment, but the others quickly lost interest. Bluefur, however, padded toward her in silence. He stopped just short of her and waited. She did not speak, either, but stepped forward cautiously until their noses touched. They stayed that way a moment, and then Bluefur rubbed his muzzle along hers. He licked the fur on her face until she responded in kind. He stepped forward again and grunted, letting his head rest on hers. Keeping his head in place, he moved the rest of his body until they stood side by side. She shut her eyes and breathed slowly as he backed up, taking in her scent as he went.

There was a long wait while he did not touch her at all, and then she grunted as most of his weight fell onto her back. She remembered the exiled one trying to do this to her several times—in the hot, sandy place, and later in the two-leggers' city—but each time was terrifying to her. Bluefur was welcome. At first they moved to their own rhythms and made clumsy sounds, but in time they began to move as one, to speak as one, and finally, to sing as one. The rest of the pack only listened. Not all songs were meant for everyone. All mated pairs found their own during mating, and now a new one was being written.

Cops did not love the full moon as much as some others might. Statistics were not written in stone, but every cop knew that full moon nights were busier, bawdier, and bloodier. They expected more violent crime and were more alert on such nights as a result. Detective Thomas, however, could not say with certainty that his department was busier on such nights. People jumped bail or even escaped from confinement no more or less than on any other night.

Still, Thomas was feeling nauseated again. Not because he expected Lieutenant Hubbard to include him as an appetizer for lunch, but because of a nagging doubt that would not go away no matter how much he tried to rationalize it away.

"Is this your way of getting back at me for confusing the lieutenant?" Agent Anderson asked as he drove. It was evening now, but the sky was still light. Dusk would come in a half hour at most. This was why they had little time.

"I don't know what you mean," Thomas said.

"Think of it as diplomatic immunity," Anderson said. "I don't blame you for being reluctant to discuss things with him. He still needs to be updated, though. Better that I do it than you, in that case."

"Okay, but I'm still wondering what you mean by 'getting back at you,' " Thomas said.

"Talking me into tailing a suspect on flimsy evidence," Anderson said. "Even I have superiors to report to, after all."

"Look, I said you weren't obligated to come."

"We both know that tailing a suspect without a partner is unwise," Anderson said. "Not to mention doing it with no reason other than a 'gut feeling.' "

"Hell, look who's talking about 'flimsy evidence,' " Thomas said.

"I didn't quite catch that," Anderson said.

"Nothing."

"Actually, I did hear it," Anderson said. "I was just hoping you'd repeat it. Don't feel too bad. You're hardly the first person to be put off by my approach. If it makes you feel better, 99.9% of the time it's a cut and dry case of a person doing something to another person, and I don't look for anything else. But sometimes—like now—you have to look at other possibilities. Sometimes the clues just don't add up."

"Try most of the time," Thomas muttered. "Turn here." Anderson did so, and the two men were silent for a few minutes. Occasionally Anderson would ask for directions, but otherwise the only voices in the car came from the police band.

The sky was getting red by the time they pulled up to the hotel. Anderson was heading for the parking area, when Thomas nudged his arm and pointed. Their subject was already leaving in a brown rental car. Anderson allowed the driver to pull away a certain distance before following.

"You know, it's been a few years since I've done this," he said. "Tailed someone, I mean. Hope I haven't lost my touch."

"You didn't tell me you were out of practice," Thomas said. "I should be driving. This lady is good."

"That's good to know," Anderson said, and gave the slightest hint of a smile before abruptly turning opposite their suspect's direction. Thomas all but stood up in his seat while trying to look back.

"What the hell are you doing?" he cried. "I thought you knew who we're after!"

"Of course," Anderson said. "Tamara Taylor. Sit back down and hold on," he added, making another abrupt turn. Thomas was jolted back into position.

"You idiot! Pull over and let me drive!" he said. "We're going to lose her!"

"You said she was good," Anderson said calmly, continuing to drive. "If so, then following her the entire way would be a bit suspicious, don't you think?"

"The point is to follow her the entire way *without her knowing it,*" Thomas said, looking about frantically for the other car. Anderson pulled onto a side street, and only then did Thomas catch a glimpse of the brown rental. Anderson did not turn, but continued crossing to the next intersection.

"Turn back!" Thomas yelled. "Didn't you see her?"

"I did. I'm following her, remember?"

"For the love of God, man, *please* let me drive," Thomas said, his arms flailing about in frustration. "You don't know this city," he said. "I do! She could be making a U-turn, a zigzag trail, anything! Some of these streets are tricky!"

"You've obviously never driven in Washington," Anderson said, making another sudden turn. Once again Tamara's car came into brief view. "Did you know it was designed by a certified lunatic?"

"Huh? What about a lunatic?" Thomas said, now busy scanning the streets for any other sign of the brown car.

"Actually, he wasn't a lunatic," Anderson said. "He just designed like one. See, the city planners held a contest for pretty much any architect, graphic artist, and what-have-you who felt like designing the streets of Washington." He made two more quick turns. Again Tamara's car was glimpsed just turning a corner. "The winner was a Frenchman—I forget his name—who didn't design something simple like a standard grid, but—"

"Look, I've been to Washington before; I know what you're talking about," Thomas said. "I just wanna know why you're torturing me like this?"

"If you want me to follow in a straight line, using one or two cars as cover, then we'll be on a wild goose chase," Anderson said. "You said she's good, and I believed you. Normal tailing tactics aren't as effective."

"But we need to be close in case she leaves the city," Thomas said.

"Agreed," Anderson said, and turned one last time onto the main street where Tamara was last spotted. Thomas peered down both lanes and saw what may have been her brown car. He pleaded with Anderson to get closer, and he did, but only by one car.

Thomas never could convince the agent to follow any closer than he did. Many times, when Thomas had lost sight of Tamara, the agent would insist that she was still within sight. Thomas had been correct about her trying to leave the city. She did not use the freeway, however, but various side streets that were likely shortcuts compared with the stop-and-go traffic of the freeway. Wherever she was going, she was in a hurry.

The sun was almost down when she finally entered the freeway past most of the traffic. It was as free-sailing as Los Angeles traffic got, and the two men followed her toward the mountains. Thomas radioed in their route and wondered how this agent could possibly see well enough to keep following Tamara.

The farther they went, the darker it became and the fewer cars hid their pursuit. Neither man could guess what her ultimate destination would be. At one point Anderson wondered out loud if he had been successful at hiding their position. Thomas had no idea how to answer.

The sun had completely set by the time she pulled onto a remote road. Anderson noted the almost total lack of lights and road signs. No other cars were present but theirs and Tamara's. Even following from such a distance, she was bound to grow suspicious. Anderson shut off the headlights.

"Oh, God, no, not on a road like this," Thomas moaned. "It's too late for that now."

"It was your idea to chase her," Anderson said, "and on nothing more than a hunch. Do you want to back out now?"

"No, but shutting out the lights will get her suspicious for sure, if she's seen us already," Thomas said. "Wouldn't you be?"

"Probably," Anderson said. "But be quiet now. I need to concentrate. I wouldn't have tried this at all if it weren't a full moon."

It was a cool night, but Thomas was covered in sweat. His lurking doubts about this agent's grip on reality no longer lurked. They were out and working overtime. Anderson was a lunatic, Thomas told himself. He probably wasn't even a federal agent, but a mental ward escapee who had killed the real Anderson and taken his place. In spite of this, something prevented Thomas from snatching the radio mike and blurting out an SOS. Perhaps it was the left side of his brain pulling in his own tenuous grip on reality.

Miraculously, Tamara's car was still in sight, albeit from a great distance, and their car was still on the road. Then Tamara's car disappeared. After catching up, both men sighted the dirt road that she had taken. They drove slowly along the road for some time, neither man spotting Tamara's tail lights. The road was surrounded by high, bushy mountain walls. Farther ahead one side sloped off into a tree-covered drop. With still no sign of Tamara's car, Anderson pulled off to one side and turned off the engine.

"Do you see her?" Thomas whispered, peering into the darkness for some sign of the sedan.

"No," Anderson whispered back, opening the door gently and sliding out. "But I believe we'll have better luck on foot."

"But she could have—"

Anderson put his finger to his lips and crouched down while Thomas tiptoed to his side. He brought two flash-lights but was not surprised that the agent left his off. Thomas had not turned on his own, either, as so far the full moon was providing adequate light. The light would also grow stronger as the moon rose higher. Anderson motioned for silence and seemed to be studying the darkness. Thomas was not one to stand around, but tried to do the same. Not very far ahead he noticed a large, dark shape, but without the flashlight a closer look was needed. He nudged Anderson and pointed, then led the way. Soon enough it was clear that they had found Tamara's car. Now Anderson drew his gun and switched on his flashlight, as did Thomas, but a quick sweep of the inside revealed no occupants. Anderson switched off his flashlight, but Thomas kept his on to sweep the area.

"She'll know we're here," Anderson whispered.

"Does it matter by now?" Thomas whispered. "She's on foot. But why? There's not a damned thing out here."

"You're the one with the hunch," Anderson whispered. "What did you expect to find out about her?"

"That she was still in contact with Loraine," Thomas whispered. "Maybe meeting her out here? Let's try down here," he added, and shined his flashlight down the edge of the hill. Anderson followed suit and swept the area slowly. Until then only the crickets broke the silence; now both men looked at each other as a different sound came from below. The flashlights failed to locate its source.

"What did that sound like to you?" Anderson whispered.

Thomas shook his head. "Animal of some kind," he said, and began climbing down the hill. There were plenty of large bushes, shrubs and the occasional tree to help his footing. Thomas was some ten feet down when Anderson finally decided to follow. Their flashlight beams swung wildly as the two men grabbed at every branch and stepped onto any ledge that would prevent their falls. After some time they reached more level ground and shined the flashlights in a steady sweep.

The sound came again, and more clearly—a grunt or bark—of an animal. Both beams focused on the same spot. Not thirty feet away was something . . . or someone, Thomas assumed. It must have been a person, because it had much lighter skin than any furry animal, and it stood on two legs. The beams focused on it, and it turned toward them. Even from this distance Thomas recognized Tamara's features, but she seemed . . . naked? And only a second before, she was standing, but was now crawling or running on her arms and legs.

She looked their way and snarled. And as she snarled, her skin became much darker, or did Thomas see hair growing? He saw her flinch, and he brought his gun up, only his gun was no longer there. Something dark shot past both men. Next to him, Anderson yelled as his footing gave way. Thomas did not see the dark shape that had resembled Tamara Taylor racing up the hill. Anderson was tumbling down the hill and into the darkness. Thomas almost tumbled after him, but managed a controlled slide.

Only when the terrain leveled off could the detective focus his light on Anderson. He heard groans from the agent, which was a good sign. Thomas slid down the rest of the way to his partner, whose head was pointed downhill. His face was covered with dirt and blood from scratches, but no serious bleeding was evident.

"Holy shit, man, are you all right?" Thomas cried. "Talk to me, Gil!"

"What the hell was that?" he heard the agent groan.

"That's not important now," Thomas said, kneeling beside him. "Is anything broken? Try wiggling your fingers and toes."

"Did you get a good look at it?" Anderson moaned.

"Come on, man, talk to me," Thomas said. "Tell me if anything's broken."

"My spirit," Anderson said with a cough, "I think. It grabbed my gun. Did it grab yours, too?"

"This habit of yours of ignoring me is getting annoying," Thomas said. He rested his hand on the agent's chest. "Does it hurt when I touch anything here? Or here?"

"I'm sure nothing's broken," Anderson said. "Help me up." He took Thomas's outstretched hand and tugged. The agent's grip was stronger than Thomas expected. Soon enough he stood on shaky feet.

"Question," Anderson said. "Is it me, or is the ground slanted?"

"The ground is slanted," Thomas said, draping Anderson's arm over his shoulder for support. "Just lean against me and try to walk together. This time *I'm* driving. We're going to the hospital."

"But nothing is broken," Anderson said.

"You're lucky your *neck* wasn't broken." Together the two men began the slow and difficult ascent to the top of the hill.

"I see that we lost her again," Anderson said.

"Looks like it."

"She really did take our guns, didn't she?" Anderson said. "Snatched them right from our hands. Too fast for either of us to stop her, either. What kind of person could do that, d'you think?"

"A 'person,' you say?" Thomas said. "I wish I could say it was even that."

"Just for the sake of clarification," Anderson said, "what exactly did you see before she—it?—got away?"

"I'd rather not s—"

Both men stopped cold as a new sound assaulted their ears. It was a distant sound, yet one that could have been right beside them. When fear strikes, some men can hear their own heartbeats. This time, either man could have sworn that he had none at all. It was a sound alien to this part of the world, yet not unexpected. Not anymore.

Thomas had heard plenty of coyote howls in all the years he had lived in Los Angeles. Even in such an over-developed place as Southern California, the wild found a way to intrude. He knew the call of the coyote, and this was no coyote. The howl of a wolf played for a full minute before fading away with the wind. For a moment even the crickets were silent before resuming their own nightsong. Looking up, the two men spied the moon just creeping up over the edge, but no sign of the beast that had been calling to it. Neither of them wanted to see it.

"My God," Anderson said, after a long silence broken only by the crickets. "What have we found here?"

Thomas's expression was grimmer than it had ever been since the beginning of his career. "A werewolf," he said, and nothing else.

Twelve

There was nothing of her other self to stop Jan's joy this night. She and the pack were free to run and hunt as their true selves under the full moon. For now they were not hunting, but simply running to the beat of the moon-song, which no mere two-legger could ever hope to hear.

She ran and ducked and leapt in perfect pace with the others, never lagging for a moment. She laughed inwardly as dirt and leaves flew up past her face. For a moment she was reminded of another run, when she was alone. A great ocean was on one side, and white specks were kicked up at her feet like dust. The water and white specks had seemed to go on forever; in fact, she never did reach the end of either before sunrise.

Jan's thoughts were not entirely of the moon. She also thought of Bluefur, who had chosen her the night before. Or had she chosen him? Not long ago she had brought him to the pack by tasting his blood. The law of the pack allowed her to choose him as a mate, also. And she had. That same law should have made her the exiled one's mate, but she had refused him. Perhaps she had broken the law, then, and the only thing saving her was that the others had banished him. Exiles did not even deserve mates. But if he had not been cast out?

The pack began to slow after reaching the heart of

their woods. A clearing—their clearing—was the one place that lay directly beneath the moon at midnight. They sat in a circle and raised their voices in anticipation of the hour. When the song ended, the pack stayed in its circle silently. Even so, the woods were not silent. A breeze whistled through the bushes and trees, joined by the hoots of owls and the skreeking of crickets. Then another sound broke in. Their other selves slept, but they recognized these sounds. Two-leggers were nearby, and invading their territory.

The pack hunted by sound and smell and soon discovered the intruders, a male and female who seemed prepared for their appearance. They must have heard the moonsong and become frightened by it. As they should have been. Most of the pack kept to the darkness and surrounded the two-leggers. The Alpha then slowly stepped out of the darkness and stopped before them, his gaze piercing the flames that separated him from the intruders. The male, already in front of the female, thought to protect her more by pushing her back and holding out a big stick. Jan, still watching from the darkness with the others, vaguely remembered that this stick could fire pellets. She wanted to warn the Alpha, but trusted him to know the danger.

The Alpha snarled, then leaped over the flame to land within a few feet of the two-leggers. The male cried out and fired his stick. Jan saw the pellet shoot out the other side of the Alpha's body. She winced as his pain was sent to her, as it was to all of the pack. The last thing the two-leggers might have seen was a blur of motion striking at them from all sides. The Alpha, having led the attack, had stepped back to let the others finish the kill.

Jan had heard the mental call of the Alpha to strike,

but had hesitated. By the time she leapt from the darkness, it was nearly over. The two-leggers had been buried in a mass of fur and flesh. Jan watched the kill with the others who had been too slow to join in. She sensed their disappointment at having missed the kill, but she did not know her own feelings.

At the Alpha's summons, the others pulled away from the two-leggers. He stepped forward to survey the remains. It would have been a miracle if either two-legger had even been twitching. Tonight there were no miracles. Jan felt satisfaction from the Alpha as he announced, *Now we feast.*

The pack converged as one on their kills. As always the elders were allowed the fleshier pieces, while the cubs gnawed on limbs and other bony parts. The feast lasted barely a few minutes, and it was hardly enough to sate the pack, but two-leggers always provided their tastiest meals.

Bluefur brought a bone away from the repast. It was then that he looked up to see Jan, immobile and staring at the two-leggers' remains. He walked up to her and dropped his meal, and waited. She seemed unaware of him, as if nothing existed but the remains of that night's kill. Bluefur leaned forward and licked her muzzle, startling her. She shook her head as though trying to wake up, then looked at him. He licked her muzzle again and gestured downward. She looked down at his offer, then sniffed it.

Have you been here all along? Bluefur asked. *Did you join the others at all?*

I . . . I was content to watch, she said.

Eat, cub, Jan heard the Alpha say. *While there's still anything left.*

I am not hungry, Jan said. *But I'm certain I will be by the next kill.*

Cub, said the Alpha, walking toward her, *you must understand that we do not find a good kill each night.*

I know, but . . .

But . . . ?

I am not hungry, she said again, lowering her gaze. *That is all.*

The Alpha watched her a moment, then gestured toward Bluefur, who bowed his head quickly and rejoined the others.

Walk with me, cub, the Alpha said. Jan felt a chill in her spine as she followed the Alpha away from the others. His words were calm, however. *You are too young to remember,* he said, *but it used to be possible to run all night without ever seeing a sign of two-leggers. But now,* he added with a sigh, *now it seems that every night their numbers double. This has been a curse and a blessing. A curse because it becomes more difficult to avoid them, and a blessing because their flesh is far better than any other animal's.*

I . . . see, Jan said.

Even you have seen this to be true, the Alpha said. *Yes, cub?*

Actually, I . . . she said, *I don't remember having eaten two-legger flesh. I do not know if this is true.*

Really? the Alpha said. She felt his surprise. *Even dwelling in the cities as you did, surrounded by them during every moon, and you never tasted even one?*

I . . . do not know why, she said. *I always found something else to hunt. Perhaps . . . perhaps it was because there were so many. It did not seem like true hunting to me. Was I wrong?*

No, cub, the Alpha said. *But tonight may be our only meal for a while. We may find nothing tomorrow. If there is any flesh left, you'd best eat it now.*

But I am not hungry, she said.

So you say, the Alpha said. *And it surprises me. Do you mean that you could truly watch the others as you did—to watch them bring down the prey—and watch them pull off and swallow the flesh, and smell the blood, and feel no hunger at all?*

I . . . no, I . . . Jan whispered, then shut her eyes.

Can this be? the Alpha said. *Can this be that on this night of all nights, when the moon becomes the sun of the night, and our other selves truly sleep, that you are still ruled by your weaker self?*

No, of course not, she said. *I am wolf. I am stronger than the other, especially on this night.*

And why not every night? the Alpha said. *Why does your other self ever control you?* She followed him back to the others, who were finishing the last of the meal, except for a small pile that Bluefur had made for her. He smiled at her return.

I saved as much as I could for you, he said.

Thank you, she said quietly, and walked up to his offering. She sniffed at it and shut her eyes as the aroma filled her nostrils. It was a dizzyingly tempting smell— one that made her lips tremble in anticipation of the feast. She felt Bluefur licking at her muzzle again, and she sighed.

Remember, cub, the Alpha said from behind her, *you are wolf once and for all now. The two-leggers think nothing but evil of us. They do not understand that we are simply hunters. Or perhaps they do understand, after all. Perhaps we remind them too much of themselves, so they seek to destroy us.*

Remind them . . . of themselves . . . Jan whispered so quietly that only Bluefur heard, and just barely at that. Then she straightened up quickly, her eyes open wide and unblinking.

Remind them of themselves, she said more loudly. Bluefur cocked his head, puzzled. Jan's thoughts spun as she looked at him, his offering, the skeletonized remains of the two-leggers, then the pack. For a moment she saw them furless and pale, standing on all fours, but their hind legs were longer than they were supposed to be. Everyone in the pack seemed to be . . . ?

She shut her eyes and shook her head several times.

Jan? she heard Bluefur say, and she looked up to see him and the others as they had always been before.

Something is wrong, she said, backing away from Bluefur and his offering. His tail wagged slowly as he followed her, but she continued moving away.

Your other self still rules you, cub, the Alpha said. *Even on this night, it makes you fight your true nature. You belong to the pack now, cub. When we hunt, you hunt. When we feast, you feast. That is our way. We are wolf!*

She mumbled something that even Bluefur did not hear. He tried to reach her, but she backed away, then snapped at him. His ears and tail straightened up in shock and surprise.

We are not wolf! she cried. *We are . . . we are . . .*

Cub! the Alpha said. *Do not be foolish! This is our way! This is—*

We are not wolf! Jan cried, and whirled around to bolt into the woods. Bluefur called out and tried to follow, only to bounce off the very solid form of the Alpha. Bluefur rolled in the dirt until he was able to regain his footing. He shook off the dirt, then glared at the Alpha.

She is my mate, he said. *You would stop me from bringing her back?*

Words will not work on her now, the Alpha said. *We must let her return to us on her own. She will always know where to find us.*

But she is my mate!

Another reason that she will return to us. Be patient. You, too, are but a cub to us. No matter what happens, your place is with us now.

Bluefur looked past the Alpha into the emptiness of the woods. It was deathly quiet. The wind had died, and the flames of the two-leggers' camp were crackling their last. After listening to the nothingness for several minutes, Bluefur turned away with a heavy heart that no other songs that night could lighten.

Jan hardly slowed her pace for a full half hour. She did not even pause when crossing the two-leggers' hard black road that cut into the woods. She heard a rumble from the side and glimpsed the light of a two-legger's giant rolling machine. She did not slow down, but leaped up and cleared the machine easily as it passed beneath her. Whether the two-legger inside ever saw her; she did not care and never looked back.

The call of the pack was as strong as it ever was no matter how far she ran from them. The strangest part of this was that she did not know what had caused her to run from them. She was as hungry as any of them, yet could not bring herself to feast on the fresh, hot meat of the night's kill. No strange images had come to her mind to make her run—or none that she could recall. There was nothing but the thought that something was wrong. Something was not right about the kill. Something . . .

The two-leggers had been a mated pair, and though they died together, should they have died? The female might have been carrying a cub, or she had borne one already, and now it was alone. Unless the pack—

The thought of it made Jan cough, slowing her run to a crawl. No, even they would not eat a two-legger cub. They had brought down many other young animals. Something was wrong. The others seemed to enjoy it so, as though feasting on that meat was the greatest pleasure they could know.

Jan shut her eyes and moaned. The wind began to pick up, and the strangest feeling came over her. Her eyes still shut, she felt a breeze on her face that then moved to her back. Again the wind shifted to her face, and stronger this time, only to blow against her back. The wind blew at her face, then her back, and on. No; it was not the wind that moved, but her. Jan opened her eyes slowly and cried out.

It was daylight. She knew this because the sun shone right into her eyes. But only for a moment as she swung away from the light to hover far above the ground. Jan's lips quivered in terror as she looked from side to side. To the right she saw a tiny, hairless hand gripping a metal chain. To the left was the same. She did not want to believe that they were hands, but moving her own made these strange ones move, as well.

It took great effort to remember to breathe as this terrifying experience continued. The chains dug into her hands, but she held on even tighter lest she fly into the ground, or worse, into the sun. She heard a female voice behind her. Not understanding the words, she looked back and glimpsed an older female two-legger behind her. Trying to get a better look, Jan turned as far as she could, then had time to cry out again before her seat slid out from under her. The chains twisted and pinched hard, causing her hairless hands to open. In spite of the sun's brightness, Jan kept her eyes wide open as it loomed larger. She took small comfort in the knowledge that, although her death would be painful, it would be quick.

The sun would go hungry today, however. The earth won the battle and slammed into Jan's body. She had spread her body as widely as possible while in flight, and hit the ground flat. Her breath was knocked from her lungs in an instant, and so she had no voice to answer the female's cries behind her, nor the strength to move.

The cries of the female grew louder and closer. Jan still did not have the strength to flee. Rough hands grabbed her limp form and rolled her over.

The night sun shone down on her through the trees. Taking her first breath in almost a minute, Jan stared back at the moon while working her breathing back to normal. After several minutes she rolled off of her back onto all fours and shook the leaves and dirt off. There was no sign of the female two-legger or the strange device that had propelled her to a painful landing, or of the sun. She sniffed the air as if it might provide answers that her eyes and ears had not. But nothing, not even the wind, offered a clue to what had happened.

Jan forced herself to continue in an uneven trot. Everything about her movements seemed unnatural to her now. Her breathing, her running. Even her ears twitched randomly, resisting her efforts to control them. She kept her head low to the ground, hoping the scent of the woods would not betray her.

She ran right into something, and looked up to see another female two-legger. Jan was not certain if she was the same two-legger who had startled her just moments earlier, but she seemed very familiar. All that was clear now was that the female was very angry. She barked and spat and waggled a finger at Jan, who understood nothing of her words. The female's tirade was a long string of nonsensical shouting and screeching to her, but she could not abandon the feeling that she was meant to comprehend all of it. The only two-legger she had ever understood was her other self, and only when they met in the imaginary forest.

The ranting female finally said a word she could understand: "Phyllis." It used to mean something to her other self. Then she remembered that her other self used to be known by that name before choosing another. This meant she believed Jan to be her other self. Jan tried to speak, but all that came from her mouth were the same nonsensical shouts and screeches. And worse, they only seemed to make the female angrier. She resumed her tirade with increased rage. Jan felt no anger in response, but angry sounds continued to come from her mouth. She felt as though she were observing this altercation instead of affecting any of it. She wanted to end this battle and escape this female, but something held her in place and made her a passenger in her own body. She and the female exchanged louder and louder gibberish, until Jan's arms threw themselves up, and her legs stormed her away from the female, stopping only long enough to yank herself free of the female's rough grip.

Jan stomped away, ignoring the shrieks of the enraged female, and passed through a wooden portal . . . into woods. Her woods. She was on all fours again and no longer hairless, but her own body seemed even more unnatural. Her hind legs moved awkwardly and stiffly, forcing her into little more than a staggered trot.

She was beginning to regret her sudden escape from the pack. Perhaps the farther she ran from them, the stronger her other self became. But this would mean the others were not following her. Not even Bluefur. The months to come would tell her if she were carrying his pups, but what then? He would want her to stay and raise them. The entire pack would raise them. She would never have been in this horrible state if she hadn't let her other self grow so strong. No wonder the Alpha was so disappointed in her.

She heard a faint rustling not caused by the wind, and that was soon followed by a scent. Jan's hind legs loosened up again; her balance returned to normal. She had all but forgotten her strange experiences of only a few minutes before; a meal was nearby. All of her senses returned to normal, as did her instincts.

Jan listened to the woods until another rustling came, but from farther away. Now she kept her body low, listening for any sound that prey would make, smelling the air, feeling the ground for vibrations, and looking for shadows.

The scent told her that food was just to her left. The moonlight revealed a small shadow trying to find its own meal of grass and leaves. She was downwind now; it would never sense her presence. She leaped, and a shriek filled the air, swiftly replaced by silence.

Thirteen

Loraine knew that she had eaten the night before. She could still smell the meal in the air and on her own breath. It took a few minutes for her to sit up beside the tree where she had fallen asleep. Jan had gone to sleep with her legs tucked up against her chest, leaving Loraine very stiff and with a sore back. She had not yet opened her eyes, nor needed to, to know that she was naked as always.

With a groan and a stretch, Loraine opened her eyes to find herself surrounded by the woods. She brushed the dirt and leaves from herself slowly, trying not to look at the rabbit carcass lying a few feet to her side. Then a noise startled her; Loraine sprang to her feet, crouched low and sniffed the air. Her ears pricked up and . . .

She straightened, forcing herself to breathe slowly and deeply. It was daylight now; hunting was over until the moon rose again. Or didn't the wolf understand this? There was no way for Loraine to know if the pack was teaching Jan strange and frightening things, such as how to make her "sleep" forever. It was then that she realized something strange: the pack was nowhere in sight. No sounds or smells or anything else alerted her to their presence. If she was finally alone, then this was good, but did it also mean that Jan had been banished?

In her heart Loraine knew this was not true. She would have felt it somehow. And she had all day to ask the wolf itself such questions. For now, let Jan rest and let Loraine find some clothing. Usually the wolf brought her near her diminishing supplies, but this area seemed unfamiliar.

Loraine walked a few miles without finding even the most meager signs of civilization, or any clothing, for that matter. She was cool, but not as cold as she could have been. Shortly after Jan had joined the pack, Loraine had learned to coat herself with just enough hair to keep warm until finding her supplies. It seemed unlikely she would ever find them this time.

The woods cut off abruptly into flat, treeless land. She kept to the trees while scanning for other people. There was a house just outside of the woods that, if the owners lived in another century, might have clothes hanging outside. With still no signs of people around, Loraine shifted to four-legged form and raced for the back of the house. Several feral cats scrambled away at her approach. Loraine smiled to herself as she thought of joining the ancient battle of dog versus cat, but then shook herself back to the business at had.

If Loraine had learned one thing about rural areas, it was that the nearest neighbors could be miles away in every direction. It seemed like such a lonely way to live, yet she had often felt more alone in the city, surrounded by people. She felt alone now, running from the law, but knew she would never be truly alone if she wished. The pack would always welcome her.

Loraine shifted quickly to human form. The morning chill set her teeth chattering, but she was determined to stay this way all day if necessary. Even when simply taking Jan's form, the wolf's thoughts began to seep in.

With still no signs of people around, Loraine continued her search for line-dried clothes. She was well in the back of the house, where a clothesline might have been strung, but there was nothing. Just her luck that these people would use a real dryer.

"Hold it!" a harsh male voice called from behind her. Loraine's instinct was to run, until clear thinking made her stay. Whoever it was could be armed.

"Keep your hands up and turn around slowly," the man said, and she did turn around, but kept her arms wrapped tightly around herself. For now, she would let the man hide behind his gun, but he was getting no free peeks.

"Roger?" she said after facing him. Joanie's ranch hand did have a gun—a rifle—but he nearly dropped it as his eyes went wide with recognition. He lowered the barrel enough to get a better look.

"Phyllis?" he said. Sheer surprise caused her to lower her guard, also, allowing Roger the free peek she had been hiding. She watched as his gaze went down to her feet and back again to her face. Only then did her arms wrap around herself again.

"Roger!" she snapped.

He started, then blinked a few times. "Jeez, Phyllis, you need to get inside. Here," he said, setting down his rifle and pulling off his jacket. He handed it to her, trying valiantly not to watch her take it.

"Thanks," she said, wrapping herself quickly. "I was just trying to—"

"What happened to you?" he said. "Don't you have any clothes?"

"I do, but I don't know where they are right now," she said. "Maybe I shouldn't go inside. Forget you saw me here. And don't tell Aunt Joanie, either!"

"What are you talking about?" he said. "Of course you should go inside. If you're in trouble, won't you let me help?"

"It's not the kind of trouble that can be helped," she said. "Really, I shouldn't stick around." She turned to leave and was stopped by Roger's firm grip on her arm. She could quite easily pull away and take his arm with it, but she was not up to resisting.

"You can't go running around like that," he said. "You'll get arrested, if you don't freeze first."

"Trust me, keeping warm won't be a problem."

"Phyllis—come inside," he said. "Have you been out all night? That was you at the ranch, wasn't it? Was that you running away that day?"

Loraine was silent for a long time. She wrapped Roger's jacket more tightly about herself and bit her lip. For now, she even resisted the urge to correct him about her name. Finally, she turned just enough to look up at him.

"I don't know why I came here," she said. "I didn't even know this was your place. I thought I was way away from anyone by now. I just don't want you hurt."

"Come inside, Phyllis," he said. "We can talk about it inside."

She said nothing, but nodded to herself and kept her eyes to the ground as Roger led her to the back door. He carried his rifle in one hand while going through the utility room, a short hallway, and then to a bedroom. Roger let go of her hand and turned his back on her in an effort to preserve her privacy.

"Um . . ." he said. "I don't exactly have your style, but you can borrow whatever fits you in here."

"Thanks," she said.

Roger hesitated, then went to the doorway. His back toward her, he said, "I guess I should call Joanie, and—"

"No!" Loraine cried. "No, please don't call her. I don't want her to know that I'm here."

"Why not?"

"Just please promise you won't call her!" Loraine said.

"But she's worried sick about you!"

"I know!" she said, then calmed herself somewhat. "I know she's worried about me. And I wish I could tell her what's going on right now, but . . . it'd take too long to explain. I plan on telling her all about this, but not 'til it's over. Will you please promise not to call her?"

"Yeah, I suppose. But I have to call her and—"

"Roger!"

"—Tell her that I'll be late today," he said. "I'll tell her my truck broke down or something. She's still my boss, you know."

"But that's it, right?" she said. "You won't tell her I'm here?"

"Right, fine, I won't tell her," Roger said, irritated. Loraine noted this, but trusted him to keep her secret. She dug through his drawers and closet for suitable clothing, which proved difficult. Roger was large and she was not, but eventually she created a wearable ensemble.

Roger was heating some coffee when she entered the kitchen. She struggled briefly with the belt which, even at the tightest notch, barely kept the borrowed pants up. Loraine sighed and let her feet drag on the way to the kitchen table. Roger left his post at the counter to pull a chair out for her. This gallant act took her by surprise momentarily, then she slumped into the seat. The microwave dinged, and Roger pulled out a steaming mug of coffee. Loraine smelled it perfectly from where she sat. She shut her eyes and breathed in deeply, savoring the memories it brought back of a more sedate time.

"How do you like it?" Roger asked.

Loraine opened one eye. "Like . . . ?" she said in a daze. "Oh, black is fine."

Roger set down the hot mug, then tended to his own brew. Loraine wrapped her fingers around the mug just to let it warm them. It was the first time she had realized how cold they had been. She would have sworn that she'd heard a crack as the blood inside thawed.

Roger sipped at his coffee while she stared at hers. "How is it?" he asked.

"Fine. Just letting it warm my hands first."

"Yeah," he said, leaning forward. "Sometimes that's the best part. On some February mornings, I just like to hold it awhile." He sipped at his drink silently. In fact, for several minutes not a word was spoken. Loraine finally took a sip of her own drink, then set down the mug and resumed her staring contest with it.

"Roger?" she said softly.

"Yes, ma'am."

"You didn't tell Joanie I was here, did you?" she asked.

"No, ma'am."

"I feel bad that you lied for me," she said. "I should let you get to work." She began to stand. "You'll just get in trouble if—"

"Sit, sit," Roger said, motioning her down. Loraine stopped halfway up and stared at his hand a while. Then slowly she followed his waving until reseated. "Don't worry about me," he said. "I'm not especially fond of lying myself, but I promised I wouldn't tell her. And I suppose you won't be telling me anything, either."

"Believe me, I'd love to tell somebody what's going on," she said. "It's just that—no one would believe me, and I wouldn't expect anyone to. So right now all I can say is thank you. Thank you for not—trying anything out there."

"Outside?" he said. "I should apologize for waving a gun at you. It's just that around here you can't always count on things being as small as a raccoon."

"Or as harmless," she said softly. "I'm still grateful for your help," she added, "but I shouldn't stick around here. You could be hurt or . . . something."

"If you say so," he said. "But at least I figure the FBI is done with their questions for a while."

"What?" she said. "The FBI?"

"So he said he was," Roger said. "For all I know, he was the dogcatcher. But the police have been by, and later a G-man to ask about what happened to Bill. And . . . some questions about you."

"Wh-what kind of questions?" she asked.

Roger shrugged. "They wouldn't tell *me* anything, of course," he said. "They wanted to know the details about Bill and the stud that had been killed, and about your own attack that night. I have a feeling no one knows yet what killed him. And attacked you."

"I do," she whispered.

"What's that?"

"Nothing," she said, then looked up. "So I guess

you're already in trouble. I mean, the cops and an FBI guy have been talking to you. Why somebody from there, though? The FBI, I mean."

"Well, I know they deal with federal crimes, and crimes that cross state lines, like some serial killers," Roger said.

"Serial killers?" she said.

"Yeah, you know how some of them go to other states," Roger said. "But I don't get it, either. That was an animal that killed him, not a person."

"What if it wasn't an animal?" Loraine said. "What if it really was a person?"

"A person?" Roger said. "But you saw it, didn't you? You said it was an animal."

"I thought it was at the time, too," she said. "But . . . it wasn't exactly."

Roger cocked his head. "Phyllis," he said, "are you saying you know what killed Bill?"

"Not exactly," she whispered. "I only know *what* did, not . . . Oh, you should get to work. I can't believe I've been saying even this much."

"Now don't do this to me," he said. "It's obvious you've been running from the cops, and maybe the FBI, too. And for what? At least tell me *some*thing. Do they seriously think *you* killed Bill?"

"No," she whispered. Her lips tightened to the point of trembling. Loraine found it impossible to keep her eyes open now. Not if it meant he could see her tears. "My roommate," she blurted out. "They think I killed my roommate! She was my best friend, Roger, and they think I killed her!"

"Hey . . ." he said. "Hey, easy . . ." She felt his hand

touch her shoulder, and wanted to pull away, but something made her stay still. Tears flowed freely now.

"I didn't kill her, Roger!" she cried. "It was somebody else. I don't know who it is yet, but I'm trying to find that out! And I was in jail, but they broke me out and killed some policemen to do it! They didn't even care! They just broke in and—"

"Who?"

"They threw people and things around and totally trashed a police station!" she said. "And I was glad that they did it! I was sitting there waiting for them and—"

"Who?"

"The others!" she cried, then stopped and wiped at her nose. Roger was holding her with both hands now. She looked up and into his eyes for the first time. Truly for the first time, as, until now, she could not have told anyone how deep and pure his brown eyes were. Her tears were forgotten as they locked gazes for nearly a minute. Loraine managed to break away only after she saw her own reflection in his eyes.

She felt his hand caressing her forehead as he pushed the hair from her eyes. She had always worn her hair somewhat short before, but now it was almost past her shoulders. She wasn't certain yet if she preferred it this way.

"Do you consider yourself to be . . . open-minded?" she whispered.

He seemed confused at first, and then shrugged. "I suppose," he said. "Depends on what I'm supposed to be 'open-minded' about."

Her instincts still told her to get away, to escape and continue her flight. Something else told her to stay with this man. She had met him during her first trip to this part of the country, but had never spoken more than a few words. He had simply been "Uncle Bill's ranch hand." She had hardly given him any thought. Or had she? Loraine's relationship with Michael had been in its final death throes at the time, and so most of her thoughts had been occupied by this. If Roger had shown her any attention before, it had no doubt been wasted. But there was no excuse for his attentions to be wasted now.

Loraine flashed a bittersweet smile. She took his hands from her shoulders and guided them to the table, where she held on to the tips of his fingers. "First, I guess I should remind you that I changed my name to Loraine a while ago," she said.

"Oh, that's right!" he said, shaking his head. "Joanie told me. I'm sorry, Ph—uh, Loraine."

"That's okay," she said softly. "It started after the attack," she began. "You know how I went to the hospital and needed stitches and . . . all that stuff. They gave me a lot of shots, too, like for rabies and whatever else you get from animal bites. The problem is, there was one type of bite they didn't have any protection for."

"Something gave you a disease?" Roger asked.

Loraine offered a smile again. "Some would call it a disease," she said. "Others would call it a way of life. The animal that attacked me—I mean, *us*—that night was a wolf. The problem was that it wasn't exactly a wolf, but a man who had let the wolf inside of him wake up."

"I . . . see," Roger said.

"I don't expect you to believe any of this," she said with a sigh. "I wouldn't, either, except that it's been happening to me, and . . . I wish there was some other way to explain what's happened to me, but the only way I can say it is . . . I'm a werewolf."

She was unable to maintain eye contact with him after her declaration. She felt his gaze still on her, however. She also noticed he was still holding her hands. She closed her eyes and relaxed, allowing the sounds of his breathing and heartbeat to reach her ears. She was surprised to find him still quite calm.

"I know it sounds—"

"It doesn't," he said. "You don't sound crazy, Loraine. If you say you're a werewolf, then you are. But maybe I should explain *my*self."

"Please don't tell me you're one, too," she said.

"Not exactly," he said, and rose from his seat. He held her hands tighter as he did, causing her arms to be yanked forward. Loraine did not let go, but now stood and let him guide her away from the kitchen table before he finally let go himself.

"So what do you mean?" she asked. "You really do believe me?"

"I guess I should," he said. "You should see something," he added, motioning her to follow. He led her outside to a shed next to the house. She sensed feline eyes watching her every move from beneath the house, but suppressed the urge to make chase. Roger unscrambled the combination lock on the shed door. He stepped inside and waved her over to a locked cabinet at the end of the shed. He had to fish around for the key to the old padlock, and needed to wiggle the key in the lock before it would open.

Inside was a single shotgun. Roger carefully removed it from its rack and wiped some dust from the muzzle. Loraine gave a nervous laugh without knowing why.

Roger only glanced at her before opening a small box inside the cupboard. He pulled out two shells and held them out for Loraine to see. She held up her hands and leaned back.

"No, thanks," she said. "I don't need to hold 'em."

"I didn't mean that," Roger said. "Can you tell what they're made of?"

Loraine peered at them now. "Metal?" she said.

"Yes, they're made of metal," he said. "I had some made a few years ago. They're silver-plated. I just hope I never have to use them."

"Me, too," she said. Roger turned away from her abruptly to return the shells to the box and the shotgun to its case. He shut the cupboard doors and snapped the padlock.

"A few years ago," he said, "my younger brother was attacked by an animal. Like you, he went to the hospital, got stitched up and had shots for rabies and everything else. The doctor said he'd be fine, and he seemed to heal pretty well. In fact, he healed a lot faster than they expected. And better, too. None of his wounds left any scars. Like yours, I see," he added, looking at Loraine's face as he spoke. She touched her cheek briefly.

"We never did find the animal that attacked him," he continued. "He wasn't sure at first what had attacked him, either, like you. Whatever it was, though, it had to have been big and strong. William was—that's his name—he was a big guy. Six foot two, two hundred pounds. He was always a little bigger than me after we'd grown. Anyway, William wasn't as well as he thought. He was never really good at controlling his temper, but I noticed that he was getting worse. He'd fly off about the dumbest things, and we'd fight for hours. And I couldn't get him to see the doctor again. Hell, I was afraid they'd missed one of his rabies shots. I didn't know what to think.

"Then about a month after the attack, William . . . changed. It was during a full moon—I remember that especially—and I saw him . . ." Roger stopped and held out his hands as though struggling to go on. "He started convulsing," he said. "He was sweating and thrashing around the room and—I thought he was having a fit, but I couldn't stop him. He was so much stronger than I'd ever seen him; he just pushed me away, and I went flying. I mean flying! I remember breaking a chair when I landed, but I got up right away and saw him . . ." Roger stopped again as though too frightened to continue.

"You saw him change," Loraine said quietly. "Didn't you?" Roger only nodded. She rested her hand on his shoulder. "He became a wolf, didn't he?" she asked. "Or something halfway between?"

Roger did not respond at first except with a nod. "I thought he was going to kill me," he said. "I looked into those eyes and . . . what used to be William's eyes, and they weren't his anymore. They were an animal's. Hungry. Evil."

"Evil?" she said. "Are you sure about that?"

"He took off into the woods," Roger said, ignoring her question. "Just took off. Flew out the window and ran off like a wild animal. I went out to find him—" He shook his head—"Never did. I remember hearing a pack of wolves howling that night. I don't know if William was part of it, but I remember thinking, wolves? Down this far south? It didn't make sense. I didn't see my brother again for six months."

"I'm sorry," Loraine whispered.

"And when he did come back," he said, "he was naked. He wasn't even in his wolf form, but just standing there, a man, and naked. I'm sure he didn't think anything of it, either. It was like he'd never worn clothes before, the way he was acting. He told me everything that night. He told me he'd been bitten by a wolf and was one himself now, and he'd joined a pack or something. He came back because he wanted me to join them, too, but— God knows I love my brother, but I'd never been as scared as that night. I told him I couldn't do it, and I tried to talk him into coming back, but he wouldn't hear it. He wanted to stay with that 'pack' of his. It was like he enjoyed being an animal, like he didn't want to be human anymore. Does that make any sense to you, Loraine? How a human being . . . a man can actually change into an animal, then give up everything like that? That doesn't make any sense!"

"Maybe it doesn't to you," she said. "It's not so much turning your back on humanity as embracing that new part of you. The wolf part, I mean. The pull of the pack is stronger than you think."

"So . . ." Roger said, "so that's what you're doing, too. You're going to leave here and run off with your 'pack,' too, huh?"

"I . . . don't know," Loraine whispered, turning away. She rubbed the back of her neck as she spoke. "You see, I wasn't there when Roxanne died. She was. The wolf was. I've been . . . communicating with the wolf— it'd take too long to explain how—and we've agreed that the pack can teach us how to find what they call 'The Exiled One.' He's the one who killed Roxanne."

"So what's his name?"

"I don't know," Loraine said. "They use their own names, not their human names. They don't even know me as Loraine, but as Jan."

"Jan," Roger said. "The wolf's name is Jan."

"Yes, they have names," she said. "That's not important right now. What is is that they want her to . . . make me 'sleep,' as they call it. I want to learn what I can from the pack so I can track down Roxanne's killer, but Jan may want to stay with them forever."

"What about a cure?" he said. "Isn't there some way to be all the way human again?"

Loraine shook her head. "It's not that simple," she said. "I've come to . . . respect the wolf. I think she's beginning to respect me, too. I wish I could explain this better." She rested her hands on his chest and leaned forward a little. "Believe me, Roger, if things were different, we could—" She pulled her hands away and turned around. "You really should get to Joanie's," she said. "Your car can't be broken down that long."

"And what about you?"

"I should go," she said. "There's another full moon tonight. You're already more involved than you should be, and I don't want you to have to lie for me anymore. The wolf . . . Jan . . . Believe it or not, I don't think she's killed anyone yet. A person, I mean. And she knows that some people are protected, meaning that they're special to me. That's how I know she didn't kill Roxanne, and I'm sure she'd never hurt you or Joanie. But . . . the others . . ."

"You think they've followed you?"

"I don't know," she said. "I think I would know if they did. But if they do, and you're with me . . ." Her voice trailed off until she gathered the strength to continue. "I doubt if just two silver bullets would be much help," she said.

He tucked his finger under her chin and brought her gaze to meet his. "I want you to promise me something," he murmured. "I want you to still be here when I get back. I think you owe me that."

"I can't—"

"I'll take the chance that your pack will come here, or that 'Jan' won't think I'm protected," he said, "but I'd never forgive myself if I just let you run off again. I'd really like you to stay. If you don't want me to tell Joanie about you, then I won't, but at least let me help you."

Answering his plea went against her every instinct. No one else was supposed to get involved. No one else was meant to be in such danger. The pack would surely kill him if they tracked her to here. But of course she would sense their approach and lead them away from him. And yet . . . his own brother was part of a pack. Perhaps because of this he would be protected from the others and be spared.

"All right," she whispered. "I'll stay. But the full moon—"

"We'll worry about that later," he said, holding her by the shoulders. She would not look him in the eyes, causing him to guide her chin up again.

"And what if you need to use that shotgun of yours after all?" she whispered, her eyes half-closed.

"I'd use it on myself first if it came to that," he whispered back, and leaned forward to brush his lips against hers. She shut her eyes all the way and let him press harder. The kiss ended too abruptly for her taste. She

kept her eyes closed as he whispered to her, and smiled
as his breath tickled her ear.

"Wait for me," he said.

"I will."

Fourteen

Loraine floated about the house for a few minutes after Roger's departure. It didn't take her long to find his old stereo. His tastes ran toward country and folk, but it didn't matter. It had been too long since Loraine had heard "two legger's" music—any music—or truly danced. The wolf could sing all night to the moon if it wished; the daytime belonged to Loraine.

She selected the most familiar group she could find, then paced the floor impatiently while waiting for the music to cue. The first song jumped right in with a quick beat and plenty of percussion. This was all that she needed. Loraine wanted to hear drums and a lot of them; the melody could be screeching tires for all she cared.

Loraine swayed and dipped and turned to the beat. It was not the best music she had ever heard, but it didn't matter. She was dancing for its own sake this time. At one point she arched back, then kicked high to make a backward flip. She leaped onto the table and held her leg up to her shoulder while turning slowly. She twirled and dipped and tumbled, not avoiding the obstacles in the house, but using them as springboards and even partners to her next spectacular moves. Her heart swelled with the first real joy she had felt in a long time. Music or no music, she could dance forever.

The first song was at its final chorus when Loraine's body hair stood on end. Her chest tightened, and one of her legs felt as though a tendon had snapped. Loraine crouched down and yelped in anticipated pain. Instead there was no pain, but her body shook in sudden fear. It was terror that she felt now, but the reason was unclear. She glanced all around the room and sniffed at the air, then leaped from the table to look out the window. Nothing. Her ears pricked to listen for anything strange, yet only the music filled the air.

She was getting dizzy from her quick breaths but felt powerless to stop them. She was too frightened to slow her breathing or stop the shaking, but why? Loraine could not even be certain whose fear she felt at this time: hers or the wolf's. Her terror was joined by anger at the thought that the wolf would still be intruding on her day life. Too many thoughts were flooding her mind now to be able to fight the wolf and send it back to "sleep."

She feared for Roger and herself. She had had to finally leave her old boyfriend Michael because of her problem, and could not go back to him now. The pack would surely track her wherever she was and kill anyone who was with her. But Roger had his gun with the silver bullets. He could very likely protect himself, unless it was she whom he had planned to use it on from the beginning. Then she'd be dead, leaving him completely vulnerable to the pack. He was in danger as long as she stayed. Roxanne had died because of her. She would cause no more deaths.

Loraine was out the front door before she knew she was running. Distant birds chittered away in the trees. As long as she heard no humans nearby, perhaps all would turn out as well as could be. Yet even their absence was not enough to calm this unexplained fear. What was causing it? What would end it? She raced back and forth in a zigzag that went nowhere, trying to catch her breath. The pounding of her heart reached all the way into her skull, sending her to her knees. It had felt so awkward, standing erect as she had been, yet crawling on hands and knees was no better.

Try as she might to calm down, Loraine could not catch her breath. She was certain her heart would stop if she didn't get one good breath immediately. She fell over onto her side, tears streaking down her cheek, and wondered if they would be the last tears she ever tasted. She was about to die and might never learn what had been her undoing.

A grey haze began to cloud her eyes, when her ears pricked at the soft mewing of a distant cat. She shut her eyes, and, just as suddenly as it had appeared, the fear was gone. She took the first of many long, deep breaths. Never had she tasted anything so sweet and cool. Her heart pounded as before, but this time from excited relief.

Loraine sat up just enough to hear better and to spot the lone feline. It was watching one of the birds and seemed not to notice her. Slowly Loraine rolled onto her hands and knees, which now seemed a very comfortable and natural position. The cat stayed transfixed on the singing birds. If any of its fellow hunters were about, they had long ago hidden themselves. Loraine inched her way toward the would-be predator, her yellow-green eyes never flinching.

The cat tried to flee when it heard something land behind it. Perhaps it felt great surprise as quick, strong hands snatched it from behind. Writhing and hissing, the terrified feline was lifted slowly, until its captor looked straight into its eyes. It vaguely recognized its captor as one of those two-legged beasts that had never come close to out-running it. Until now. A low, long growl coming from the two-legged giant's throat made the feline thrash violently. Loraine's yellow-green eyes flashed, and she smiled at the thought of silencing this howling, useless creature. She had never liked cats, but their meat might be very tasty. There was only one way to find out.

Loraine's hand splayed open, allowing the cat to drop to its feet and scramble away before its paws had hardly touched the ground. She watched the cat disappear and made no move to stop it. She looked at her hands, and then felt them as if not believing her eyes. They had never changed shape or appearance at all, yet in that moment, they seemed not to belong to her. Not to Loraine at all, but to . . .

Anger replaced her fear—a growing anger that sent her shooting back to Roger's house, slamming the door behind her and almost causing her to punch the wall. Loraine paced and fumed and shouted for the next few minutes before finally calming herself enough to think.

"Okay, okay," she whispered to herself. "She's gotten stronger now, that's all. The others are trying to make her stronger than me, that's all. But it's not going to happen. No, not going to work that way. Jan!"

Loraine grabbed a chair at the kitchen table, then turned it around before sitting. She propped her arms on the table and shut her eyes.

Jan, get out here! she thought to the wolf, not both-ering to create the park for their usual meetings. *Jan, I don't have time to think up trees and ponds for you. We have to talk.*

She listened to the silence, which remained just that.

Jan, we have to—!

Roger's kitchen was replaced by the darkness of the woods. Loraine tried to cry out, but no sounds emerged. She looked about and saw no one else present, neither two- or four-legged, and meant to run from this place. Something held her back, though . . . something heavy. She felt something heavy, but warm, on her back, keeping her from moving. Or rather, it was not the heaviness that made her stay, but something else. So far she had been unable to control her movements, as though she were paralyzed. In time she did move, but not of her own accord. Her body was moving on its own.

Loraine's head lowered itself until she looked at the ground, and finally her feet. These were not her feet, however, but the wolf's. Again her head moved up, and not at Loraine's command. The heaviness at her back had not gone away, and in time she realized that another wolf—a male, no doubt—was on her back and answering its call of nature. The earlier assault on Loraine's mind had failed to generate the sheer terror that this new experience did. One of her worst fears was now being realized: a strange, large male was raping her, and she was utterly powerless to stop him. It did not matter that she happened to be trapped in the body of a four-legged animal, unable to even cry out for help.

Her own scream woke her from this nightmare. Loraine kept her eyes shut and flailed her arms about, hitting nothing but a leg of the kitchen table. She opened her eyes and pushed herself to the wall, taking the next ten minutes to bring her breathing back to a more normal level. No one and nothing else was in the kitchen with her, and so she finally accepted that she had struck only the table and not her unnatural assailant.

Finally Loraine gathered the courage to stand up again. It was clear to her now what Jan meant to do. The wolf finally imagined itself strong enough to force its will upon her permanently. Jan was finally trying to make her "sleep."

Jan! she thought loudly. *We need to talk, and you know it!* Silence. *Don't you pretend you're 'asleep,' I know what you were trying! I'm ready for you now, so don't think you can—*

I'm here.

The words came from inside Loraine. This was the first time she had heard the wolf so clearly without the creation of their usual meeting place. Their connection seemed to be growing closer. Loraine had no choice now but to follow wherever this might lead. Now was the time to learn if the wolf understood this.

I know what you're trying to do, Loraine thought to the wolf, *and you have no right!*

Do you?

Loraine was quiet for a time. *I admit that I once thought that I had, but no longer,* she responded. *I let you run with the pack, and do whatever you like with them, and you still try to make me 'sleep'?*

The others have done this to their other selves.

And that makes it right? Loraine thought. *Because the pack killed their human selves, you believe this is good?*

They are older than I . . . Wiser . . .

Bullfuck! Loraine thought. *They're fooling themselves, and they're trying to fool you! Do you know what I think? I think they're afraid to remember that they were human once! They're afraid to admit that they'll never be all-wolf any more than they can be all-human!*

The pack fears nothing!

The hate and anger from the wolf was so strong that it hurt Loraine. She groaned and held the sides of her head, fighting the searing pain that emanated from the beast. And beneath this was the disturbing thought that the beast could be this strong during the daytime. If she won now, could she do so again at night, when the wolf ruled them both?

It does! Loraine thought over the pain. *Think about it, Jan! How could they not be afraid? They think humans are the scum of the earth, and only worth being eaten, and why? Because they were all human once! All of them! That means me, too!*

Roger's kitchen turned black. The pain was gone, but she was alone in a black void. There was no sign of the wolf here at all. She reached out and tried to feel her way around the darkness, unaware that she could see her own body perfectly, as though she herself were the only source of light here. As she groped in the darkness, Loraine had the unsettling feeling this was what the wolf's imaginary park had become. The once green park filled with trees and grass now reflected the blackness of the wolf's rage and hatred. Loraine decided to strike first.

I won't let you do the same thing to me, she thought. *You hear? I won't 'sleep,' or whatever it is the pack really did to their other selves! Haven't you figured that out yet? Didn't even one member of the pack figure that out? I can never be completely human again. You can never be completely wolf!*

She was given enough time to hear the roar behind her before something large and furry smashed into her from behind. Both Loraine and her attacker fell to the floor, but the wolf was on its feet first. As Loraine stood the beast leaped again, this time sending her flat onto her back.

She remembered the wolf as having reddish-brown fur, but she appeared almost as black as the void now. Only the whites of the eyes and teeth were visible, and the teeth shone more clearly than the eyes. The wolf snarled at the pathetic two-legged bitch pinned under its paws. There was an unmistakable gleam of pleasure in its eyes as it snapped at its prey.

Loraine knew that her defenses would last only so long against the beast. She could keep it at bay with her hands for a time, and possibly manage a kick or two, but the wolf was built to hunt . . . and kill. But it couldn't possibly kill her. The wolf would surely die with her. Wouldn't it?

Loraine screamed as the wolf clamped its jaws around her forearm, and shook it hard. She pummeled the top of its head with her free hand, which only strengthened its grip on her arm. Loraine felt she would save it the trouble of killing her by dying from fear.

Fear which suddenly left her. Loraine gritted her teeth at the pain, but kept her eyes open wide so she could look right into her attacker's eyes. She stopped flailing at the wolf, which glanced up at her, then shook her arm again. Loraine grunted and gritted her teeth. The wolf loosened its grip, but not enough to release her.

Kill me, Loraine grunted. The wolf's eyes widened. Its ears stood straight. *Kill me, Jan,* she thought again. *It's the only way you can be free!*

Jan loosened her grip on Loraine's arm even more. Loraine waited for the wolf to release it completely before pulling it away. She rubbed it as she "spoke."

The pack is right, she thought. *I'm just a weak human.*

A two-legger who could never survive in the woods, as you have. I'm weak and helpless. Be a wolf, Jan! Kill me!

You . . . Jan thought, taking a small step back. *You wish to die?*

I'm holding you back, Loraine thought. *If I can't even beat you in combat—just a cub amongst the others— what good am I to you? It's no wonder the others haven't accepted you.*

I . . . I ran from them, Jan thought. *The others do accept me.*

Then go to them, Loraine thought. *Go with the others. My job really is finished; the others exiled the one who killed Roxanne, and that's good enough for me. I just didn't realize it until now.*

Your friend . . . Jan thought, *she no longer matters to you?*

Of course she does, Loraine thought, able to sit up now because Jan had backed farther away. *But justice has been done. My job is done. I can't go back to what I was, so now I release you for good. Why are you taking so long?*

But—but killing is . . . Jan thought, taking a last step backward, then shaking her head. *How do I do this? They did not teach me this.*

You were doing a good job of it before, Loraine thought, holding out her arm. *One snap at the neck and—*she made a motion across her neck—*Shkshkshkshk! It's done. But I do have one request. I think you owe me that.*

A request?

That you do it quickly, Loraine thought, and waited. The wolf stared at her a long time, then looked away. Even that animal face showed the confusion that ripped through its thoughts. Loraine was certain she was beginning to sense Jan's feelings. It had happened before, but had never been consistent.

Do it quickly . . . Loraine heard Jan mutter to herself. *Quickly . . . Yes . . . Open her throat, and she would die without—* Jan looked up at her. Loraine could have shut her eyes and still known the fear rushing through her other self.

Why did you attack me? Jan thought. It was Loraine's turn to be confused.

Attack you? she thought. *You attacked me, remember?*

Jan shook her head. *Last night, you attacked me,* she thought. *You tried to make me sleep last night. You tried to put me into your world and frighten me into giving you control!*

I don't know what you're talking about, Loraine thought. *You're in charge during full moons. You always are. I don't even remember what you do all night. How could I attack you?*

I do not know, Jan thought. *You tried to drive me mad with strange pictures of flying back and forth into the sun, then flying until I hit the ground and then growling at another female two-legger who tried to grab me.*

Flying back and forth . . . Growling at a two-legger . . . Loraine thought to herself.

None of this would I have experienced with the others, Jan thought. *You tried to drive me mad!*

A swing! Loraine thought. *I remember dreaming about being on a swing. I used to swing all the time as a kid. For some reason I got scared this time and fell off. Then later I dreamed about fighting with my mom just before I left New York. You weren't being attacked. For some reason you were . . . well, you were having a waking dream!*

You wish me to sleep as much as I wish you to sleep! Jan thought, baring her teeth.

Then kill me! Loraine thought. *I'm tired of arguing with you! Do it!*

The she-wolf's ears flattened. She lowered her head and showed her full set of fangs. All four legs shook with renewed rage, and with a yelp, she leaped. Loraine made only minimal effort to resist, and lay on her back, her throat bared. The she-wolf growled and snapped at her throat, but never connected.

Loraine locked gazes with the beast. *Kill . . . me . . .* she "growled."

The wolf's posturing stopped. Her ears straightened, her teeth were again hidden behind her black lips, her growl was silent. *I cannot,* Jan thought, almost too quietly for Loraine to hear. She began to sit up, forcing the wolf to move back.

No, you can't, she thought. *There's no need to be ashamed, Jan. We don't have to fight each other anymore. Can't you see that? You don't have to believe everything the pack says. You don't have to follow everything they do!*

How can I not? Jan thought. *They have done so much for me . . .*

Yes, they have, Loraine thought. *Yes, be grateful to them. But listen to what your own heart says, not what they say. There's no shame in not being a killer!*

Loraine covered her ears as the wolf sat back and howled. What surprised her was how long it lasted—so long, in fact, it allowed her to slowly uncover her ears and listen. Truly listen for the first time to the song of the wolf. Her wolf. She heard more than just a single note or word. There was a song here—a full, living song

of betrayal, of pain, and somehow, love, as well.
Loraine's lips quivered, and tears welled up in her eyes
even in this strange land of the mind. The tears rolled
down her cheeks as she sat down and joined in. For a
moment the wolf stopped and watched her, then resumed
the song, but with a different meaning. There was a glad-
ness now that replaced the pain and sorrow.

Detective Thomas caught himself fingering his holster
as Agent Anderson pulled up to the security gate. His
badge gained them entrance, and they spent the next fifteen minutes trying to find a parking spot. Thomas rubbed
his gun's handle with his thumb, and looked over slowly
at the agent. Anderson felt the gaze and returned it.

"Something wrong?" he said.

Thomas shrugged. "Just wondering if we should've
brought silver bullets," he said.

"I did," Anderson said, and climbed out of the driver's
seat. Thomas sighed and hustled to catch up to the agent.
They did not speak as he kept pace with the taller man.
Thomas had given up trying to figure out whether Anderson was joking or not.

The elevator ride up was also silent, but each man's
reason was different. Anderson felt little but grim re-
solve, while Thomas doubted his own sanity. They had
seen the same thing that night. A woman had changed
into an animal before their eyes, disarmed them both,
and escaped into the darkness.

They exited at the proper floor and reached their destination at the end of the hall. A light above the door
served to warn away the usual traffic: "Recording in
Progress." Anderson knocked loudly. A large man with

long hair and a torn T-shirt opened the door a crack. Anderson held his badge inches from the man's face.

"FBI," he said. "And Detective Thomas of the Los Angeles Police. Is Tamara Taylor in?"

"Uhhh, yeah."

"We need to speak to her."

"Well, okay, but she's recording and stuff," the man said, opening the door enough to allow the two men to enter a small lobby. They heard a haunting melody from the speakers leading from Taylor's session. The control room was partially visible from their position. Their escort signaled them to wait while he opened the soundproof door cautiously. The monitors inside the control room mixed with the speakers in the lobby to create an odd echo effect.

A squat, balding man emerged from the control room. The flash of badges did not assuage his ill temper.

"Look, we're recording right now," he said. "You're just going to have to wait."

"We're only here to ask Ms. Taylor a few questions," Thomas said.

"About what?" the man said. "She's answered enough questions from you guys."

"If you don't mind, we'd like to decide when she's been asked enough," Thomas said, putting his hands on his hips. "We're very sorry about this interruption, but you haven't been returning our calls."

"She's been very busy lately," the man said. "As you can see, we've got an album to put out, and time is money. You're welcome to make an appointment."

"Sir?" Thomas said. "May I ask your name?" The man straightened up.

"I'm Ms. Taylor's manager, Paul," he said. "And if this is about her old choreographer—"

"Okay . . . Paul?" Thomas said. "We're not here to hang out backstage and get autographs. This is police business that we need to discuss with Ms. Taylor. Now we understand that 'time is money,' but the sooner you let us talk to her, the less of it is wasted. Is that clear to you?"

"Look, unless you've got a warrant or something, Ms. Taylor has nothing else to—"

They were interrupted by a dull rapping from inside the control room. The three men looked inside to see Tamara knocking on the double window separating her from the rest of the world. Once she got Paul's attention, she made a quick slashing motion across her throat. He held out his hands and pointed to his watch, but she waved him off and headed for the door leading to the control room.

"No, Tamara, it's all right," Paul said. "I'm just seeing to these—"

"I know these guys," she said. "It's okay. You can take five."

"Tamara, no," Paul said. "Not without your lawyer."

She smiled quickly and tapped his cheek in mock affection. "I said, I know these guys," she said. Paul blew out his breath through his teeth and shrugged. He could manage her, he could do his best to protect her, but he could never control her. That had been made clear from the time she hired him.

She led them down a narrow hallway, turning at least three corners before arriving at their destination. It was another studio, much smaller than the first, but just as soundproof. She gestured at two seats, which the two men used as Tamara seated herself at the end of the control room. She leaned back and rested her feet on the edge of the control board.

"Like he said, time is money, so state your piece," she said. Anderson cleared his throat, then reconsidered and nodded at Thomas.

"Yes, ma'am, we understand how busy you are," Thomas said. "We appreciate your speaking to us. There's something we need to discuss. You see, we think you really do know what's happened to Loraine Turner."

"It's just Loraine," she said. "She dropped the 'Turner' part."

"I see," Thomas said. "The fact of the matter is, we'd like to ask you about last night."

"Oh, yeah, when you were following me again," she said, letting her feet drop from the control board and leaning forward. "Did I bore you as much as the other times?"

"Actually," Thomas said, throwing a nervous glance at Anderson, "we, uh . . . we saw something that was a bit difficult to explain, and . . . we were hoping that you could help us on that."

"So you admit that you were following me."

"Ma'am, it's our job to check every lead," Thomas said. "You and Loraine were rather close, and—"

"How would you know something like that?" she asked. The two men exchanged looks, and Thomas cleared his throat.

"Well, you gave such an appearance, ma'am," he said. Tamara watched him with an implacable expression that slowly shifted to a smile.

"You have good instincts," she said.

"Thank you, ma'am," Thomas said. "But we're wondering if you can explain why you drove so far out of town just to run around in the bushes?"

"I'm an outdoor type."

"Could the full moon have had something to do with it?" Anderson asked. "Or do you go out every night?"

"Doesn't have to be a full moon," she said. "But I definitely 'go out' on those three nights." The two men exchanged another look. Thomas shifted in his seat and seemed to be considering his next words.

"I just thought I should say," Tamara said, "that you're not tricking me into revealing anything. If I didn't want to answer anything, believe me, you wouldn't get a word out of me. Maybe you should just ask what you really want to know, then let me get back to work."

"Ma'am, there's no need to take that tone—"

"What do you want to know, guys?" she said. "And don't call me 'ma'am.' I hate that."

"We want to know—" Thomas began, then glanced at Anderson, who nodded grimly. "Tamara . . ." he continued, "we want to know . . . if you're a werewolf."

"Yes."

Even Anderson was struck dumb by the quick answer. He watched her face for some slight change in expression, but it was neutral. Either she was telling the truth or she was a flawless liar.

Tamara glanced at her watch. "You have thirty seconds to wrap this up," she said.

"What?" Thomas said, the first to snap back to reality. "Thirty sec—? This could take all day now! Days!"

"Why? Is it illegal to be a werewolf?"

"Well, no, but—but—" Thomas sputtered.

"Loraine was assisted in escaping lawful confinement by a pack of werewolves," Anderson said with seeming calm. "Considering how rare such creatures are, you do understand that admitting your . . . condition makes you a suspect in her escape."

"So you came here to arrest me," she said.

"No, Ms. Taylor, we did not," Anderson said.

"Bringing a charge like this into a courtroom won't get us very far," Thomas said.

"Oh, surely, with the proper evidence, our case would be just as legitimate as any," Anderson said.

"Oh, come on, Gil—"

"I see that you boys have something of a dilemma," Tamara said. "If it helps, I didn't help her get away. At least, not from jail."

"Are you saying . . . ?"

"I'm saying that Loraine is innocent of killing Roxanne," she said. "Maybe it doesn't mean jack to you when I say that she was Loraine's best friend, and she loved the girl. As friends, I mean. She doesn't love women the way Roxanne did."

"I see."

"And she didn't want to get out of jail," she continued. "Not like that, anyway."

"Then why didn't she turn herself back in?" Thomas asked. "Or is that how you helped her?"

Tamara sighed and shut her eyes while smiling. "Turn herself back in," she murmured, then louder: "How come cops always think that's such an easy thing to do? 'Turn yourself in.' Have you ever been on the run before? Don't answer that. I'll tell you how I helped her. But first, some advice for you whether you think you need it or not. You're not dealing with some everyday fugitive. Loraine's like me: living in two worlds, and they intertwine more than you might think. She's not a killer, but there are others around her who wouldn't think much about ripping out a grown man's throat if it meant they'd have a meal that night."

"The pack, you mean," said Anderson.

"You're perceptive."

"Your pack?"

"I don't run with a pack anymore," she said. "And I was never part of the pack that busted her out."

"Do you know where they are?" Thomas asked.

"This would take forever to explain, but I couldn't help you find them," she said. "I seriously doubt if they're in the neighborhood anymore, either. Packs don't much like cities."

"In the hills, then," Thomas said. "Or the mountains?"

"I meant, not in this state at all," she said.

"Wisconsin?" Anderson offered.

"If you want to go that far, be my guest," Tamara said. "Packs like northern country. That's all I'll say."

"Yet you live in Southern California," Anderson said. "In Los Angeles, yet."

"I don't actually live here," she said. "I have a ranch in—" she cut herself short and smiled. "But that's nothing you couldn't find out from any tabloid," she said. "I've already said that I don't run with a pack anymore. And time's up, boys. I let you go a lot longer than thirty seconds."

"Why don't you let us decide when we're done," Thomas said.

"And how will you make me stay?" she asked. "Shoot me?"

"Ms. Taylor—"

"Take my advice, detective," she said. "Let Loraine

solve this herself. You're up against something much
more than human. You think doped-up gang members
on a drive-by shooting are scary? Go ahead and shoot
one of us point-blank when one of our claws is clamped
around your throat, and the other one is ready to rip off
your face. I'm not threatening you, detective. I'm warning you. I want this to end as much as you do, but your
chances of surviving this are much slimmer than hers,
and she's just a cub. Still learning what it is to be a
werewolf."

"You know we can't just sit back and let her solve it
herself," Thomas said. "More than human or not, she's
broken the law. And forgive us if we don't know werewolf laws. We only know that she's compounding her
trouble by staying out there. You're asking us to give her
permission to be a vigilante."

"Your funeral," Tamara said. "I can't tell you anymore."

"But, Tamara, we have a million questions," Thomas
said. "Where is she now? If she didn't kill her friend,
then who did? Is that person also a werewolf?"

"I don't *know* the answers to those questions!" she
said. "What the hell do you think she's doing right now?
Chasing her tail and sniffing dogs' butts? She's trying
to find out all those things herself. And she has *not* been
contacting me!"

"And after she finds these things out?" Anderson
asked.

"She'll bring in the real killer, what else?" she said.
"Wouldn't you?"

"Yes, I would," Anderson said.

"Unless you plan on arresting me, you both have to
leave," she said, standing and walking between them to

the control room door. *"Now.* Pick a better time to talk if you still have a million questions, but until then, I've told you plenty." She turned toward them; her eyes all but glowed a brilliant yellow-green. Her voice became extremely low and guttural. *"Don't you think?"* she added.

Both men shot to their feet and were at the door. Anderson paused to shake her hand.

"ThankyouMs.Tayloryou'vebeenveryhelpful," he rattled off. "Please understand that we do intend to continue this discussion, however."

She allowed them a glimpse of unusually long and sharp canines as she smiled. *"I'm sure you do,"* she said.

Agent Anderson kept up a brisker pace than before on the way to the parking lot. Detective Thomas had little trouble keeping up with him this time, though.

"How do you think that went?" Anderson asked as soon as they exited the building.

"I'll let you know after I've changed my underwear," Thomas said.

"Really?" Anderson said with only the slightest arch of an eyebrow. "I wish I could boast a similar reaction."

"Huh?"

Anderson thrust his hands into his pants pockets. "Only that I asked what you thought of our interview," he said. "Because I'm not sure myself. I couldn't read her at all."

"You couldn't read her?" Thomas said. "You couldn't see her eyes change color or . . . or hear that voice? Or wonder which was sharper—those teeth or a scalpel? Gil, we're in over our heads here!"

"Now don't lose yours over that," Anderson said. "If it makes you feel better, I could use a change of underwear myself. On the other hand, I'm convinced that that was just a scare tactic. If she ever wanted to kill us for knowing too much, she could have done so very easily last night, and gotten away with it." He whipped out his keys as they reached the car and unlocked the driver's side, then climbed inside. Thomas gripped the door handle on the passenger side as though it were a lifeline. He wasted no time climbing inside after his door was unlocked.

"How do you know she's not just toying with us?" he asked. "You know, playing with her food?"

"Do you think she was part of the pack that freed Loraine?" Anderson asked, beginning their drive toward the exit.

"She has to be," Thomas said. "Except that her alibi checked out when this whole business started. But how many werewolves can there be running around out there?"

"You're the local. You tell me."

"Be serious."

"When haven't I been?" Anderson said, successfully dodging traffic enough to pull out into the street. "In spite of what she said, I'd think that a city would be a perfect place for a supernatural being. Like those clippings you showed me of a big ape-guy running around the streets a while ago. That didn't even make the front page. By the way, I'd lay even odds that that ape-guy was one of our wolves. Yeah, cities are perfect for monsters. They're big, crowded, and have great night lives."

"And plenty of prey," Thomas muttered.

"Unfortunately," Anderson agreed. "Tonight's another

full moon. We can't leave Ms. Taylor alone tonight, wouldn't you agree?"

"Oh, God, not again," Thomas whispered. "What about last night?" he said out loud. "We didn't even get a chance to shoot, let alone find out if your silver bullets work."

"We have the advantage now of knowing what we're dealing with," Anderson said. "We can take her if we remember that we're not dealing with a human being. We'll remember how fast and strong she really is. She had the advantage last time."

"And if the rest of her friends decide to join in the fun?" Thomas asked. Anderson seemed to consider this a moment, then nodded.

"Then she'll have the advantage again this time," he said. Thomas watched him, hoping to find the slightest crack of a smile. At worst, he expected Anderson to burst into hysterical laughter and pinch him until he finally woke up from this bizarre nightmare. But the agent was as deadpan as ever.

Thomas turned away and pinched his eyes together, letting his breath blow out between his teeth in more of a hiss than a sigh. He was feeling cursed himself at this moment—cursed to be forever saddled with humorless people. The only difference was that one was as straight-arrow as they came, and the other's shots flew like a rollercoaster. If Anderson ever hit his targets, Thomas feared he would never know.

Fifteen

It was already dark when Roger pulled into his driveway, and it concerned him that he could see no lights in his house. He left the truck's headlights on half a minute after parking. He heard and saw nothing from inside the house, and gathered his courage to tiptoe to the front door.

"Loraine?" he called before resting his hand on the knob. A glance over his shoulder revealed a full moon just beginning its ascent among the stars. Still hearing nothing, Roger decided that Loraine had grown tired of waiting, and headed off to God only knew where. She had forgotten to lock the door, however. Roger stepped inside and was about to flip on the main light when he noticed a flickering glow coming from the next room.

He approached the room cautiously until a silhouetted figure stepped into view. He recognized it as a woman . . . he hoped.

"Welcome back," she said in a sultry voice.

Roger continued his cautious approach. "Loraine?" he said.

"Thanks for not turning on the light," she said, meeting him halfway. "The candles are doing the job well enough."

"Oh," he said, peeking around the corner. Four candles were set in a square on the living room table. The fireplace was also at full flame. "I didn't even know I had any."

She smiled. "I thought you'd be tired and wanted to keep it quiet when you got home."

"Oh," he said, letting her take his hands and guide him into the living room. "Yeah, quiet is good." He sat on his old couch while she sat across from him and tucked her hand under her chin.

"Are you hungry?" she murmured.

"No, not really," he said. "I grabbed something at Joanie's. Are you?"

She smiled again. "I already ate," she said.

Roger swallowed. "I see," he said. "You know, I—" he shifted in his seat—"I see that tonight's going to be a full moon. It's rising already. You remembered that, did you?"

"Of course, silly," she said. "We talked about it this morning."

"So . . ." he said, waving his hand in a circle, "so . . . do you feel like something's happening? Like you're changing at all?"

She showed her biggest smile yet, then stood halfway to scoot over to his side of the room. Roger moved over as she sat beside him and put her hand on his thigh.

"I've already changed," she murmured. "I won't be going anywhere tonight."

"But it's a full moon," he said, leaning away slightly. "You know, how you said that full moons make you . . . change?"

"We'll talk about this later," she said, leaning over and touching his shoulder now.

"So . . . you're saying that you really *don't* change into—"

"—A werewolf?" she said, pausing a moment in her subtle pursuit. "That hasn't changed. I'll never be completely human again. But that's my choice now. I still am, and always will be, a werewolf. But you don't have to fear me during full moons anymore. Or ever."

"I don't follow you."

"Oh, Roger," she said, scooting closer to him now, "it's strange how I hardly even noticed you when I was first here. I didn't see what a good man you were."

"I'm . . . much obliged," he said, holding her away gently by the shoulders. "But that boyfriend of yours? You're sure you're not—?"

"We talked about that this morning, too," she said with a giggle. "He's no longer a part of my life. He can't be. Don't worry; fidelity is very important to us."

"Us?"

"To me," she said. "And to you, too, I hope." She had managed to get close enough to warm his face with her breath. Roger was frozen in place as she leaned even closer. Then suddenly he pushed her away gently and stood.

"What's wrong?" she asked.

"Nothing," he said. "I'm just not sure if—well, maybe we shouldn't. You're Joanie's niece—my boss's niece, you know, and—"

"And *that* is what's making you nervous?"

"No, 'course not," he said. "It's just—well, hell, we hardly know each other, and . . ."

Loraine smiled as she rose slowly from the couch. "You don't have to explain it," she said softly. "You're still not sure about this little problem of mine. If it's real, or if I'm just a few llamas short of a ranch?"

That brought a small chuckle from him. It was also not until she was facing the light of the flames that he noticed how light her eyes appeared. He remembered them as darker, not the sparkling light green that reminded him of his mother's favorite jade crystal.

"You know that werewolves are real," she continued, pulling him back from his reminiscing. "And you wonder if I am, too. I am. But . . . no longer the way you might think." She sighed. "Maybe this is too fast, or confusing. Will you dance with me, then? It won't hurt just to dance with me. I haven't danced in so long."

"I'm really not much of a dancer," he said, as she took both of his hands and tried to lead him to an open area. "I'll just step all over you. Really, I don't—"

"You don't have to," she whispered. "You asked earlier if I was hungry. Well, I am. But not for food. For music. It's just as important to me as breakfast, lunch and dinner. Is there anything you feel that way about?"

"Uh . . . I'm not sure," he said, as she leaned over and clicked on his stereo to her preferred selection. It was music that Roger had never listened to until now. He had never appreciated classical music as much as his mother had wished; in fact, he had no love for it at all, but had never brought himself to throw away her gifts of several tapes.

"That's too bad," she said, facing him again. Her eyes appeared more yellow than green in this light. They seemed to flicker with their own luminescence. Roger found himself unable to turn away from them.

"Everyone should have something that gives their life meaning," Loraine whispered. She held out his right arm, then rested her left hand at his waist. Roger responded stiffly, shaking his head gently.

"Uhhh . . ." he said, "I'm really not so good at this kind of dancing. I can kind of do a line dance, but—"

"Shhhh," she said, quieting him. She let her head rest against his chest. "Just relax and let it take you wherever it wants."

He had never waltzed before, not even at his sister's wedding, and so his feet kicked at Loraine's several times. Eventually she stopped moving. Roger forced a smile.

"See?" he said. "I just keep—"

"I'll lead," she said. He thought it best not to argue, and nodded, then was suddenly swept away to the other side of the room. She was only half his size, but Roger felt his feet dangle in midair more than once as she led them around and around the room, and then through the other rooms of the house. The kitchen table became a centerpiece to their dance, and it was then that Roger pulled away and tried to let go. But Loraine held on tightly and pulled her stiff, nervous partner even closer to her.

Her appearance had changed. Before his eyes her body had covered itself with fur, and her face had stretched and pulled itself out into something very much like a wolf's. Her nails had grown longer, and a tail had begun pushing its way out of her clothes. Even her feet had stretched themselves to twice their length. In all of this, she had never stopped dancing and never stopped looking into his eyes. And all that Roger could think of then was a childhood memory of being frightened by a cartoon about The Three Little Pigs and their nemesis The Big Bad Wolf.

"Don't be afraid," said the wolf-beast with a gruff, but oddly gentle, voice. *"I would never hurt you. That's a promise."*

It took all of Roger's courage to stay where he was and let her continue their waltz around the house. He could feel her changing again, her balance shifting. Her fingers seemed to pull away from his, until he no longer held fingers, but paws. Her face was no longer half-woman and beast, but all beast now. He looked down to see a wolf's body struggling to stay erect as they spun around the living room. Then, her body changed again without missing a step. She appeared as before—the half-human beast—and continued the change until she appeared as Loraine.

His fears were dissipating as rapidly as her transformations came. With almost each step, she shifted from woman to beast to half-beast and every point in between. Roger's hand stopped sweating, and he held her closer even after the music had stopped. They wrapped themselves in each other's arms and swayed gently in the silence that followed. The heat of the flames and their own breath warmed them.

The silence was then broken by the distant song of the wolfpack. Loraine's ears pricked, and she closed her eyes and leaned against Roger. He wondered if she knew that her features were changing to match the other beasts.

"That's . . . the pack, isn't it?" he whispered.

"Yes."

"They sound close," he said. "They're coming here, aren't they?"

"No," she said. *"I don't want them to come here. They know that. They just . . . want me to know that they're near."*

"And what about you?" he asked. "Do you want to go with them?"

"Yes," she whispered, then looked into his eyes. "But I can't. They banished Uncle Bill's killer, believing it to be the worst punishment possible. In their own way, they were right, but they don't care about the human world. They don't care about the people that he'll be killing on his own. We can't allow that."

"We?"

"Jan and I," she said. "You see, we've joined. That's why I won't change, even during full moons, unless I want to."

"You've lost me completely. I mean, the dancing . . . You were changing . . . or was that me?"

"I was changing," she said, taking both of his hands and leading him to the nearest chair. "Thank you for not being afraid."

"Speak for yourself!"

"All right, then not running away, or getting that special rifle of yours and . . . Just thank you for not doing those things," she said, then knelt down and rested a hand on his. "Actually, I could tell that you were afraid. But my promise stands. I would never hurt you.

"This morning," she continued, "the wolf came to me. It's hard to explain what I mean by this, but for the first time I could really feel what she was feeling, and she could, too, although I didn't know until later. We . . . came to an understanding, eventually. Perhaps the wolf sensed that it was time."

"Time for what?"

"That we could no longer live in constant battle with each other," she said. "That it was time to do something that no other werewolf has done that we know of. Even

the pack hasn't made peace with their other selves. They
hate their human sides. They want to be full wolves, and
refuse to admit that they never will be. I guess . . . I
guess we both realized that wasn't right. Jan has just as
much right to live as I do. My point is that maybe there
is a cure. Maybe I could 'kill' the wolf in me and be
completely human again. But I don't want to do that.
She isn't evil. Yes, she hunts for her food, and will kill
for it, but that isn't evil. No more than any animal who
kills its own food."

"But—but I thought werewolves eat . . . people,"
Roger said.

"The pack does," she said. "They destroy their human
selves more with every human they kill, but they don't
realize that their human selves will never be completely
destroyed. Or maybe they do. Maybe that drives them
crazy, knowing that."

"But not you."

"I couldn't afford to be battling myself any longer,"
she said. "I need Jan to do what I need to do. Another
werewolf killed my best friend, and I don't think I could
find him alone, or fight him, for that matter."

"You're not seriously going to try to take on another
werewolf, are you?" Roger said. "That's ridiculous!"

"Am I supposed to go to the cops and tell them what
they're *really* looking for?"

"You don't have to tell them you're looking for a
werewolf!" he said. "Just tell them you know who did
it, and—"

"I *don't* know who did it," she said. "The only one
who's seen him long enough to identify him is Jan, and
only when he was in wolf form himself! I caught maybe
a glimpse of his legs one time before blacking out, but

that's it. She'd know him by the smell, too, so I couldn't tell the cops anything. In other words, he needs to be hunted."

"But you must be wanted," Roger said. "Aren't you?"

"Yes, I am," she said. "The pack thought they were doing me a favor by busting me out of jail."

"So they should help you do this, too."

"Tch," she said contemptuously. "Been there, tried that. No, they just want me to run with them forever. No matter how tempting that is, it wouldn't be justice. And the cops would just lock me up again. Maybe they'd believe that someone else did it, but they sure as hell wouldn't let me out to help them! And I shudder to think what would happen to the cops who thought they could kill him with bullets alone. No, I'm doing this on my own."

"The hell you are."

"Look, I appreciate that you're worried—"

"I'll go with you," he said.

She was taken aback a moment, then touched his cheek and shook her head. "I'd worry even more about what he'd do to *you*," she whispered. "I can't let anyone else be hurt because of me."

He took her hand from his cheek and held it. "Nobody's been hurt because of you," he said. "Sounds to me like some other wolf has been trying to mess you up bad. I *will* go with you. You're going back to L.A., right?"

"Well, yeah, but what about Joanie? She needs you."

"I think you need me more right now," he said. "I'll have to make sure Joanie will be okay without me for a while. But the more I think about this, the more I wonder if . . . maybe this werewolf was the one who took William. I don't know. But I couldn't let you do this alone."

"The police will be after you, too, if—" she said, when Roger stopped her with a finger to her lips. This seemed to calm her down. She shut her eyes and sighed.

"Now enough talk from you," he said, then reached down to pull her up. She stood enough to sit on his lap and lean against his chest. He wrapped his arms around her and kissed the top of her head. She responded with a long, languid gaze before meeting his lips halfway. By now the moon had risen to nearly its full height, filling the house with a soft blue glow bested only by the orange flickering of the flames in the next room.

Loraine's ears pricked at the others' mournful song. They were too far away for her to tell if the song was meant just for her, but tonight it would go unanswered, whatever its message.

Agent Anderson hung up the phone and pulled on his coat. Detective Thomas, in the middle of his own call, looked over at him. Anderson waited patiently as Thomas succeeded in hurrying the call to its conclusion.

"We're going somewhere?" he asked.

"I am," Anderson said. "I'm afraid we must part ways. They found two more bodies with the same m.o. as our furry friends."

"No shit. Where?"

"Wisconsin."

"What? I'm going with you," Thomas said, holding out his hand as he shot out of his own seat. "Wait here."

"That's up to your lieutenant, but I have to leave now," Anderson called as Thomas raced around the corner.

* * *

"But, sir, this is just where I've been expecting this to go!" Thomas said. "You've heard me talk about that possibility. That's two—no, three bodies now in Wisconsin with the same m.o.! You've got to let me accompany him as the arresting officer!"

"I don't 'got to' let you go," Hubbard said.

"I meant, please let me go with him," Thomas said.

"This case has been under federal jurisdiction since both locations were established," Hubbard said. "If I could spare you, I'd let you go, but I'm sure Agent Anderson and his partner are quite capable of wrapping things up. I realize that you've been working closely with him, which is unusual enough as it is, but we have to leave it in their hands."

"We don't *have* to leave it in their hands," Thomas said. "Look at the circumstances. A lot of good men and women were killed or hurt because of that girl!"

"There's no reason to take that kind of tone," the lieutenant said. "Now I've already said that I can't spare you, so we'll just have to trust the feds to handle this from now on."

" 'Take that kind of tone.' Come on!"

"Hey!" the lieutenant said. "Do you need to take the day off? I hope not, because you're needed here. But if you can't—"

A knock interrupted the lieutenant's lecture. Agent Anderson shuffled his way into the office. "I hope I'm not interrupting anything," he said.

Hubbard walked over to him, his hand extended. "Oh, not at all, Agent Anderson," he said, pumping his hand briefly. "I've just been told that you've been called away.

I wanted to thank you for all your assistance. Good luck on this latest lead."

"Thank you," Anderson said. "Detective Thomas expressed interest in accompanying me. Even though the case didn't begin here, I think there'd be no objections to his going with me to Wisconsin."

"Thank you, but he needs to stay here with us," Hubbard said.

Anderson needed only a glance toward Thomas to see that this feeling was not shared. He shrugged. "I'm sorry to hear that," he said. "Detective Thomas, it was a pleasure, and if it helps, there's no guarantee the case will end there, either. Maybe we'll work together again."

"I'd like that," Thomas said, offering his hand. They shook hands heartily before Anderson pulled away and glanced at his watch. He waved to both men and disappeared around the corner.

The two remaining men exchanged nothing but silence now. Thomas tucked his hands into his pockets and threw the lieutenant one last look before leaving the office. He stopped at his own desk, where a dozen other unsolved disappearances awaited him, as always.

Sixteen

She had been hunting for them this time. It was a chill night, and the darkness had fought and won against the fading moon. Loraine was not blind from the lack of light, but did need her other senses to find her way to the pack.

They had run far since the night before, when they had been so dangerously close to the two-leggers' territory. Now she sensed they meant to travel as far north as possible. Much of the land there was still hospitable to their kind.

The others were resting when Loraine pushed her silent way into the clearing. Most of them looked up, then relaxed at the sight of one of their own. She walked on four legs while amongst them. She searched for, then approached the Alpha, who lay so as to relax and be ever watchful at once. She bowed her head slightly, and he did the same. His mate, the female who had led the pack in his absence, watched her silently. She seemed more content in this new role than to forever lead the others. Jan wished to speak, but opted to allow the Alpha to begin. She needed to know first if she were still welcome amongst them.

I sense there is still great turmoil within you, cub, the

Alpha said. *Even your form betrays the presence of the two-legger within you.*

Actually, she said, glancing around before continuing, *the two-legger will always be within me. There is no longer a torment. I . . . came to bid good-bye. I have a task to perform, and I would not ask you to help me. You've done your part already.*

And when this task is completed . . . ?

Jan sighed and looked about solemnly. *Even then, I could not run with you. Loraine and I have peace. For good. You choose to live as you do, but neither of us could survive that way. You make your two-legged selves sleep for all time. We cannot. We must both be awake, always, if we hope to succeed. Does this . . . anger you?*

The Alpha exchanged a look with his mate, then returned to Jan's attention. *We cannot be angry with you for this. It is agreed, though, that running with us as you are now would be . . . uncomfortable for the others. And I sense that this is no fleeting condition.*

It is not, Jan said. *We will always be one. But the price is that neither of us can ever take our true forms. A two-legger may look at me and see a wolf, but you know better. In the same way, a two-legger will notice something different about me when I walk amongst them, though the wolf may see nothing amiss. I do not yet know whether I will be accepted amongst them, either, or scorned as an outcast.*

Know, cub, that you would always be accepted amongst us, the Alpha said.

Would I?

The Alpha watched her a moment, then made to speak, when Jan was distracted by a sound off to her side. She looked, and saw the muzzle of a familiar wolf peeking out from the dark bushes. Forgetting her manners, she broke away from the Alpha and approached Bluefur, who remained motionless all the while.

They stood nose to nose, the tips almost touching. Bluefur brought out his tongue to kiss her muzzle, then widened his eyes and leaned back slightly.

Something is wrong, he said. *Are you feeling well, mate?*

She smiled as best as her thin black lips would allow. *I feel better now than I have in too many moons, mate,* she said. *But you can see well. I am sad now, and it pains me that you, too, will be the same.*

You mean to leave us, he said. She nodded once. *Why would you do this?* he asked. *You cannot leave the pack and me, your mate. You carry my cubs!*

I carry . . . no one's cubs, she said, her head still down. *I know that someday, I would have, but now that will never be.*

Because of the two-legger's stench that you carry with you? Bluefur said. She looked up. *Yes, I smell the other male on you.*

This is not as simple as you think—

A two-legger male, Bluefur growled. *And* after *we had mated!*

And what of your own mate? she countered. *I came to bid the pack—and especially you—a thankful farewell. Yes, I am grateful to all that you and the others have done for me. Yet now you spit venom upon me before I've spoken a word! Do not snarl at me about loyalty to one's mate, when you left your own human—yes, a two-legger!—wife and children to run with the pack! What of them?*

And would I have heard their call had you not changed me that night? he hissed. Jan curled her lips tight into a snarl, then let them slowly relax. For creatures who prided themselves on being so different from the humans, they imitated them well. She lowered her eyes and took in a deep breath.

Your words are true, she said quietly, then looked up. *But hateful, also. I was not then what I am now, that night when I brought you over so brutally. Perhaps I left you with no choice but to leave your old life and everything that was in it. Including family. Not rejoining them is your choice. And not remaining with the pack is mine. I would not ask you to leave the others and join me, nor would I expect you to come if I did ask. But I must have justice. We have run and hidden from our troubles for most of our lives, and can do this no more. Farewell, Bluefur. Though I leave you and the others now, I will always feel your presence within me.*

Bluefur said nothing as she leaned forward and licked his muzzle on both sides. She pressed her nose against his for a few minutes, then parted and walked past the others without a glance back. She broke into a run shortly after clearing the surrounding bushes. The sounds of the night woods were momentarily drowned out by the pack's mournful song of loss.

Joanie hugged her niece long and hard, afraid to let go for fear of losing her forever. Chances were good that this would be true, but she did not know how good. Loraine forced back a bitter tear for not telling her aunt the whole truth. Joanie only knew that she needed to return to California, and that Roger was going with her.

"I'll write to you more than I had been," Loraine said.

Joanie smiled. "I suppose I've been bad about that, too," she said.

Roger stepped forward to offer his own embrace, which Joanie took gladly. "I feel terrible about leaving you," he said. "You sure you'll be okay?"

"I'll manage," Joanie said. "It shouldn't take but a few days to find a new hand from around here. Until you get back, that is. Besides, Loraine seems to need you more than I do right now. At least, that's the impression I get . . . ?"

"It'd just take too long to explain, Joanie," Loraine said. "I promise you that I'll tell you everything when I'm done in L.A."

"Well . . ." she said, "you know what's best."

Roger drove while Loraine rode beside him. Her knees pressed deep into the cushion as she waved frantically at her aunt. Only after Joanie had dwindled to a mere speck, and a bump almost threw Loraine out of her seat, did she turn around and sit properly in the passenger seat.

Roger's radio wailed away at his choice of music, which Loraine scarcely heard. Her thoughts were on things far away. She pushed the seat back until it was almost horizontal, and lay back to lose herself in the clouds. Roger sensed her need for silence, but offered her a gentle pat and rub on the thigh as a small offer of comfort. She acknowledged it with a sigh and a nod, then shut her eyes and tried not to think about what was waiting for them down south.

Agent Anderson met Agent Davis, his partner, at the airport.

They flew in silence. Anderson hated flying no matter how much of it he'd done as part of his work. For a time his nickname in Washington had been "Rain Man" due to his annoying tendency to quote airplane crash statistics as casually as his cinematic counterpart. Davis also suspected Anderson hated airplanes because of the possibility of someday flying into the waiting maw of an alien mother ship. Anderson himself had never voiced such a concern, but Davis had known his little quirks for a long time. Perhaps too long.

Anderson rarely gave a second thought about any of the local lawmen he worked with in the past, but he did spend some time wondering how poor Detective Thomas was faring, now that he had accepted the existence of werewolves. Those nonbelievers could be a stubborn lot at times, but Thomas had been gifted with an open mind, at least. Anderson silently wished him well in convincing that lieutenant of the real murderer's identity.

Davis, at his partner's insistence, skipped their stop at the hotel to head for the crime scene. The local authorities had picked it clean, but Anderson preferred viewing the scenes for himself. There would be time enough later for poring over photos, notes and tape recordings.

It was night by the time they arrived. The gruesome discovery was many miles out of town. Davis knew better than to try to convince Anderson to wait until dawn, when visibility would be substantially improved. Armed only with a flashlight, Anderson stepped out of the car and made a slow circle around the area. Davis followed him as far as the edge. The only sounds he heard were the crickets and the crunching of leaves under the agent's feet. Davis stopped and shoved his hands in his pockets, watching his friend and partner shine his light first onto the main area, and then into the nooks and crannies of the surrounding plant life. As Anderson searched, sometimes walking, sometimes stopping to kneel for a closer look at something, Davis noticed an odd silence. The crickets chirped merrily away, but the crunching of the leaves was gone. The ground where Anderson walked was covered with leaves, but he moved as silently as a breeze. This led Davis to two conclusions: either his partner had been raised in a Shao-Lin temple and forced to walk on rice paper without leaving a trace, or he had already flown into the waiting maw of an alien mother ship long ago.

"Find anything?" he asked, hoping to steer his thoughts back to reality.

"Not yet," Anderson murmured, bringing his flashlight up to shine almost into Davis's face. "You're probably right. We can try this tomorrow morning."

"I thought we could go to the m.e.'s office first thing tomorrow," Davis said as they headed back to the car. "We can compare notes with what you've seen in Los Angeles." He walked to the driver's side to fish around for his own flashlight. "What is it?" he asked after pulling it out.

"Shhhhhh," Anderson said. "Listen."

Davis listened, and after a long silence, a familiar sound wafted in from far in the distance. It was the sound of many voices raised into one mournful cry, or the wind. Davis had been trained to expect the worst, however, and opted for the former.

"Let's get into the car," he whispered. "It sounds like it's coming from that way."

Anderson was ignoring his partner's advice. His flashlight beam continued its dance on the bushes and trees, but never pierced the darkness enough to reveal anything. He took a few small steps forward and listened. Soon enough it came again—that low, sad song, but not quite as distant as before. Anderson wavered back and forth as if contemplating his own investigation, then looked back at his partner, who was fingering his holster.

Anderson clicked off his flashlight and went back to the car. He heard Davis's sigh of relief quite clearly, but never voiced this. He would humor his partner by looking at the local authorities' photos and reports after a sleepless night, knowing that the real answer waited in the darkness.

Roger and Loraine met no opposition at the train station. Taking the train instead of an airplane had been Roger's idea. His reasoning had been it would be cheaper and there was probably less security than at airports. After all, people didn't hijack trains or try to sneak bombs on board that he knew of. He confessed to a lifelong desire to take a long train ride, and this was his first real opportunity. Loraine had grumbled at the plan, then decided she was too tired to argue. The trip would be long, offering both of them the chance to rest, get their bearings, and most importantly, form a plan.

They attempted this after the train had left the station and they settled into their car. It was only here that Roger saw Loraine's true face. Her recent transformation allowed her to alter her features with hardly the effort that it had been before. She could probably hold them indefinitely now, but was reluctant to test this.

They sat side by side on the small pull-out couch and watched the landscape fly by as the train reached its highest speed. They did not speak for a long time, and were almost motionless but for their breathing and Roger gently rubbing her hand with his thumb. They had tried to discuss a plan for when they reached Los Angeles, but fatigue won for now, though it was barely the afternoon. After a time, Loraine moved from her spot and looked Roger in the eyes. Their lips met in a kiss and a brief embrace, then both stood as one and tugged at the sofa until it formed into a bed.

Little else occurred that day. They both slept soundly, their bodies pressed into each other and providing more warmth than any of their blankets. Loraine ate heartily that night, but Roger spent much of his meal watching her, wondering why he had hardly noticed her the first time they'd met. He felt a tingle every time she looked up at him and smiled, her eyes glistening as bright as the stars. Later they took a walk through the narrow corridor, still without words between them, she wearing her altered face whenever they left the safety of their sleeping quarters.

After they finally went to bed, Loraine lay on her back and stared at the ceiling. Even with the moon as weak as it was, its call was unmistakable. Half of her wanted to tear the sheets off, leap through the window and run off into the night. Joining both of her selves was good for both, or neither side would have agreed, but there would be more adjustment needed than Loraine had realized. As long as it was done before they reached Los Angeles.

She heard something outside the train even above the noise of the engines. She sat up slowly so as not to disturb Roger, and pressed her face against the glass. Her eyes were already accustomed to the darkness and could make out a number of familiar shapes . . . racing the train?

Loraine leaned closer and wished she could open the window, when the shapes snapped into better view. They were wolves, or rather, werewolves like herself, and they were running to keep pace with the train. For a moment Loraine thought it was her own pack, trying yet again to bring her back. Then she realized that she felt no bond with these wolves. They were strangers to her.

She watched them race for some time, until the Alpha broke away from the pack and disappeared over the hills. The others followed, and she saw them vanish, too. Something on her shoulder startled her; she yelped, then looked to see Roger's hand there. Shutting the curtain, Loraine lay back down and turned toward him a little. He caressed her shoulder and arm.

"Something wrong?" he whispered. Even in the darkness Loraine saw the glint of his eyes. Most likely he could see nothing at all, but she resumed staring at the ceiling to avoid eye contact.

"No," she whispered. "No, just a little nervous, I guess. Sorry if I woke you."

"No problem," he whispered. "It's gonna be fine. We'll find him."

"Yeah, we probably will," she said, patting his hand. "But who'll win?"

"We will," Roger said. "Just keep telling yourself that."

Loraine meant to express other doubts, but she was tired, and the gentle rocking of the train was finally making her eyes heavy. All she could manage for him was a quiet moan as he leaned over to kiss her. She lay still and shut her eyes, letting his breath warm her face. Calm as she was then, though, her sleep was broken often by troubled dreams.

Seventeen

Detective Thomas was feeling particularly lonely. With his temporary federal partner gone, the lieutenant was free to push any preexisting cases upon him. Certainly the detective was determined to see every one of them solved, but he knew the answer to one case, and could tell no one. He had spent much of that morning pondering just how to phrase the answer to this case so that he wouldn't be removed from it immediately. The lieutenant was almost comfortable with the fact that animals had been a part of Loraine's escape, and that was the problem. He was *almost* comfortable.

Intelligent dogs . . . he mused to himself. *No, maybe a government experiment. A super race of animals. Maybe Loraine is a mad scientist. Jeez, those are no better than the werewolves!*

Thomas threw down the pencil he had been fingering while thinking, then stood and walked determinedly around the corner. The lieutenant's door was closed, so Thomas knocked. He stepped inside slowly after gaining permission to enter. The lieutenant was on the phone, but almost done, by appearances. Thomas had noted early on that Hubbard always started phone conversations seated at his desk, then stood, then paced as much as the phone cord would allow when he was trying to

wrap things up. He was pacing when Thomas came in.
The lieutenant gestured at a chair, but Thomas opted to
stand and wait.

"What's on your mind, Thomas?" Hubbard asked as
he hung up the phone. "Have a seat."

"I'd rather stand," he said. "But thanks. Sir—" he began, then looked down and began pacing himself. "I
wish there was a decent way of saying this."

"Just say it, then."

Thomas laughed once and ran his fingers through
thinning hair. He changed his mind about standing and
sat in the chair. "You see, it's about Loraine's case. I
may have figured out what we've been missing. But not
only won't you believe it, I doubt if you'll like it, either."

"So try me."

"I guess the best way to do this," Thomas said, "is
to sum up what we've got so far, from the beginning."

"Look, I'm aware of all the evidence—"

"But just think about it when I go over it," Thomas
said. "Please, just—just keep an open mind for a second." *If it's ever been open at all,* he thought. "Her
friend was found dead at their apartment. Ripped to
pieces, a bloody mess. Loraine was found naked and
covered with blood, and heavy pieces of furniture had
been moved all over, indicating a massive struggle.
Loraine is brought in—and we've been overlooking this
point—she disappears for one night, leaving a wild animal in her place. That animal is supposedly killed when
an officer fired repeatedly into it, but when the animal
control arrives, it's alive and very, very pissed off. And
the next morning, Loraine reappears and the animal is
gone!"

"We haven't exactly been overlooking that, detective," Hubbard said. "We just have no explanation for it."

"But we do, sir," Thomas said. "Just hear me out. It's all right in front of us, but we've just been too . . . I don't know, too unimaginative to realize it! It was the night after that incident with the wild animal that Loraine was freed by a pack of even wilder animals. They ran through here like a hurricane. They tore up the place and killed several men and wounded a mess of others, and moved too fast for even the cameras to see clearly! What kind of animal can do that?"

"Well—"

"There *is* no animal that can move that fast or do that, lieutenant," Thomas said. "There *is* no animal that can tear off a cell door with its bare hands. Or paws, or whatever they used. And then there's the jogger we found recently. Killed by the same m.o., and partially eaten to boot."

"Then what exactly are you saying *did* do all that?" Hubbard asked. Thomas made a beeline for the lieutenant's wall calendar and removed it. He dropped it onto Hubbard's desk and flipped back a page.

"Look there," he said. "This is the day Loraine was brought in, and the day after that. Notice anything?"

Hubbard glanced to where Thomas was pointing, then leaned back again. "Not particularly," he said. "Will you please make your point? I'm on a tight schedule today."

"They're full moons," Thomas said, tapping the dates for emphasis. "Both of those nights were full moons. The night before she was brought in was a full moon, too!"

"You know, cannibalism is not unknown," the lieuten-

ant said. "If this is about how weird things get during
full moons . . ."

"Not weird," Thomas said. "Hairy. Hairy and clawed
and fanged. I'm begging you to have an open mind
about this, sir, but Agent Anderson and I came to the
same conclusion that night that we tailed Tamara Taylor.
We're not dealing with human beings on this case. We're
dealing with werewolves."

"Werewolves."

"The evidence is all there!" Thomas said. "And I've
left out the most crucial evidence until now. During the
last full moon, Agent Anderson and I tailed Tamara Taylor. It was my idea, and please don't ask me why I talked
him into it. I don't even know why I kept having this
feeling about her. I just knew that she knew more than
she was telling us, but damned if I knew how to prove
it. So, Anderson and I tailed her, and . . . well, she led
us on a merry chase, all right. It was like she knew we
were following. I didn't think that was possible, because
Gil was better at tailing than I've ever been."

"Let me guess: because he's a werewolf," Hubbard
said.

"He may be the weirdest G-man I've ever seen, but
he's no werewolf," Thomas said. "Please, just bear with
me. As God is my witness, that night we saw Tamara
Taylor turn into a wolf. An honest to God four-legged
wolf with hair and a tail! She's the one who disarmed
both of us; now you know the real reason I needed to
requisition another gun. And that led us to the only answer to this case: she, and Loraine, and whoever helped
her escape, are all werewolves."

It didn't surprise the detective to be met with silence.
The lieutenant picked up a pen and clicked on the tip

over and over. After a moment he tired of this and set it down, meeting Thomas's gaze.

"Peter, I understand that this has been a very difficult case for you," he said. "You've been telling me about your frustrations with sorting through the clues, such as they are. But . . . this . . ."

"Look, I know you haven't known me all that long, but haven't I always taken the realistic approach to my cases?" Thomas asked. "Maybe I don't do everything by the book, but as Anderson himself said, 99 percent of the time a crime is just a matter of somebody doing something to somebody else. But what if it isn't? We can't ignore the one percent either! What other explanation is there for all of this?"

"To be honest, I wish I knew myself," Hubbard said. "But werewolves? Come on, man, that's not even part of that one percent you were talking about. Using wild animals is out there, too, but that's as far as I'll go, not to mention anybody else."

"Are you saying that a pack of wild animals pulled off a cell door with their bare hands? Paws, I mean. How? A dog couldn't hold onto something and pull. But an animal that could change into human form, or even just human enough to be able to grab hold of—"

"All right, that's enough," Hubbard said. "You've made your point, and you were right: I neither believe it nor like it. So do me a favor and find another explanation, as long as it *actually could have happened.*"

"Then how am I supposed to explain what Gil and I saw?" Thomas said. "Do you need to hear it from him personally?"

"*Please* tell me you haven't confronted Tamara Taylor

with this . . . evidence of yours," Hubbard said. "You didn't accuse her of being a werewolf, did you?"

Thomas thrust his hands into his pockets and swallowed, but said nothing. The lieutenant sighed and covered his face with his hands.

"Oh, God," he said.

"Sir, she—" Thomas began, then stopped. Hubbard looked up, his eyes reddening, and waited.

"She what?" he prompted after a time.

"Nothing," Thomas said. "Never mind. But I understand how you feel about this now, so all I'm asking is that you look at this evidence. Look at all of the evidence—every bit of it, and *then* tell me it was just a bunch of well-trained dogs that are responsible. Hell, if even well-trained gorillas could've done this. That's all I'm asking, sir."

"I don't have time for that, and you know it," the lieutenant said. "I've already reviewed the evidence. I've reviewed the evidence of all the cases, but if I can't count on my detectives to sweat the details and keep their heads on straight, then what am I supposed to do? When the commissioner wants updates, what do I tell him? Do you think he'd be very understanding about how the Big Bad Wolf tore up the station and killed and wounded some fine police officers?"

"Sir—"

"I'm sorry, but I can't in good conscience keep you on this case if you can't come up with a realistic solution," Hubbard continued. "I want you to pursue your other cases, but not this one."

"Look, we've exhausted all realistic solutions," Thomas said. "This is the first time that any of this has made any sense! The mystery animal that first night, the pack tearing up the place, and the nature of the murders themselves! Loraine couldn't do what she did as she is now. She had to change. She had to become something else—something bigger, stronger, and meaner than any human could be! She—"

"I said that's enough!" Hubbard said. "I don't need to hear any more of this crap. The only thing I can agree with you on is that the case is stranger than anything I've seen so far, but that's it! Now if you insist on continuing on that line of investigating, then I'll have to find someone who's still in the real world."

"No, please, sir, I've almost wrapped this up—"

"I'm afraid you've done just the opposite, detective," Hubbard said. "I'm sorry. Like I said, you're free to pursue all your other outstanding cases, but not this one."

"So who is going to find a realistic solution?"

"I haven't decided," Hubbard said. "Daigle, maybe."

"Daigle? He wouldn't know his own—!"

"Hey!" Hubbard said, leaning forward to lock gazes with Thomas. "All that's settled is that you're off the case! Whoever's on it is no longer your concern! And whoever it is, you'll cooperate with him when handing over the files, all right?"

". . . Of course . . . sir," Thomas said through gritted teeth.

"Let's not be a baby about this," Hubbard said. "Did you really expect to be kept on the case after a story like yours?"

"After putting all the evidence on the table like that and—" Thomas began, then bit his lip and looked away. "I suppose that was a little foolish of me, wasn't it, lieutenant?" he muttered.

"Or something," Hubbard said. "Peter, you must realize that I've got the department to think about, too. You know how hard it's been to fend off the media because of the odd nature of the case. It's bad enough for us that the breakout occurred in a full police station. Am I supposed to call a press conference and give them your story as an explanation?"

"You've made your point, lieutenant," Thomas muttered. "My sincerest apologies for taking up your time."

"I'll allow that bit of sarcasm now, but I'd better not see it again," Hubbard said. "Sulking about this won't help the case."

"May I go now?"

"Yes, you're dismissed. Oh, and one other thing," Hubbard called as Thomas was leaving. "I plan on contacting Tamara Taylor and apologizing to her."

"For what?"

"Borderline harassment, that's what," the lieutenant said. "Come on, man, tailing her not once, but twice, and on nothing more than a hunch? And getting a federal agent to help you the second time? And you didn't answer my question earlier, which leads me to believe that you really did confront her about being a werewolf. Unless I'm wrong, and I hope I am."

Thomas responded with silence.

"Wonderful," Hubbard said. "Well, maybe I can convince her that we're not *all* psychotics here."

Thomas glared for barely a second and had many fine words to say to the lieutenant, then simply nodded and left Hubbard's office. It warmed his heart to know that the department's image meant more to the lieutenant than those who had lost their lives trying to defend the station. Yes, he had many fine words for the lieutenant, but there was no need to add insubordination to his growing list of offenses.

"Again, I can't tell you how sorry we are for any inconvenience Detective Thomas may have caused you, Ms. Taylor," Hubbard said.

"Tamara."

"Very well, Tamara," the lieutenant said. "I won't take up any more of your time, so thank you for allowing me the opportunity to explain the situation. We have another detective investigating the case at this time."

"Oh, no, don't tell me you fired Mr. Thomas because of me?"

"No, no, not at all, Ms.—uh, Tamara," Hubbard said. "He's still with us. Just not on the Loraine case."

"I see," Tamara said. "Well, it was a pleasure speaking with you, lieutenant. Keep up the good work and all that."

They concluded their conversation quickly. The lieutenant was quite pleased with his bit of public relations; later he would send a written apology also. Of course, there was no guarantee the singer would not press charges anyway. She seemed to be quite good-natured, but again, there was no guarantee.

Detective Thomas spent the rest of the day looking into old files, but his mind and heart were clearly elsewhere. Not long ago he had had a great passion for each and every mystery that had come across his desk. Some had been solved, and so many more were still waiting to be, but something was missing from all of them now.

Thomas could almost feel the passion for solving them draining from his body, and the worst part was he knew why. No case was the same as any other, and yet now all of them were. They were all part of that 99 percent Anderson had described. Thomas's only one percent case had been taken from him. He tried not to fault the lieutenant for not believing, but did fault him. Was he really so devoid of any imagination? Or was he himself simply devoid of reality? Who amongst his coworkers would not have laughed him off the force over his werewolves?

He spent much of his time wondering about Anderson and how he might have handled the same situation. The lieutenant would have—could have done nothing to him, but his own superiors were another matter. He wondered if Anderson had gone to his boss with the same story, but who was to know what a fed could get away with?

Agent Anderson failed to inform Davis of his whereabouts that night. This was not uncommon for either agent, although Davis was much more inclined to follow Standard Operating Procedures than he. To be fair, Agent Davis did know that Anderson was out doing some field investigating that night. Davis was content to pore over the coroner's report and other materials back at the sheriff's office. This he did in spite of the sheriff's obvious dislike of the presence of federal agents. This, too, was not uncommon, but neither man had time to concern himself with the egos of local authority figures.

Anderson was back at the crime scene. It was not a full moon, necessitating the use of his flashlight. Ordinarily he would think it much safer because of the lack of the full moon, but the dead couple had been killed during some other phase. This made the situation much more dangerous than he preferred.

A familiar sound nearly caused him to drop the flashlight. He whipped out his gun and listened for it again. After a long silence, it began: the sound of many voices raised into one mournful cry. It was a sound that could have been mistaken for the wind. Anderson knew better.

His first thought was to head back for the car and drive to the safety of their hotel room. Instead he managed to swallow his fear and take tentative steps in the direction of the wailing. The fact that there seemed to be many voices raised the stakes of his little outing. He had brought two full clips of silver bullets—an extremely expensive effort that would pay itself off if it saved his life. With any luck, no one or nothing would be hurt. There was no way to predict how werewolves would react to an intruder in their midst.

Anderson advanced cautiously into the wilderness. The mournful cry started again, this time slightly louder. He moved with a silence that had never ceased to amaze his partner, and if he were there, he was certain to have commented on it. This was only a small part of why Agent Davis was not accompanying him tonight. Anderson had already expressed his belief that werewolves were the culprits, and Davis had nodded and promised to look into it. This was their understanding. Anderson could espouse any theories he wished about their cases, and Davis would give them serious consideration, as long as he didn't have to do any of the field work. In Anderson's case, field work involved anything from swimming in the sewers to traipsing around in unknown woods in the middle of the night, as he was now.

The wolfsong began again, and much closer this time.

So close that it caused Anderson to stop and turn off his flashlight. He listened to the silence that followed, until a very loud, and very near growl from the darkness sent the agent stumbling into the bushes for cover. Anderson found shelter quickly, and listened as he steadied his gun in the growl's direction. He saw a shadow moving into the spot he had just left, then stop. Even in this near absence of light it was clearly an animal that sniffed at the ground. The faintest crackling of the leaves first alerted him to the presence of other shadowy creatures. There was no way he could count how many of them had joined their companion without turning on the flashlight, which he dared not do.

If these animals were the killers he sought, it could only be a matter of time before his presence was detected. As silently as he could, he pulled his gun loose from its holster and touched the base of the clip. It was in place as well as any clip ever was. In all he had a total of sixteen shots, if he were allowed time to use them.

A very large shadow passed directly in front of him, allowing him to see its definite wolf shape. It was by far the largest wolf he had ever seen. He knew enough about the animals to know that a large wolf might reach 100 pounds or so, but nothing like this beast. It was possible that, if these beasts had truly been men, they lost none of their mass when transforming. Things were not getting more comforting.

Anderson strained to watch the dark shapes milling about his last position. He heard some of them sniffing at it, then exchanging grunts and growls that were unusual for any dogs that he'd heard. He knew more about wolves than most, but had never actually heard one up close. These could be normal sounds, or something unusual even for wolves.

Something touched him from behind. Anderson cried out, shot to his feet and turned around, but even at this range the things behind him appeared as nothing more than dark shapes. He backed up and was tripped by the bushes near him, causing him to flip over onto his stomach. His gun stayed firmly locked in his hand, but the flashlight rolled away and stopped at the front feet of the largest wolf. Anderson rolled back onto his own feet and tried to aim his weapon, cursing his foolishness at choosing such a dark place to search.

He was momentarily blinded by a brilliant light aimed directly at his eyes, but he quickly focused past the light and kept his gun steady. At least now the light provided him with a true target. The light shone upward from about waist height, then slowly rose to reach his chest. The beam swung away from his eyes and back onto its wielder. This allowed the first true look at his quarry, and it was no comfort to him whatsoever.

The huge wolf had become something more like a huge man. It was somehow lingering halfway between wolf and man. It stood like a man, and would have been naked but for the full coat of fur on its body. Its face was more like a wolf's than a man's, with a longish snout, hair, green eyes and wolfish ears. Its black lips parted just enough to reveal sharp white teeth.

Anderson struggled to keep the gun steady. Folklore told him silver was a weapon against nearly any supernatural menace. Folklore had been known to be wrong before. The wolf-beast, who Anderson knew now to be the leader, handled the flashlight as though seeing such a device for the first time. Then he swung the beam around in a slow arc, offering the agent his first, and perhaps only, opportunity to see the rest of the pack. One by one the light passed over their faces. Some of them shut their eyes just as the light passed by, and others endured it boldly. None but the leader had changed its shape from wolf form. Yet he saw in all their eyes the same human feeling: hatred.

With a snarl the leader tossed the flashlight in Anderson's direction. He ducked, then let off two shots. His eyes were shut in spite of his training, so he had only the startled cries of the mortally wounded leader to indicate his bullets met their mark. He opened his eyes to see the flashlight had landed with its beam still pointing towards the wolves. He watched as the leader seemed to fall in slow motion, his body limp and his face locked in an expression of mute surprise.

The others also watched in silence as their leader fell. They waited as if expecting him to rise again unharmed, until a smaller wolf stepped forward. It leaned forward to peer at the dying wolf more closely, then sniffed at him. The two wounds in its chest showed no signs of healing. Finally the other wolf looked up at Anderson, its eyes aflame with rage and hatred, and growled a long and deep growl. Anderson's instincts finally shot into play; he turned and raced into the darkness.

For a long time he heard no sounds of pursuit behind him, making him wonder if the others were too shocked at their leader's death to act, or too frightened, or both. He glanced over his shoulder and still saw no dark shapes following, then looked forward just in time to see a tall figure right in front of him. Anderson slammed into the wolf-beast at full speed, yet he might as well have slammed into a tree. The werewolf did not budge from its spot as Anderson was sent flying backward. The light from his flashlight once again blinded him, but not enough to keep him from aiming and firing at the source. The wolf cried out, then dropped without any further sound. In a panic, Anderson stood and fired in a circle until the clip was spent. He dropped the used clip and fumbled for the other, then was sent flying by an impossibly strong throw. By some miracle he avoided hitting any solid objects and rolled along the ground until he had enough traction to stand once again. The new clip was still in his pocket. He clicked it into place and aimed at the darkness.

"If you haven't figured it out by now, these are silver bullets," he said to anyone who could hear. He had no doubt they could, but understanding him was another matter. "I have many more where those came from, too." Silence. He knew they were all there now, though he heard nothing. They could very well have been within a few feet from him, using the darkness to conceal their motionless shapes.

"I did not come to destroy you, but to speak with you," he said. More silence. "But know that I will defend myself if I must." He strained in vain to see, hear, or smell anything that would indicate their location.

"If any of you can understand me, I only want—" Anderson was cut short as his gun was snatched away by an unseen hand. Only then did he realize that one had been standing beside him all the while. He stepped away and caught only a flash of metal, then the sound of that metal being snapped in two.

"I only came here to see if you were real," he said, still backing away. He had no doubt the pack was following his moves. "I'm sorry that I shot your companions, but it was in self-defense. Can any of you understand me? Any of you?"

The wolf that had destroyed his gun stepped forward. The flashlight's beam illuminated her path as she stepped in front of him. Anderson swallowed in a vain attempt to wet his dry throat. He heard a sound coming from the she-beast's throat that seemed like a growl at first, and then became more familiar.

"Tonight . . ." it said in a quick grunt, *"we feed."*

The others grunted, growled and murmured in eager agreement, and took a step forward as a whole. Anderson stepped back, then realized there was nowhere to go. They had formed a tight circle around him.

"You can speak?" he said, his voice wavering. "You understand me? Then please let me speak with you. All my life I've . . . I've wanted to know if you were real. Your secret will be safe with me, if it's what you wish, but please . . . all of you. You were human once, weren't you? Is this true?"

"You killed my mate," the she-beast growled. The others joined in her anger.

"I was frightened," Anderson said. "I didn't understand. Forgive me for hurting any of you."

"Forgiveness," she said, *"is not our way."* She began moving toward him slowly.

"Then let me join you," he said. She stopped, as did the rest of the pack. He had not meant these words, but at least it had bought him some time. "I could join you," he said. "I could . . . we could work at living with other humans and not destroying them. There's so much we could learn from your kind, and you from us. Where did you come from? How did you come to be? How do you live, and how long do you live? Humans don't have to be your enemies!"

A sound almost like human laughter burst from the new leader's lips. She held onto her sides and let her head roll back just a little. He forced a smile, hoping to ease the danger that grew more terrible at every moment. It sent a chill down his spine to think this moment of mirth was only making matters worse.

Finally the lead wolf-beast calmed herself enough to look him square in the eyes. The others had joined briefly in the laughter, in their own way. Though they seemed to possess human intelligence, their four-legged shapes did not seem to allow for human speech or sounds.

The she-wolf wiped her lips and leaned forward, her smile now replaced by a stern look. There also seemed to be a touch of pity in her expression, but Anderson could never have known for certain.

"You," she said, *"are a fool."*

Some of them had heard the agent's last words. Those who had did not remember them long, save the female Alpha. She had chuckled to herself as she thought of the two-legger offering a peace between them. The human beast had killed their Alpha—her mate—and one other with that hated metal. He deserved to die, as did all of his kind. But that time was not yet right. Someday all of the packs might be rid of the two-leggers for good, but only someday.

The next morning another skeleton was found spread over a fifty-foot radius, only a mile from where the first two had been found. The sheriff organized an all-out

search party, which discovered nothing. Agent Davis had
no trouble identifying the remains of his partner, sparse
though they were. His investigation was interrupted only
long enough to see to proper shipment of the remains.
He was asked if he needed time off, but Davis declined.
Anderson would have insisted that he remain on the case
and not concern himself with the pomp and circum-
stance of some mere funeral. The FBI wasted no time
in assigning a new partner for him. He was a younger
man with only one case under his belt. He was eager
and seemed ready to tackle any problem. Davis's only
concern was how open-minded the new man could be.
He would find out in time. Meanwhile, no trace of the
wolfpack, or any other animal pack, was found.

Eighteen

Lieutenant Hubbard often counted himself fortunate that he had no wife or girlfriend. Not that he never wished for one at times, but he had seen too many relationships destroyed by the nature of his work. It took a very special kind of spouse to put up with the abysmal hours and stress, not to mention the danger that existed at every moment of their day. Even the supposed safety of police headquarters was no longer a given. Crazed suspects had broken free of restraints before and tried to run amok, but always with little success—until now.

The lieutenant rarely thought about things besides his work, and tonight was no different as he trudged through the underground parking garage. He never had trouble locating his car, which was new and equipped with a remote-controlled alarm that indicated its position with a touch. He clicked off the alarm and pulled his keys from his pockets.

"Lieutenant Hubbard?" a gentle, feminine voice said behind him, but it startled him enough to make him nearly drop his keys. He whirled around to see a young woman with a very familiar face.

"Are you Lieutenant Hubbard?" she said again.

"Uh, yes, I am. How did you . . . ?"

"I'm Tamara Taylor," she said, stepping forward and

extending her hand. He hesitated, then took it and offered a limp handshake. "Sorry if I scared you," she said. "I just wanted to talk a minute."

"Oh, yes, right, Ms. Taylor," he said. "I mean, Tamara. But may I ask how you got in here? This garage is for police only."

"You may ask," she said, then smiled. It faded when she saw the lieutenant did not respond in kind.

"That's not really important," she said. "I won't give away your secret. I don't have much time, so I'll just say what I came to say, and let you do the rest. It's about my friend Loraine."

"She's contacted you?" the lieutenant asked.

"No," she said. "Nothing like that. It's what you said earlier about Detective Thomas being off the case and all that. About me not being bothered anymore."

"That's still true," he said. "Unless you came to say that he's still trying to contact you?"

"No, he's been a good boy," she said. "By your standards, I suppose. You wouldn't tell me why he's off the case, though. I was just a touch curious."

"I'm afraid that's not something I can discuss."

"Then we'll play Twenty Questions," she said, smiling again. The lieutenant still did not return the smile. "You strike me as a pretty open-minded kind of guy," she said. "You probably like a good joke as much as anyone else."

"Actually—"

"You don't have to tell me what Mr. Thomas may have said or done to get kicked off," she said. "But I'll tell you this: he was getting there. It took him a while, but he and that FBI guy were on the right track."

"Actually, there may be some confusion here," Hub-

bard said. "He was not demonstrating progress in a realistic manner. That's all I can say."

"Well, when you're dealing with the supernatural, it's
hard to define what a realistic manner is, isn't it?" she
asked.

"Come again?"

"I want you to see something, lieutenant," she said,
stepping back a few steps and opening her coat. "In
some ways I feel it's my fault that Mr. Thomas got in
trouble. Yes, his questioning was an interruption at times,
but in the end, he was asking the right questions."

"Ms. Taylor, I appreciate your concern for the man,
but sometimes this happens in our line of work," Hubbard said. "It's late, and my day is done, so—"

"Just keep an open mind, lieutenant," she said. Her
voice sounded strangely hollow as she spoke. Hubbard
barely turned toward her at first, then faced her all the
way as something began to happen.

Her features began to shift—seemingly the face alone,
and then he noticed her whole body changing. She quivered slightly as if tensing every muscle, but there was
nothing tense about what followed. Her body now
seemed to be made of mercury as it stretched in some
places and shortened in others. Halfway through, her
balance shifted enough to make her drop onto all fours.
She gritted her teeth and shut her eyes as most of her
face stretched itself into an animal-like snout. Her face
then turned brown as fur covered her face. She sat up
on her haunches long enough to pull off her clothing,
revealing a body completely covered in brown fur, then
stood on all fours again. A tail that had been mashed
up inside of her pants now unfurled to its full length.

She wagged it slowly back and forth as two non-human eyes peered up at Hubbard through a wolf's face.

He pulled out his gun now and held it unsteadily. He brought his other hand up to hold it in place, which helped only a little. The she-wolf cocked her head but made no moves, threatening or otherwise. She leaned back now, letting her front legs stick out, and pushed with her back legs. In a moment Hubbard realized she was trying to stand on her hind legs, which was difficult for any four-legged animal. He watched as she compensated by altering her shape once again. She stood now on wolf-like legs, but with a much more human-like upper body to aid in balancing.

"Just keep . . . an open mind," she said in a growl of a voice, *"lieutenant."*

"This isn't happening," he whispered, his gun still aimed directly at the creature.

"Silver bullets kill," she said. *"Steel bullets . . . only hurt."*

"What?" he stammered. "Silver? Wh-what do you mean?"

"No harm to you," she said, and leaned over to pick up her coat from the ground. Hubbard followed her actions with his gun but did not fire. He watched the she-beast put on her coat as her features shifted once more. In time brown fur was replaced by tan skin. Only the hair on her head left any reminder of her former persona. The coat effectively concealed her now-human body.

"It's hard to speak in that form," she said. "Our vocal cords and lips aren't quite in the right shape."

"Our . . . *our* vocal cords?" Hubbard said.

She nodded. "Loraine isn't the one you want," she said. "She needs your help, not your bullets. I can't tell

you who the real killer is, because I don't know myself.
All I know is that there's a werewolf out there who
thinks nothing of ripping people up for food, or sport,
or whatever kind of satisfaction he's getting. And unless
you accept that—unless you stop going after a normal
human—you'll just end up another victim. You can shoot
him all you like with those bullets," she said, pointing
to Hubbard's own gun, which was still aimed at her,
"and you'll end up dinner. Do yourself a favor and get
some silver bullets."

"How can . . ." the lieutenant said, "how can this be
happening? How did you do that? I'm not in the mood
for games, Ms. Taylor!"

"Neither am I," she said, walking forward until her
chest was right against the muzzle of his gun. "You can
keep on going to work every day with your head firmly
up your ass, seeing nothing but what you keep up your
butt. Or—" she began, and Hubbard saw nothing but a
blur as his gun disappeared, and so did Tamara. He saw
something move away from him, and looked around
frantically, until something touched his shoulder from
behind. He started and whirled around to see Tamara
again, his gun dangling from her fingers. She held it out
patiently. He snatched it from her and put it away, his
eyes never leaving her.

"—You can see what else there is in the world," she
finished. "Good night, lieutenant."

"Wait!" he called, but she was already walking away
and did not stop to hear any more. "I said hold it!" he
called again.

"Just keep an open mind!" she called without looking
back or stopping. Hubbard rushed after her, believing
himself to be catching up, until she turned a corner. He

prayed not to see what he'd seen in a hundred different
bad films, but his prayers were not answered. She was
nowhere in sight. The corridor leading outside did have
some places that a small person could squeeze into and
hide, but they were so far away the person would have
to move impossibly fast to make it. On the other hand,
he had already seen her do just that.

Back in the main part of the garage, Hubbard scanned
for any others who might have been there at the time,
but he was alone. His footsteps echoed as if confirming
the lack of others in this concrete cavern. Out of habit
he pressed his car alarm remote again, even though it
was already unlocked. Nothing else out of the ordinary
interrupted his drive home, his nightly routine of pre-
paring for bed, nor even his dreams. But his sleep was
not as relaxed as usual this night.

Roger allowed Loraine to lead the way now that they
had arrived at the outskirts of their destination. He had
balked, however, at the idea of finding the absolute
cheapest motel in the city. He did not need any city
experience to know that the cheaper the room, the more
dangerous the area. She had assured him that anyone
who threatened either of them would be ripped apart
personally, but inevitably they found a motel that was
more to his liking, and checked in as Mr. and Mrs.
Wolfe.

"Did you have to use that name?" Roger asked after
tossing his duffel bag onto the bed. She had suggested
his packing something larger, but Roger had insisted that
little more than an overnight bag would suffice. She had

not pressed the point, encumbered as she had been with an even smaller bag.

"Plenty of people are named Wolfe," Loraine said. "Don't tell me: you would have said Smith, wouldn't you?"

"No, but we're not supposed to draw attention to ourselves, remember?" he said, zipping open his bag and dumping the contents onto the bed. Loraine watched with growing amusement.

"Do you always unpack that way?" she asked.

"Huh?"

"Never mind," she said. "Sorry you thought it was dumb, but I'm trying to keep my humor about this. Besides, I am a 'Wolfe.' And who else but you knows that, anyway? Well someone else does, too."

"Who?" he asked, heading for the bathroom with his toothbrush.

"I shouldn't tell you," she said. "It's another werewolf. Don't worry; she's a friend, but I shouldn't blab her secret to everyone."

"Another werewolf?" Roger shouted over the running water. "Here in the city? How many of you are there, anyway?"

Loraine followed him to the bathroom before answering. She stood in the doorway and kept her voice low as she spoke. "I wouldn't start yelling about werewolves," she said. "You can probably hear everything through these walls. And I don't know how many of us there are. I only know of my own pack. It's difficult to explain, but there's a . . . type of bond that allows me to sense them. I don't have this bond with other packs, only my own, so I really don't know how many others there are."

Roger spit out the last of the toothpaste. "Very few, I hope," he said, shaking out the water from his toothbrush. "Oh. I'm sorry. I didn't mean to—"

"No offense taken," she said, reaching out to caress his arm. He set down the toothbrush and took her hand, using it to pull her closer to him. He began nuzzling her neck and humming, until she pushed him back just enough that the tips of their noses almost touched.

"I'll wait for you to get ready," he murmured. "Would you like the window side or the wall side?"

"Neither," she said. "You get some sleep. I need to get started."

He leaned back and looked at her wide-eyed.

"We can't afford to stay here night after night," she explained. "Besides, I'm sure he's still out there, so I have to find him as soon as possible."

"But we just got here," he said. "It's late; let's get to bed. We can find him tomorrow."

She shook her head vigorously. "No, you get some rest. I can't afford to be tired. Looking for him in the daytime would be too difficult."

"I'm not gonna let you go out there alone in the middle of the night," he said, squeezing her hands as if in warning. She seemed to sense this, and pulled her hands away.

"It's not the middle of the night," she said. "And I never planned for you to come with me on these hunts, anyway."

"Wha—?" he said. "What do you think I came with you for? I'm not going to sit and watch cable movies while you go out and . . . and hunt for him. We're looking together, remember?"

"Roger—"

"I tried to bring my gun with us, but you wouldn't let me," he said. "How am I supposed to help if all I have is something with regular bullets?"

"Roger, I thought I made this clear to you," she said. "This is my fight, not yours. I'm very grateful that you're with me, but I never intended to let you hunt with me. And maybe daylight is safer, but the night is . . . well, the night is for my kind. All my encounters with him have been at night. Jan remembers what he looks like, but only when he's in wolf form. Still, his scent— the way he moves—everything about him would be closer to his wolf side at night. That's why I have to go now."

"Fine," he said, shrugging and taking a step back. "I still say we need the rest, just for tonight, but if you can't wait, we'll go now."

"I will go now," she said. "And I'm not going to argue with you on this."

"What, are you going to force me to stay?" he said, then stepped forward and held her by the shoulders. "I love you, Loraine. Maybe you think I'm only saying this to make you change your mind, but it's true. I won't let you fight him alone. From what you've said, he must be twice your size as it is, so . . . well, you just can't do it alone."

"I'm not alone," she murmured. "And I love you, too, Roger," she said, "and that's why you're staying here. It's in my nature to be protective of my loved ones, and especially . . . my mate. I don't even want to think about what he'd do to you if he found you. I'm terrified that he'd just tear you to bits like—" her voice cracked, and she brought her hand to her mouth. "Like Roxanne," she finished, then let Roger take her into his arms as her tears flowed freely. "Oh, God," her muffled voice came, "even after all this time I keep seeing her in my head. I keep remembering what she looked like . . ."

"Shhhh," he said, patting and rubbing her back as they embraced. "It hasn't been that long. You'll always remember what she looked like; you know you could never forget her."

"But I've been trying to remember her when she was alive," she sobbed. "And all I can think of is that . . . that bloody mess he made of her!"

"That'll pass," Roger said. "It won't always be like that. You'll be able to remember her the way she was in life someday. We'll find this guy, and when we do, he'll wish he'd never bitten you or anyone else."

Loraine forced herself to move her face from his chest. She looked at him with reddening eyes. "Please don't come with me," she said. "If the same thing happened to you, I'd—I don't know what I'd do!"

"It's not going to happen," he said. "And did you ever think what would happen if you went out alone, but he killed you instead? I don't know what *I'd* do if that happened, either. And you know why else I have to go with you. Maybe there's some way we could talk to him first. Maybe he's from the same pack that my brother was in, or at least knows which one."

Loraine was feeling quite tired suddenly; exhausted, in fact. It may have been that their long days and little sleep were finally catching up to her. She shook off the fatigue angrily. There really was no time to rest. The exile was out there somewhere, if he was still in the city, and there was no tracking him through the bond of the pack. She would not sense him any more than the others would, now that they had severed their link to him. Finding him in a city this size, and this dangerous, at night would require all of her hunting skills. Since their joining, Loraine and Jan shared not only thoughts and memories, but abilities. Loraine could summon the strength, speed and senses of Jan at any time, but even she was but a cub to this larger, stronger and more experienced adversary. Perhaps she could not do this alone after all . . .

"If anything happened to you," she said, "I doubt if I could let myself live any longer. But I do need you, Roger. I need your help. And if you're willing to start tonight, then let's go. If we don't find him tonight, then we try again later after sleeping in the daytime. We'll have to do that every day until we find him. Sleep by day, I mean."

"I understand," he said, then pulled her toward him into a kiss. She caught herself beginning to nod off in his arms. She told herself the thrill of the hunt would surely awaken her. She would either be fully alert and ready, or dead.

Detective Thomas had had a very long and frustrating day by the time the lieutenant called him into his office. As always he could not tell Hubbard's mood by the look on his face, so Thomas had gotten into the habit of assuming the worst.

"Have a seat," Hubbard said, and Thomas complied. The lieutenant was already involved in his habit of clicking his ball-point pen. He did this for a few moments as if searching for the right words.

"How was your day today?" he asked finally.

"Well enough, I suppose," Thomas said. "I was looking into a lead on the LeRoy case."

"Oh, really? Any luck on that?"

Thomas shook his head. "Dead end," he said. "In fact, I'd say it was almost a red herring."

"I'd like to hear more about that," Hubbard said, then leaned forward. "But later. Right now . . . Right now I was wondering . . . What exactly did you and Agent Anderson see that night that you followed Tamara Taylor? During that full moon?"

Thomas straightened up in his chair slowly and cocked his head. The lieutenant had lowered his pen and was looking him right in the eyes. Somehow, some way, he was ready to listen.

Nineteen

One of the reasons Roger was so reluctant to go looking for the werewolf that night was that Loraine had made him leave both his rifle and its silver bullets at home. But she had pointed out, and rightly so, that traveling with a rifle was no easy task, and walking around with a loaded weapon on L.A. streets was even harder. He had no trench coat to help him conceal the thing, but he was determined to be with Loraine during her search no matter what the cost. He would have preferred having some kind of weapon, even a knife, judging by the population of the streets at night. A silver knife would kill a human monster as surely as a supernatural one.

It was still a few weeks yet before the next full moon. Roger thought to lead the way by suggesting places to begin, until he noticed an odd look in Loraine's eyes. She had been responding to one of his questions, when she stopped midsentence and straightened up, sniffing the air. Her expression was almost crazed—wide-eyed and unblinking—but Roger thought better of questioning her. She began to move with great determination in a particular direction, and Roger found himself having trouble keeping up with her.

For a while she kept to the sidewalks, and then sud-

denly cut across the street. Roger called out as a car
swerved to avoid her, honking as it went by. Loraine
hardly gave it a glance. He rushed to her side and
grabbed her arm, but this only slowed her down a bit.

"Loraine!" he cried. "Didn't you see that car? You
were almost killed!"

"But I wasn't," she muttered, and continued dragging
him to the other side of the street. Bystanders stared at
her, some shaking their heads at the foolish woman who
shouldn't be allowed on the streets.

"I have a scent," Loraine said, slowing down enough
for Roger to catch up. "It's faint, but . . . if I get close
enough, I should be able to tell if it's our friend."

"You smell him already?" he asked. "You might not
catch him if you don't watch where you're going. Didn't
you see that car?"

"I did, but it wasn't necessary to dodge it," she said.
"Stay back here. I think something's down the alley."

"It's dark down there," he whispered. "I better go with
you."

"If I need help, I'll shout," she said. "Wait for me."
It took barely a second for the darkness to swallow her
up. Roger took a few steps to follow, then hovered at
the entrance, trying in vain to pierce the darkness. He
would have felt safer with her, facing down a werewolf,
than fending off any of the unsavory characters who
passed by.

An uncomfortably long silence from the alley was
broken by the echoes of several large dogs—or wolves,
for all he knew—and Roger rushed into the darkness. A
shadowy figure materialized just long enough for him
to smack into it. The figure was small, but sturdy as a

brick wall. Roger went tumbling backward. He was then hefted to his feet and dusted off.

"I told you to wait for me," Loraine said. Roger squinted and finally made out some of her features. "It was just some dogs."

"Yeah, I can hear that," he said, trying to ignore the cacophony of barks and howls.

"Are you okay?" she asked, finishing her tidying job on him.

"Yes, yes, I'm fine," he said, backing away. "I didn't realize you were so . . . sturdy."

"This may take longer than I thought if I keep sniffing out dogs," she said. "I can only hope my tracking skills improve, and pretty soon. The longer it takes to find him, the better the chances the cops will find me. I can't afford for that to happen before I've tracked him down. One way or another he'll pay for what he did."

"What's next, then?" he asked.

"You go back to the motel," she said. "There's no reason for you to stay with me. If the cops find you with me—"

"We've already been through this," he said. "I'm going to help you no matter what happens."

Loraine crossed her arms and glared at him. Roger did the same; they stood in silence until Loraine sighed. She shook her head and ran her fingers through her hair in frustration.

"Let the record show I don't want you to do this," she said. "You're making it harder for me. Okay, then: the next plan is to get a cab."

"A cab?"

"I think we're in the wrong area entirely," she said.

"We're in the wrong . . . place. Maybe the bond wasn't entirely broken."

"You know where he is?" Roger asked.

"Not exactly," she said. "More like, I know where he isn't. Maybe that'll be the best way to track him." She checked her pockets. "Damn, I left my money at the motel," she said. "Do you have any?"

"No."

"Okay, we'll just have to find an ATM. I can't believe I still have my card," she said, and stepped away from the darkness of the alley. She ignored the disreputable passersby, not all of whom were ignoring them, and made a beeline for the cash machine of a bank across the street. No cars threatened their lives this time. Loraine reached the cash machine and fumbled with her card. Roger stood to the side and kept an eye out. It took longer than usual to retrieve any cash since Loraine had forgotten her PIN number. Eventually she guessed correctly, retrieved the money, and turned to look down the barrel of a semi-automatic gun. There were three teenaged boys there making it very clear that they, too, wished to use their own "cash machine."

"The money, bitch," the armed one said. "Now."

Loraine could not see if the others were armed, and did not care. Before anyone—certainly not Roger—could react, something flashed out at the young man, and now he stared down the barrel of his own gun. Loraine's anger was too great to be satisfied with this display of speed. She continued with a low growl and let her lips curl back into a long-toothed snarl. At the last moment she lunged forward and howled at the would-be thieves, showing them the face of a wild animal for just a moment. The three boys all but rubbed

the soles from their shoes in their haste to leave. Roger
could only watch in disbelief as Loraine turned back to
him, her face now quite normal as she handed him the
gun. He took it hesitantly.

"I think we should go, too," he said, looking around
for any witnesses.

Loraine nodded. "We'll call a cab at a liquor store,"
she said. Roger had less trouble keeping up with her
now that his adrenaline was working overtime. They
ended up at a gas station and waited inside of its con-
venience store. Roger tried to question her about their
incident with the three gangbangers, but she answered
with very little. Her thoughts were clearly elsewhere,
and it concerned him. She really seemed to have no fear
of them or their gun at all, which was admirable, but
what if somebody had the wrong kind of bullet? Would
she always be fast enough to protect herself, and him?

Roger was as silent as she after a time. During the
wait he became aware once again that he was carrying
a loaded weapon in his coat. Why he had taken it from
her at all, he did not know, and now getting rid of it
safely and quietly would take some doing. His other op-
tion was to use it—if he could get his hands on some
silver bullets. That would take even more doing.

Detective Thomas nearly knocked over the mail clerk
on his way to the lieutenant's office. He mumbled an apology without breaking step, and came upon Hubbard in his
office, on the phone as usual. Thomas was in no mood to
wait for the conversation to end, and straightened out his
computer printout on Hubbard's desk. When the lieutenant
merely glanced at the paper, Thomas leaned over and

poked a spot on the page over and over. Irritated, Hubbard covered the phone and frowned.

"Look, do you mind?" he said.

"She's back in town!" Thomas said, poking the same spot with such vigor that Hubbard wondered if his finger would break.

"Who?"

"Loraine!" he said, and pushed the information under the lieutenant's nose: a bank record. Very recent and very local activity had taken place at an automatic teller.

Loraine and Roger were unaware of the All Points Bulletin in effect. What they were particularly unaware of was that both Thomas and Hubbard were a part of it. Using the ATM as the hub, they searched every hotel and motel in a five-mile radius, fully prepared to expand the area should their efforts prove fruitless.

Loraine made it a point of staying in the motel room all day while Roger ventured outside for the occasional errand. She saw no use in hunting during daylight hours, nor was she keen on maintaining her disguise all day long. It also seemed a little easier at night, when Jan's power was more focused.

However, Jan's power could do nothing to dispel the incredible boredom of waiting in a no-frills motel room. There was no cable, and TV reception was challenging at best. She left the set on and caught herself drifting off into a brainless stupor as talk show after talk show played out their sordid dramas. Loraine remembered when there used to be nothing but game shows, soaps, and rotten sitcoms. Worst of all, she used to find them all entertaining. Now she was seeing everything around her with new eyes. These strange humans on the screen, acting or not, were displaying the worst that humans were capable of. They spurned their mates, stole from each other, lied for the barest of reasons, fought with, spat at and even killed one another.

The pack, arrogant as it was, still respected and even loved one another. They did not kill their own kind, and despite Jan's rejection of them, she was always welcome amongst them. When they killed, it was for food and nothing else. That was the greatest of the exiled one's crime, she had learned. He had come to enjoy killing for its own sake. He had been sent to bring her back to the others, but had become drunk with the pleasure of so much prey in so many places. Bringing her back was scarcely even his concern by the time he had killed her friend, leaving the corpse to rot and Loraine to pay the consequences.

She knew he could not have left L.A. with so much more "fun" to be had. He might even have been enjoying his exile, knowing he was free to hunt and kill as he wished without the pack's laws to bind him. Loraine had blamed them once for this—unleashing a monster upon innocent lives with no intention of stopping it. In time she came to understand that human laws or concerns were nothing to them, nor should she expect them to be. Their punishment was exile, and to them it was the harshest of all. The two-leggers could slaughter their own kind until the end of time, but it was not the way of these wolves.

Roger had returned with a feast catered by the nearest Colonel Sanders. Part of Loraine had hoped for something a little less cooked, and the other part remembered about the dangers of raw meat, especially chicken. She

swallowed her meal before Roger had finished his bis-
cuit, then stared at more of the human degradation on
the small screen.

"How's O.J. doing?" Roger asked at one point, forcing
a smile. Loraine did not react for a few seconds, then
straightened up, her eyes wide.

"Sorry?" she asked.

"Nothing," he said. "I was just wondering how your
day went. Sorry I've been out so much, but . . ."

"Oh," she said, touching his cheek, "don't worry
about that. I got in some naptime, even though my
dreams weren't very cheery."

"Nightmares?" he said.

"Something like that," she said, rising from her seat
and gathering the remains of their meal. She picked up
the chicken pieces, and stopped as she grabbed a leg.
There was little left that could be considered meat, only
strips of fat, gristle and blood vessels, but Roger looked
up just in time to see Loraine slip the leg into her mouth,
clamp down, and pull. The leg came back out minus
everything but the bone itself. Loraine examined it further as if considering swallowing even that, and did not
notice Roger throwing his thigh piece into the box and
downing the rest of his drink.

"There's still a few hours of sunlight left," she said,
turning around. Roger crushed the cup and shoved it into
the bag, then closed up the box holding the remaining
chicken pieces. Loraine pointed at it.

"You're not tossing all that, are you?" she asked.

Roger pushed the box at her quickly. "No, you can
have the rest," he said. "I've had my fill of chicken."

"At least they have a fridge in this dump," she mumbled, taking the box and putting it away there. She

cleaned up by licking her fingers, then plopped onto the bed. "So," she said, spreading out her arms, "any ideas on how to kill some time until moonrise?"

"Maybe," he said, standing and moving to the edge of the bed. "But I thought it was dangerous to exercise right after eating."

"Could be," she said, sitting up slowly. "But what a way to get a charley horse."

"Why, lieutenant," Tamara announced from her hotel door, "what a . . . surprise." Thomas tried to peek over her shoulder. For some reason he was more concerned that her obnoxious manager was around than the dangers of provoking a supernatural beast. She was alone, though.

"May we come in, Ms. Taylor?" Hubbard asked.

"No," she said. "But I might have let you if you hadn't called me 'Ms. Taylor.' "

"I see," Hubbard said. "In that case, I'm afraid—"

"It's a joke," she said, opening the door wide. "It bugs me when I have to explain them. But, I've been told I have an odd sense of humor. Well, come in, then."

"Tamara," Hubbard said, stepping inside. Thomas followed close behind. "We have reason to believe that you may be in contact with Loraine Turner, if you haven't been already."

"Why? Because I'm 'one of them'?" she asked. "We werewolves can smell each other no matter where we are or something?"

"Ma'am, this would be much easier if you'd cooperate—"

"I've been cooperating with you boys plenty," she said. "Loraine hasn't talked to me since she left L.A., so I don't know any more than you do. I don't know how many times I have to explain this to you."

"We have reason to believe that she's returned to Los Angeles, and that she may attempt to contact you," Hubbard said. "You two worked together, and you're both of the same . . . ilk. We were hoping you could give us some help. Quite frankly, ma'am, we're . . . We don't know how or where to start looking. Where do people like you go or live? We'd be very grateful for any help you can give us."

Tamara folded her arms and lowered her gaze until she seemed to be glowering. "What's with the 'of the same ilk' and 'people like you' crap? Why don't you just say what I am? You sound like a racist the other way."

"All right, if it'll make you happy," Hubbard said. ". . . You're a werewolf." Thomas noted that the lieutenant had hesitated before speaking, as though it required summoning his strength and his will to do so. And when he did speak, his words were much quieter and more uncertain than Thomas had heard so far from the lieutenant.

"And we need your help," Hubbard said, stepping forward. Tamara folded her arms.

"The only help I can give you is this advice," she said. "Stay away from them. Both of them, or I guarantee somebody's going to get hurt."

"Both of them?" Thomas said. "What are you saying?"

"That Loraine never killed anyone," she said. "Certainly no people. There's another wolf out there, and he probably never even left the city."

"How do you know this?" Hubbard asked. "How do you know it's a 'he,' for that matter?"

"I'm just passing on what Loraine's told me," she said, shaking her head. "Her own pack broke her out of jail. I doubt that they're here now, but I wouldn't count on anything at this point. As far as I know, another pack member had been following her around—probably to find her and bring her to them—and must have botched up the job but good to get himself exiled."

"Exiled?"

"Exiled," she repeated. "You know—kicked out? When that happens, all bonds are broken. The others don't acknowledge whoever's kicked out, nor can he or she track them anymore through that bond."

"You're losing me," Hubbard said.

"Not me," Thomas said. "Keep going."

"That's it," she said, holding out her arms. "He's on his own, whoever it is. And that's why I advise you to stay far away from this, if you know what's good for you. Call off your dragnet."

"Is that a threat, Ms. Taylor?" Hubbard asked.

"Not from *me,* it isn't," she said. "But it will be if you don't stop calling me 'Ms. Taylor.' Seriously, you guys have no clue what you're dealing with, or you wouldn't be coming to me for help. I disarmed *two* of you the other night. What do you think two werewolves could do, then? It's not Loraine I'm worried about. I don't think she would deliberately harm any of you. But the real killer? He killed her roommate, and not by just some accidental hit on the head. She was torn to pieces. Or so Loraine told me. Am I right?"

"That's . . . about what the condition of the body was, yes," Hubbard said.

"So you're dealing with a wild wolf," she said. "They're the ones who come to enjoy killing, and to do it for sport and not food or self-defense. They stop becoming true animals and turn into megahumans."

"Don't you mean the other way around?" Hubbard asked. "They become more like animals?"

"Name one animal besides human beings that kills for sport," she said. "Just for the sheer pleasure of killing," she added, and waited. Both men looked at each other, then back at her.

"Ever owned a cat?" Hubbard asked. Tamara frowned.

"I don't get along with them all that well," she said. "You're right about them, though. Most of the time they'd rather play with their food than eat it. But that's not *our* way."

"Okay, so it's not *your* way," Thomas said. "But why won't you help us?"

"It should be obvious that I'm not going to help hunt down one of my own kind," she said. "Especially one who's a friend. And don't give me any b.s. about how turning herself in would be the smartest thing to do. *You* try being a fugitive sometime and see how easy it is."

"You sound like you're speaking from experience," Thomas said. "You know, how do we know that you haven't been responsible for this all along?"

Tamara smiled and stifled a chuckle. "All what along?" she asked. "You mean that I killed her friend and framed Loraine for it?" She sighed. "Shouldn't you be wondering why I would jeopardize my career—one that I've spent decades on—not to mention my first major tour, by killing the best friend of my choreographer and forcing her out of town? Finding Loraine was a big break for me, guys. I knew from the start what she was, but that didn't matter. She was exactly what I needed in a choreographer, and her being a werewolf, too, was a little bonus is all. In fact, she was the first one I'd met since leaving my own pack."

"How many packs are there, anyway?" Thomas asked.

Tamara shrugged. "A few dozen, I suppose," she said. "Could be hundreds for all I know. But are we through here? I've got a big day tomorrow. I have to break in a new choreographer."

"You don't seem terribly concerned about her safety," Hubbard said. "If you say you're her friend, wouldn't you want to help her by helping us find her?"

"Of course I want to help her," she said. "But helping you hunt her down isn't how I'll be doing it."

"Really?" Thomas said, moving toward her. "And how *would* you be helping her?"

Tamara kept her arms folded as she moved toward the detective. She stopped less than two feet away and locked gazes with him. "Any way she asks me to," she said.

"Tamara," Hubbard said, pulling Thomas away from her, "may we remind you that assisting her would be an obstruction of justice and a felony offense. She's been charged with murder and is wanted for escape from lawful imprisonment."

Tamara pointed her thumb at the lieutenant while speaking to Thomas. "Do you have trouble understanding him sometimes?" she asked. "Oh, yeah, you're a cop, too. Never mind."

"Tamara, we are very serious about this!" Hubbard said. "Will you assist us or not?"

"Not," she said, raising her hand.

"I see," Hubbard said, straightening his coat. "Then

we'll remind you again that you're still under suspicion and will be under surveillance."

"Is that so?" she asked, her eyes flashing yellow-green. Both men backed away and fingered their guns. "I have a job to do, boys. Are you saying a bunch of cops are going to be hanging all over me?"

"Tamara, you're only making it worse for yourself," Hubbard said. "We just need to make sure that you don't attempt to assist Loraine if she contacts you. And if she does," he added, stepping forward now, "you *will* let us know, won't you?"

Tamara was silent for a long time. She looked from one man to the other. *"I make no promises,"* she said.

Loraine rolled away and stared at the curtains that barely kept out the fading daylight. Roger stayed on his back and sighed. He glanced at Loraine several times, then fidgeted while thinking of his next words.

"Sorry," he whispered. When she didn't move or speak, he caressed the back of her head and let his hand rest against it. She still did not react. "Loraine?" he said. "Are you mad at me?"

"No," he heard her murmur. "Not mad. Just . . . thinking, is all."

"Yeah," he said, now scratching her shoulders slowly. "I've been thinking, too. In fact, I've . . . got a question for you."

She turned toward him slightly. "What's that?" she said. It took him a while to respond.

"Well, it's about your change," he said. "I just noticed we haven't really talked about it much. Hell, we haven't talked about much of anything, so I don't know what's going on most of the time. I guess my question is . . . are you still human? At all?"

Loraine was quiet a moment, then rolled over so that she faced him again. She forced a smile and touched his cheek. "Yes," she whispered. "But what I said before hasn't changed. I'll never be a hundred percent human any more than I'm a hundred percent wolf."

"So what 'percent' are you, then?" he asked. "Ninety-nine? Fifty? Two?"

Her smile wasn't forced this time. "Well, I'd hope that I *look* more than two percent human right now," she said. "But I don't have an exact number. Out of fairness to Jan, I'd say fifty percent. We're on equal terms now, remember?"

"And other werewolves aren't?" Roger said. "That's what I don't get about this. First you were worried that something would happen to me last full moon, then you said it's not a problem anymore, then you say the other wolves made their human sides 'sleep,' or some damn thing, then—"

"Shhhhhhhhh," she said, putting a finger to his lips. "It's not as confusing as you think, Roger. I wish the others would want to be just like me, but for whatever reasons, they choose to suppress that human part of themselves permanently. They wanted Jan to, too, but they could never convince her that this was the right thing to do. I'll always be a part of her, and vice versa, but the pack doesn't see things that way. You know," she said, rolling closer to Roger and letting her finger run across his chest, "in a way, I pity them. Some of them are hundreds of years old, maybe even older, but they insist on believing that they're all wolf."

"But they're not."

"Right," she said. "You know, Jan had a mate in the pack. He called himself Bluefur. I never knew his human name, but he used to be a cop that I—well, just Jan alone at that time—attacked and brought over to the pack. When I met him later, I was surprised that he wasn't angry. In fact, he was grateful for what I'd done. I guess joining the pack was the best thing he'd ever done."

"So . . . he's waiting for you to go back to him."

"No," Loraine whispered, and shut her eyes. "I'm afraid that we're no longer mates. He thought I carried his cubs, too, but I don't."

"Cubs?" Roger said. "As in little werewolves? They can have kids?"

"Yes, *we* can," Loraine said. "But the time just wasn't right when we . . . Anyway, it was clear that he couldn't accept what I'd done. He's part of the pack, and accepts their ways and their thoughts completely. They said I was always welcome, but I wouldn't really be. Not as long as that two-legger part of me is around."

"Two-legger, huh?" he said. "That's pretty silly."

Loraine chuckled and shrugged. "Oh, that's their thing, I suppose," she said. "But it's how I thought of you, too. Even of how *I* am now. I can't think that way anymore, though."

"So . . . you don't have a mate anymore," he said. "Or do you?"

"Of course I do," she said. "You."

"I'm your mate?"

"Well . . . my boyfriend, I mean," she said. "In a way, I like the word 'mate' better. It's more appropriate, I think. It—I wish I could explain it to you. It just says more."

"Like husband, you mean?"

"No," she murmured. "I mean, yes, it can mean that, too, but I don't want to think that far ahead. I can't," she added softly. "I just want things to happen the way they happen. Maybe someday, when this is over, we can think about . . ." Her voice trailed off, and she rubbed his arm. "Like I said," she continued, "whatever happens, happens. Let's just stay together now and worry about tomorrow when it comes."

They were both quiet for a while. Roger lay on his back, his arms tucked behind his head. Loraine caressed his chest and shut her eyes. After a time he wrapped an arm around her and pulled her closer, then scratched her back. She moaned and arched her back as he scratched harder and faster. He scratched in different places, until reaching her shoulder blade, then stopped as she kicked at him.

"Ow! Watch those toenails," he said.

"Hnh?" she said in a sleepy daze.

"Nothing," he said, and tucked his arms under his head again. Loraine's breathing was getting slower and deeper; she was almost asleep. He envied her this. It was too early yet for that, and he had never been one to nap. Still, they both should be asleep if they were to be alert for tonight.

There would be more hunting that night. He had a weapon now—a gun—but no silver bullets for it. Unless he could find something else more useful, like a silver knife, Loraine was right; he could not help her once they found this "exiled one." And if they did find him, Roger wondered if they would be able to talk to him before the bloodshed began. He didn't need to ask Loraine what she intended to do if they finally found the other were-

wolf. He didn't want to know *how* she intended to exact
her revenge. Perhaps his purpose would not be to help
kill the other werewolf, but to keep Loraine from falling
into the abyss of murder.

She seemed so peaceful in sleep. Her breathing was
deep and free of trouble; her face had just a hint of a
smile. After a time he watched her moan and stretch,
then swipe at an imaginary pest near her nose. After this
she sighed and curled up into a tight ball.

He couldn't help but remember a puppy he'd had as
a kid that used to sleep the same way. *Stop it,* he thought
to himself. *She's not a dog.* Unfortunately, she almost
was. And like his puppy, Loraine was just a cub to the
one they were after. She was just a kid, period—barely
in her mid-twenties. Too young to be wanted for murder
and a fugitive. All she ever wanted was to be a dancer.

Roger fought a lump in his throat. Loraine hadn't lied
to him yet; she had told him right away what she was
and what she intended to do. What she needed to do.
So why was he here, really? He could have just kissed
her on the cheek, wished her well, and stayed with the
llamas where it was safe. He needed to decide if he
simply pitied the poor little wolf on her own against the
law, or if he really loved her. If he only pitied her, he
needed to do her a favor and go back home before making her suffer even more.

He listened to her breathing again. It was deep and
full and musical—almost like a song. He thought of letting her sleep. It might have been the last moment of
peace either of them would know before the hunt resumed. Even with his help, the outcome was unknown.
The other wolf was nearly twice her size and at least
that much stronger. Loraine herself was physically supe-

rior to Roger—faster, stronger, more agile. They needed a better plan than simply hunting the other wolf. What came after he was found?

Roger made a decision. He reached over and nudged Loraine gently until she moaned and began to stir. She uncurled from her ball and scratched her belly, then opened her eyes. The curtains were drawn and the lights were out, but her eyes seemed to glow like little yellow-green globes. Roger knew this was only a reflection of what little light there was. Or perhaps they glowed of their own light. He leaned over before she could speak and kissed her. She smiled to herself as he pressed next to her and draped an arm across her.

"Is it nightfall yet?" she whispered. "Do we have to go?"

"Not yet," he whispered. "We still have time."

"Oh," she said, rubbing her eyes. He moved her hands away and kissed her. She hummed as he rolled onto her and held her tight, then widened her eyes as he began a low, amorous growl before pouncing.

Twenty

Detective Thomas slapped his steering wheel hard. "Dammit!" he yelled. "Are you sure we can't just shoot her and get it over with?"

"Now there's a novel idea," Hubbard said. "What else are we supposed to do? We can't point a gun to her head to make her help us."

"Couldn't we just plant evidence or something?"

"You'd better be joking about that, detective," Hubbard said, adjusting the radio.

"Of course I am," he muttered. "And why can't we get ahold of Anderson? You'd think the feds would Fed Ex him down here after what we've found."

"We can only pass on the information and let them handle it," Hubbard said. "But, yes, I'm surprised that no one has contacted us or arrived to assist us. Until then we'll have to act on our own."

"How many men do we have watching Tamara?" Thomas asked.

"Two units," the lieutenant said. "It's all we can spare, I'm afraid."

"We both know she could probably get past four units," Thomas said. "Maybe even more. If she wants to leave, how could they stop her without silver bullets?"

"There *are* other methods of detaining people than

just shooting them, Thomas," Hubbard said. "Besides, it wouldn't be wise of her to blow her cover more than she has. We can't force her to help us, but if we catch her assisting Loraine in any way, her butt is ours."

"Yeah. Until her pack comes," Thomas said grimly.

Roger stood near the curtain and watched Loraine pull on her only pair of sweats. She had brought others with her from Wisconsin—filthy things that could not have smelled worse if they'd been rubbed in compost. Roger had tossed them in the Dumpster himself and made a special run to Kmart for new clothes.

"Next time we'll find something tighter for you," he said.

Loraine looked up. "Hnh?" she said, then smiled and waved him off. "Yeah, right, and have it rip right off as soon as I flex an arm."

"Yeeaahhh," he said. She finished tying the pants and joined him at the curtain. A peek outside revealed the sunlight would last only another half hour. She let the curtain drop and gave him a playful slap on the cheek.

"You animal," she said. "We better go now."

He led the way to the door. Loraine paused to alter her features before emerging into the fading sunlight. It had been all day since she'd stepped out into fresh air and seen real light; dimmer though it was now, she shielded her eyes until they got used to the brown and grey sky. She took a deep breath, and coughed.

"Oh, boy," she said. "Have some oxygen with your smog today?"

"Yeah, I noticed it, too," Roger said. "I don't know how you guys can stand it."

"You get used to it," she said as they walked to their rental car. "At least, I *was* used to it before I became more . . . sensitive."

"And you're going to keep living here?" he asked. They reached a blue-grey sedan. Roger fished for the keys and unlocked the passenger side first. Loraine grabbed for the door, but he held it open until she was completely seated, then shut it.

"Oh," she said. "Thanks. Few guys will hold a door open anymore."

"It's how I was raised," he said matter-of-factly. "But sometimes it's a pleasure and not just a habit," he added, smiling and patting her thigh.

"Mm," she said. "That's nice to know. You have to be careful around here, though. A lot of women hate it when guys do stuff like that. But *I* like it. I like anything that's chivalrous. That's all it is, really—just being considerate."

It helped to talk about other things than the real business for the night. Roger turned on the radio but had trouble finding any country western, and so left it on a mildly inoffensive rock station. Soon enough it offended Loraine, though, who channel surfed for a full five minutes and found little except commercials and traffic updates. If there were any news items about the renewed search for the killer lady with the wild animals, she did not stay on any station long enough to find out.

Less than a minute after the two had pulled out of the motel lot, another nondescript car pulled in. Two men left the car to confer with the manager, who allowed them a peek at his guest card file. He was used to men like them coming in and asking for the very same thing, and he had already spotted them as undercover police as soon as they walked through the door. The manager knew many of the permanent residents led disreputable lives. They always seemed to find their way out of jail, though.

Detective Thomas flipped through the names, then stopped and flipped back a few cards. He pulled one out and showed it to the manager. Hubbard, curious, leaned closer, too. "They just arrived the other day?" Thomas asked. The manager took the card and shrugged.

"If it says that here, then yeah, they did," he said.

Thomas pulled out a small wallet and flipped it open to a photograph.

"Did one of them look like this woman?" he asked.

The manager peered at the photo a moment, then shrugged again. "Don't know," he said. "Don't remember."

Thomas snapped the wallet shut and tucked it away in his breast pocket. "We'd still like to see their room, if you don't mind," Thomas said.

"Yeah, sure, whatever," the manager grumbled, and wandered away to find the keys. He waved at the two policemen to follow. They did, and Hubbard caught himself resting his hand on his revolver handle nervously. He pulled it away and thrust his hands into his pockets as the manager led them to the door of "Mr. and Mrs. Wolfe."

The door swung open to an empty room. Thomas and Hubbard were careful not to touch any of the personal items within, although Thomas did spot the remains of their early meal in the trash. The only thing to catch his eye was a completely fleshless drumstick. No meat, tendons, gristle or anything but the bone. He held it out to Hubbard.

"Hungry, weren't they?" he said.

"What's that?" Hubbard said from the bathroom. Thomas shook his head and tossed the leg back into the trash.

"Nothing," he said, wiping his hands on his pants.

The two men conducted their best superficial search and discovered only one other interesting item than the bare bone: train ticket stubs, except their origin was difficult to deduce. They had been torn in half, leaving only a few letters to indicate their departure point: "IN." Thomas showed it to the lieutenant, who agreed it could indicate Wisconsin. If the "Wolfes" had brought any ID, they had taken them with them. They had left no wallets, money, or other clue to their identities. Thomas hoped to continue the search, except that Hubbard called it off. The lieutenant thanked the manager for his time and cooperation, and they were on their un-merry way.

"What do you think?" Thomas asked. "Assign a stakeout? I'll bet those tickets *are* from Wisconsin."

"If one were assigned, it'd have to be to us," Hubbard said. "We're out of units."

"Then let it be us," Thomas said. "Mr. and Mrs. Wolfe? It's got to be them."

"Well, I suppose that's as close as we've come," Hubbard said. "I'll do it. We've been out all day, and you have a wife to go home to. I'll get Daigle to sit with me."

"Sir, this has been mine from the beginning," Thomas said. "Well—with a brief hiatus, anyway. If we've finally caught up to her, I want to be there. Besides, what the hell are you going to tell Daigle? He has no clue about what we're up against."

"You'll be notified as soon as we know anything,"

Hubbard said. "Head back to the station. You've been out enough nights already. And Daigle doesn't need to know anything other than we're staking out a suspect."

"Sir—"

"This kind of work can wreak havoc on a man's life, Thomas," Hubbard said. "The best we can do is minimize the damage." He looked over at the detective. "Go home and watch some TV. Sleep. Talk to your wife. Whatever helps you relax."

"Relax," Thomas muttered. "I'm supposed to relax in the middle of an All Points Bulletin?"

"That's exactly why I'm telling you to try," Hubbard said. "*Some*body has to be rested if this lasts past tonight, and I think it should be you. Have you gotten any sleep at all since this began?" he added. Thomas tensed and made sounds as if trying to think of a response, but Hubbard waved him into silence. "I thought not," he said. "I said you'd be notified if your hunch is right. And if it really is Loraine," he added, reaching to his belt and pulling out an antique, but well-maintained six-shot revolver, "I can only hope this does the job."

Thomas whistled once. "Where did you get one of those?" he asked. He wanted to take it and handle it himself, but was driving.

"I've had it for years," Hubbard said, turning it back and forth to catch the light. "I have a small collection of antiques, but this was always my favorite. I used to watch *The Lone Ranger* as a kid and wanted my own six-shooter. With silver bullets."

"No shit," Thomas said. "Do you mean that you've had silver bullets for years, too?"

"Actually, no," Hubbard said, reholstering the pistol. "I never got around to them until . . . just recently. I know someone who makes custom firearms and their various projectiles. He could only manage two silver bullets on such short notice. I intend to get more, though."

"How about enough for the whole force?" Thomas said. "I managed to get some of my own, but what's going to happen if some other cop tries to take her down with regular bullets? He'll be torn to pieces like the others."

"We can't afford to outfit everyone with silver bullets," Hubbard said. "You know that. We just have to make sure no one else does take her down."

Thomas nodded in grim agreement.

Loraine had her window rolled all the way down. She rested her head on her arms, which in turn rested on the door. She shut her eyes and breathed in deeply whenever a breeze picked up on her face. It let her pretend that she was running like she used to for so many nights. The others never seemed to walk anywhere—they always ran—and although she kept up with them, she had often thought to ask just what they were running to. Or from.

Something startled her at a stoplight. She almost hit her head on the ceiling, then straightened up quickly. Roger took his hand from her shoulder.

"What?" she said. "Something wrong?"

"I was about to ask you that," he said. "Did I scare you? You kind of jumped. I just wanted to make sure you weren't letting your tongue hang out, too."

"Why would my tongue be hanging out?" she asked.

Roger glanced over and smiled, then shook his head. "Never mind," he said. "I was just joking. It's just that sometimes you act kind of . . . you know . . . like your 'other self'?"

Loraine flipped open the vanity mirror on her side and checked her features. She seemed satisfied with her disguise, and closed the mirror. "I thought you were saying I look like Jan," she said. "Are you saying I'm acting like a wolf, then?"

"Noooo—"

"You have to be honest, Roger," she said. "I don't want to start scratching behind my ears with my legs or something while talking to someone. Right now it's . . . kind of hard for me to sort out what'll look strange to people."

"You're kidding," he said. "Are you saying that you're *forgetting* what people act like?"

"I'm not forgetting," she said. "It's what I've been telling you for a few days now. Jan and I are on equal terms. Let's just say that she's being nice right now by letting me walk on two legs. I'll have to return the favor sometime."

"Um . . . like when?"

"Probably tonight," she said, pulling down the vanity again. "If we find the exiled one, Jan will have a better chance of talking to him than I will. I have a feeling that he prefers staying on four legs whenever possible, if you know what I mean."

"So . . . when you've changed and all that," Roger said, "will Jan recognize me? Or will I be in the middle of a werewolf movie?"

"You're already in the middle of a werewolf movie, you silly two-legger," she said. "And I've told you, you're safe around me in both of my forms. When you talk to me, you talk to Jan, too. You can't talk to us separately."

"I can't?"

"Not that I'm aware of," she said. The music on the radio irritated her again, so she channel surfed. After a time she found something more tolerable—an unknown, slow, haunting melody—and Loraine sat back in her seat.

"I think you should know," she said, "that I can't speak in Jan's form. The vocal cords aren't made for that, and the mouth is no better. Maybe someday I'll be able to change and keep the throat I have now, but I wouldn't count on it yet. I wish two-leggers were better at body language. I mean humans. Sorry."

"I think we do well enough with body language," he said. "At least, I can always tell when someone's happy to see me or wants me out of town by sunrise."

"Sh!" Loraine said, having failed to ask for his silence with a subtle hand signal. She pointed to an upcoming intersection. "Turn left here." Roger complied after some minor difficulty changing lanes.

Loraine was not much for conversation now. He made a few attempts to talk, but was only met with a sharp bark. The sun was almost down; apparently she didn't need the full moon to succumb to its effects. He gripped the steering wheel harder and prayed silently that she spoke the truth about being harmless to him.

Loraine barked out directions like a woman possessed. Roger managed to catch glimpses of her face as he drove. Her eyes, wide and almost glowing, were locked into a steely gaze that never flinched from the streets ahead. Her lower lip was curled back to reveal her bottom teeth jutting out. They were not sharp, but Roger knew that could change at any time. He wasn't sure if he wanted to be around when they did. The only thing he was certain of now was that the hunt had begun, and it could end in any number of ways, few of them pleasant.

Meg Thomas was in a generous mood that night and allowed her husband control of the television remote. The tradeoff was that she had control over use of the kitchen, meaning that no food went in or out without her permission. He'd been putting on a few pounds lately.

Peter Thomas wasn't actually watching any of the programs that clicked into place for a millisecond or so. It was only by chance that he finally rested on an episode of *Cops* before he rose from the couch and paced in front of the phone.

Meg came into the room, sighing loudly at her husband's viewing choice. "I thought you liked to leave your work back at the office," she said, reaching for the remote.

Thomas had his back to her and kept it from her reach unintentionally.

"Hnh?" he said, turning around. Meg snatched it from him and clicked off the television. "Why'd you do that?" he asked, snatching it back. "I was watching that."

"You don't even know what it was, I'll bet," she said as the glow of the television once again lit their living room. "Honey, is it something you want to talk about?"

"What? This?" he asked, indicating the program.

Meg stared at him. "Yes, what's on the TV," she said. "I think we need to talk about it. No, it's whatever's been bothering you at work. Is the APB over? You haven't been home this early for weeks now."

"No, it *isn't* over," he said. "That's just it. I'll never

figure out that damned lieutenant. What purpose is there to send me home now? We could be *this close* to closing it up, and he sends me home to 'relax.' Relax how?"

"I can think of a few things," she said, laying a hand on his shoulder. "At least, there was a time when they used to work."

"What?" he said, only just noticing her touch. His gaze had been on the telephone, as if staring at it would magically induce it to ring. "Oh," he said, now facing Meg. He only sighed and rested his hand on hers. "I appreciate what you're trying, hon, but— God, I don't know anything anymore. I've *never* seen a case like this. I can't get my mind off it, and Hubbard sends me home!"

"Are you the only one who can work on this case?" she asked, moving close to him. She brought both of her arms lightly around his waist.

"Believe it or not, yes," he said, eyeing the phone again.

Meg brought up a hand to guide his chin toward her. She leaned in and kissed him gently. "I know you've never liked the new lieutenant," she murmured. "But I'd like to thank him for sending you home tonight. I know I'm supposed to be oh-so-understanding about your work and all the time it takes up, but sorry if I get a little sick of it sometimes. Peter, for once you're home *before* I've gone to bed, and I'd like to see the TV off, the phone off the hook, and you talking to me. *Talking* to me. You know, that thing we used to do a long time ago?"

Thomas finally tore his attention away from the phone, and briefly, from his thoughts on the case, and looked his wife square in the face. He had always loved her, always been grateful for her patience and understanding, but sometimes forgot she was human and had limits.

A smile crept along his face, and he yanked her toward him into a long, full kiss. She was no fool who would waste the moment, and held him close as long as they were able to stand. But standing was no way to spend an evening like this. When they finally parted, it was on Meg's terms. She took her husband's hand and guided him to the floor, then bade him wait. She looked back and waved once, then slinked to the nearest linen closet. Inside was a large quilt, which she dragged across the floor before tossing it onto Thomas. He laughed as he pulled it off, then helped his wife spread it onto the floor. She rolled onto it first and relaxed every part of her body, and waited.

Thomas all but tore off his coat and shirt before lying beside her. He thought it strange that she made no attempt to undress, but then remembered a particularly wonderful night of passion, a night which had begun with the simple, but sensuous act of undressing her. She remembered that night, too.

Their outer garments soon lay in a single heap at one end of the room. Meg giggled as he struggled to undo her bra clasps, an action he always preferred left to her, but Meg offered no assistance. She made it clear that even his struggles were quite seductive, and wrapped her arms around his neck when he finally held up the lingerie in mock triumph. Now man and woman were free to roll about in the quilt, letting it wrap them together like a cocoon meant only for lovers.

It had been a long time since they had surrendered so totally to their passions. Perhaps too long. Thomas was mildly disappointed that they were not moving in sync with each other, but was determined to make up for lost time with her. He could so easily have lost her, this remarkable woman who had been far more patient than he had deserved. Tonight he would make it up to her, and never let himself be pulled from her again. Not like he had been.

A horrible chirping and ringing assaulted their ears. Thomas ignored it at first. Let their machine get it; whoever it was could wait. The phone made its four rings before the machine did answer in Meg's voice. They had neglected to turn down the volume. *Oh, well,* Thomas thought. *Let them say their piece and get off.*

"Peter? It's Daigle. If you're there, pick up the phone. If not, get to Fairfax and Packard as soon as you hear this. We've got another body. See ya there." *Click.*

Thomas stopped. He pulled out and rolled to Meg's side, groaning. She turned toward him and rested her head on his chest.

"Tell them I died," he groaned. "Call them back and tell them I left town."

Meg kissed his chest, then let her hand rest there. She rubbed it slowly and gently. Thomas wanted only to lie there and listen to her breathing.

"You have to go," she whispered.

"No, I don't."

"Yes, you do," she whispered. "It's your case. They need you."

"So do you," he murmured. "Dammit! I was on my way to . . . to really spending some time with you again, and now this."

"Shhhhh," she said, her finger on his lips. "Don't think I'm happy about this, either," she said, sitting up and reaching for her clothes, which were too far. She stood up and walked over to them. Thomas sat up and watched her move. He had almost forgotten how desirable she could be. The way she moved. The way her arms and hips swung just far enough to—

"Here," she said, throwing his shirt on his face. He pulled it off, but was not smiling this time. She squatted beside him while pulling on her own shirt, then hesitated. "Or . . . should I leave this off for when you come back?" she said with a wink.

Thomas frowned. "He said another body," he grumbled, fighting to pull on his pants now. "This could be all night. Dammit! Sometimes I really hate this job. And you've been so good about all of this. Meg, will you marry me?"

"Sorry," she said, eyeing her wedding band. "I'm taken already. He's a cop. I just love men in uniforms."

"I don't wear one."

"I know," she said. "Couldn't you just put one on at home every now and then?"

Thomas forced a smile, then touched her chin. She grabbed his hand there and held it in place so she could lean forward and meet his lips in a long, but gentle kiss. Finally she let his hand go and watched silently as he fixed his clothes and gathered up his wallet, keys, and gun.

He paused at the door, then looked back to Meg, who was still squatting on the quilt. She offered him a sad wave. He returned it, then threw a kiss. "I love you," he murmured.

She smiled and closed her eyes. "I know," she murmured back.

Twenty-one

Loraine and Roger watched the bustling scene from a hidden corner of a store rooftop. Roger was still having trouble believing how she had literally run up the side of the building—all thirty feet of it—and then taken only seconds to pull him up with a long aluminum pole. He had tried to make a light comment about it, but she was never in a more humorless mood than this night. She peered down at the murder scene with unmoving intensity. Roger did his best to match her stillness.

"Why are we watching this?" he whispered. She did not answer right away, but stared at the individuals who seemed to be in charge of the investigation. At the center of the scene lay the remains of the victim, which even at this distance were a gruesome sight. Roger avoided looking any more than he needed to. He believed they had seen all there was to see by now. What he did not realize was that Loraine was also listening to every word, which were completely indiscernible to Roger's ears.

"—m.o. as the others—"

"—what I needed: another all-nighter—"

"—hey, we've all lost it after seeing stuff like this—" and other words filtered in and out as she worked at finding something truly relevant to latch onto. Finally a name triggered her full attention. She focused on two plainclothes policeman who had been standing together.

"—Tamara?" one of them said. "Who's with her now?"

"We've checked her already," the other cop said. "She hasn't been out or in all night."

"Being a good little girl, huh?" the first cop said. "Do you believe that?"

"We'll check it out when we're done here," the second cop said.

"How about I go now?" the first cop said. "You don't need me."

"Not without backup you don't," the second cop warned. He might have been the first cop's superior. He did appear older.

"Why are they wondering about Tamara?" Loraine muttered to herself.

Roger leaned closer. "What's that?" he whispered.

She held up her hand to silence him, and tilted her head to follow the two men as they walked and talked. They both piled into an unmarked car and gunned the motor loudly before pulling away. Loraine almost stood up to follow, then remembered herself and squatted back down. "She can take of herself," she whispered.

"Who?" Roger said.

"It doesn't matter," she said, and gestured at the crime scene. "That's our boy's handiwork, all right. It looks like a fresh kill. He didn't even try to eat him, either."

"This is getting disgusting," Roger groaned, slumping against a ventilation shaft.

"Think of it as a nature film," she said, her attention always partly on the activities below. "If an animal hunts, it should be for food. I'm no more likely to eat a person than you are, but the others . . . Well, they're a little less discriminating. The exiled one has been killing without reason. I can see why the pack kicked him out, but that leaves him free to slash his way through the city, and for what? He must be getting his jollies out of this."

"I don't think I can handle this," Roger said, his complexion two shades lighter than usual. Loraine smiled and touched his cheek. "Why don't we just leave this to the cops?" he asked. "We're after a total psycho, if you're right."

"Yes," she said, "but one that's immune to bullets, unless they're silver. How many cops have those? I may be the only one who can stop him, unless . . ." she added, her gaze drifting off in the direction the two policemen had followed. Then she shook her head and looked back at Roger. "No, I'm the one who has to do this. He hasn't paid for what he did."

"Yeah, I guess he hasn't," Roger said. They were quiet after this. Loraine crawled back to the edge of the roof. The body was just now being removed, but too many cops, photographers and bystanders lingered. She lay back and groaned.

"Damn," she whispered. "I just need to get down there for a *second*. How long are they going to hang out there?"

"Can't you, I don't know, sense his presence or something?" Roger asked. "They took the body away. What else can you do but just start looking around the area?"

She turned only her eyes to look at him. "I thought you'd hunted before," she said. He shrugged and nodded at the same time. "Well, most of it requires patience," she said. "I wish I *could* sense his presence, but it hasn't been very reliable, as you've noticed. I picked up on the murder *scene,* not the murd*er*er. His scent should still be in the area even after the body is gone. The best we can do now is wait until everyone leaves. Unless you really *want* to start driving around with no clue where he is."

"Not really," he said. "I just thought you'd be able to pick up on him is all." He lay down beside her, where they tried to watch the stars. The city lights and airborne pollutants made the sky a hazy, dull grey filled with the blurry lights of airplanes and helicopters. She had lived in cities her entire life, and thought she loved them more than the most beautiful mountain home. Now she doubted her sanity at even tolerating this place.

Hubbard and Thomas had already relieved the two squad cars responsible for making sure Tamara stayed put. They were parked across the street from the hotel now. Thomas punched in the numbers to the hotel on his car phone.

"Yes, room 1200, please," he said, and waited. Then: "Say that again? You don't say. What if I told you this was an emergency? Tell her it's her manager, Paul . . . Look, I'll explain it to her when she answers; I won't even *tell* her who called. If she doesn't get this message, there'll be hell to—! Oh, thank you." While waiting he looked at the lieutenant and rolled his eyes. The lieutenant didn't see, because he was busy pinching his nose and wondering how this was going to be explained if it didn't work. After half a minute Thomas's attention snapped back to the phone.

"Say that again?" he said. "Well, how long did you

let it ring? Are you sure you dialed the right number? Tamara Taylor, room 1200. Well, try again, she has to know this! Wh—? I *am* on my way there. I'm in the middle of the freeway; you ever drive in L.A. traffic? Try again!" Long pause. "Well, where the hell did she go, then? Look, I'm going to be there in about ten minutes, and somebody better let me in with a skeleton key when I get there!" He folded up the phone with a loud snap and shoved it back into its cradle. He looked over at Hubbard, whose face was locked in an expression of absolute bewilderment. He opened his mouth to speak, then thought better of it and waved it off.

"Sorry," Thomas said, opening his door. "I guess you never met her manager."

"We are going to talk when we get back," Hubbard said. They walked across the street quickly. Thomas reached the door first and held it open for the lieutenant. They strolled through the lobby and reached the elevator call button.

On the 12th floor, Thomas led the way to Tamara's room, but Hubbard did the knocking. First he rapped lightly a few times, then pressed his ear against the door. After a pause, he knocked again, this time much louder. Still no sound came from inside, nor did the door budge. Hubbard leaned in close.

"Tamara Taylor," he said. "This is the police. Open the door, Tamara." He glanced at Thomas, who swayed back and forth from nervous energy. "Tamara Taylor," Hubbard said again. "This is the police. Open the door."

A door did open, but from behind the two men. A curious guest peeked out, then zipped back inside when Thomas looked at him. Hubbard sighed in frustration.

"Well, we have two possibilities," he said. "She's in

and won't answer the door or the phone for whatever reason, or she's not here."

"And which one do you believe?" Thomas asked.

Hubbard glanced at the door. "I have no idea," he said. "Either way we're wasting our time. Let's get back out there and get Loraine. If Tamara's out there, too, we take her in."

"You're serious?"

"Am I ever not?" Hubbard said, his expression implacable.

Thomas watched him a moment, then cast Tamara's room one last look before heading for the elevator. "You know, sir . . ." Thomas said as the elevator doors spread open, "after this is over, I was wondering if we could have a talk about my hours . . ."

Tamara was very tired. She really did have a big day planned tomorrow, but was loath to leave Loraine at the mercy of those idiot two-leggers who may have gotten ahold of some silver bullets. It didn't make sense to underestimate them anymore, not even that humorless lieutenant. Loraine might not even know they were looking for her, concentrating as she was on the exiled one, and could get caught in some nasty business. At worst, they could arrive just as she found the exiled one, mistake her for the real killer, and pump her full of silver.

Tamara drove with no real indication of where Loraine could be, although she kept all of her instincts and senses at full alert. There would have been no difficulty at all if they belonged to the same pack, but they did not. The last time she had found Loraine, she had caught sight of the pack as they raced out of the city, and had followed at a safe distance. Now she had nothing to go on.

Loraine rolled onto her stomach and peeked over the edge of the roof. The last of the investigating team was leaving. She nudged Roger and crawled away from the edge until it was safe to stand. Roger copied her movements. They reached the alley side of the roof and peered down.

"Um . . ." Roger said, looking about, "how are we going to get down? What if we lowered that pole and slid down?" he added, grabbing at the long pole that had earlier been used to pull him up.

"Sure, why not?" Loraine mumbled, and took it from him. "Grab the end and hold on tight," she said. "I can lower you down."

"Shouldn't I be—? Oh, never mind," he said, gripping the end with all his might. Loraine lifted him up effortlessly and slowly brought him over the edge. Roger fought the urge to look down and held on for life. Eventually his feet touched the ground, and he let go and waved. Loraine pulled the pole back up in spite of Roger's efforts to grab hold again. He had thought of holding it in place while she slid down. Loraine disappeared from the edge for a moment, then Roger's eyes widened in horror as he watched her shadowy form leap up and away from the edge. There was nothing in the alley that could break her fall, save his open arms, but it happened too quickly for him to judge her landing.

She hit the ground just long enough to roll into a tight ball and keep going, using the momentum to send her spinning across the pavement for a good five yards before stopping. She rolled onto both feet and seemed quite unfazed as she brushed off the dirt. Roger chased after her.

"Loraine!" he cried, grabbing her shoulders. "What were you doing? Are you okay?"

"Shhh!" she said angrily, and tiptoed to the edge of the building and stared at the street beyond. Apparently satisfied, she turned back to Roger. "Don't yell my name!" she whispered. "They probably think I killed that guy!"

"But maybe they know you didn't do it," Roger whispered. "They couldn't really still think you did that? They couldn't know that you're back. Do you think they know about the other wolf?"

"Who knows?" she whispered. "As far as I'm concerned, we're on our own. Come on," she said, motioning for him to follow. She altered her features again and stepped out into the street. The investigating team had all left at last. Passersby stopped and stared at the bloody stains on the sidewalk, satisfying their morbid curiosities until it was cleaned up. Loraine and Roger blended in easily with them, and met no opposition at the crime scene other than an ineffective yellow tape barricade. Once there she knelt down and touched the dried blood, then rubbed and sniffed at what little came off on her fingers. Looking about, she used Roger for partial cover as she fell to all fours, sniffing the ground closely. Roger tried to obscure her actions as best he could, but was mostly reduced to simply smiling and shrugging at puzzled pedestrians.

"Uh, Loraine," he murmured. She ignored him and lingered at one spot, her face all but flat against the concrete. "Come on, hon, you asked me to . . . remind you of certain things?"

She looked up now, and seemed aware of her position for the first time. She shot to her feet and brushed off her pants. "Oh," she said. "Yeah. Thanks. I think I've got a scent."

"Really? Great," he said, taking her by the arm and leading her away from the bloodstains. "So you think you can track him now?"

"I think so," she said, and turned to face him fully. She held both of his hands. "This could be it, Roger. If I pick up on his trail and find him, well . . . You're not properly armed. If I have to fight him and protect you at the same time—"

Roger stopped her with a hand to her lips. "Don't worry about me," he said. "No matter what, don't let your concentration split. If it comes down to it, I'll get out, but not before I've done whatever I can to help you. And how do you know you can take him on alone?"

"I don't," she said. "I just couldn't bear to see something happen to my mate."

"Well . . . mate," he said, "I don't want to see you hurt, either. So . . . do we go after him or not?"

"Yes," she said, straightening up. "Let's go." She turned and made to leave, but he grabbed her hand. "What?" she said.

"Well, the car's that way, remember?"

She shook her head. "It's on foot from now on," she said. "I couldn't track him from a car. I need to be close to the ground."

"Oh," he said. "Great."

* * *

Hubbard and Thomas returned to the station, where the lieutenant ordered Detective Daigle to obtain a warrant for Tamara's arrest. After a phone call to Meg, Thomas resumed the dragnet with Hubbard riding shotgun.

"This is going to sound strange," Thomas said, "but I have no idea how to even start looking for these people."

"Why not?" Hubbard asked.

"Think about it, sir," Thomas said, turning a sharp corner. "We're looking for people who can change their appearance. It's hard enough finding normal people; now we have to find a chameleon."

"Maybe it won't be as hard as you think," Hubbard said. "I see it this way: either they look human, or they look like a wolf. We see them, we take them in. We see a wolf running around, we take that in, too."

"With silver bullets," Thomas mumbled. "What if they don't work? What if all that stuff about silver is bullshit, and we really need wooden stakes or something?"

"Aren't those for vampires?"

"Who knows what they're for?" Thomas said. "My point is that we have no proof that any of this works. Just stuff from the movies, really, and you know how realistic *those* are."

"That's true," the lieutenant said. "But we have to go with something."

"I don't think we'll get a second chance if it doesn't work," Thomas said. "And then what?" Hubbard offered no answer, nor was Thomas especially interested in hearing one. He looked at his picture of Meg on his side of the dashboard, and brushed against it once. Hubbard was paying attention to the road. The city lights were as bright as they had ever been, pouring up into the sky to dim the stars, but tonight the sky seemed darker than usual.

Roger wished he could have followed in the car. Keeping up with Loraine while she was on a trail was more than he could handle at times. He had always considered himself in fairly good shape, but was disappointed in how little stamina he really had. Loraine was concentrating too much on the hunt to realize he was lagging behind most of the time, nor did he expect her to stop just for him. This was her fight, and although he wanted to help, it would do no good to slow her down.

Somehow he managed to always keep her in sight, even if distantly. After a good half hour of the chase, she began to slow down, and dropped to the ground at one spot. Roger caught up to her and wheezed against a tree as she sniffed in different places.

"Is there—a problem?" he gasped. "Lost—the trail?"

"There's some confusion here," she said. "He might have passed this area a few times before. Part of it is . . . Sorry, Roger," she said, and began pulling off her clothes. "We *won't be able to talk from now* . . ." Her voice devolved into an incoherent growl as Jan's four-legged form replaced Loraine. Jan kept her nose to the ground as she swayed back and forth. Her new form was better suited to the task at hand, and she picked up the trail quickly. Roger scooped up her clothing and ran after her. Unfortunately, his chances of keeping pace with a four-legged animal at full speed were now next to nothing. The best he could hope to do was to keep following in the direction she had bolted off to.

He emerged from bushes onto the street. Jan's path, if strictly followed, would cut diagonally across a busy intersection. He saw no signs of any accidents that a rampaging wolf might have caused, so he jogged along the sidewalk to the nearest intersection. The wait for the signal allowed only a moment to regain his breath. He ran across the crosswalk and could only guess as to her whereabouts. He tried to use his own senses like Jan might have. He tried to block out all other sounds except those an animal in full flight might make, with little success.

Roger crossed many intersections with no sign of Jan—or Loraine, for that matter. He came upon a dark corner whose other side seemed to lead to a heavily wooded area with even more shrubbery to block whatever lay beyond. He ran across the street and squeezed through.

He emerged onto the grounds of a huge complex. A large parking lot dominated most of the area, with many dark buildings in the distance. It reminded Roger of a school or a college campus. He would probably have as much luck finding her here as out in the city, unless she had made turns miles back.

There seemed to be no one else on the grounds. Still, it was not that late, so there could be others nearby. He could only hope that no one else but Loraine had made any other contact with the "exiled one." He slowed down his pace out of necessity, lest he pass out. It amazed him how far he had been able to go without collapsing. He did have a sideache he would never forget, however.

Roger had been on a college campus only once before,

when visiting a friend, and noticed how shamefully space was wasted. It seemed not a single building was closer than fifty feet away from any other, but at the time he had assumed only that school had been guilty. Now he knew better. It was bad enough approaching exhaustion without having to hike that much farther to reach any part of the campus.

He staggered along the semi-lit walkways, unable yet to call out for Loraine, if she was anywhere near this place. Some distance away he spotted two shadowy figures strolling along the grounds. He picked up his pace as best he could, and saw he was following two women. In spite of his aching muscles and lungs, he was able to draw closer and could almost make out their animated chitchat.

"Excuse me . . . ladies?" he called. One of them shrieked and jumped forward, while the other whirled around. Roger stopped and held out his hand while fighting for his breath. "I'm sorry," he wheezed. "I didn't mean to scare you. I'm looking for somebody. Have either of you seen any big animals running by here? Large dogs?"

"No," one of the girls said, shaking her head. She looked at her nervous friend, who also indicated a "no." "Sorry," she said. "Did you lose your dogs?"

"Something like that," he said. "You didn't hear anything, either?"

"I didn't hear anything," the first girl said. "What kind of—?"

All their hearts froze as a long, low howl seemed to come from everywhere around them. The two girls drew closer to each other and began backing away from Roger, whose attention was on this song of the night that lasted for a full ten seconds.

"Loraine?" he called out, and headed in what he believed to be her direction. His excitement renewed much of the strength he had lost, not to mention fear. The songs of the wolf were alien to him; she might have been calling him to her side, or crying out for help. There was only one way he would find out.

As he ran, a pair of inhuman eyes watched him from the bushes.

Tamara rolled down her window and pricked her ears. There was no mistaking it. From beyond the roar of motorcycles, boomboxes, the grinding, screeching, and belching din of the city came a sound like the purest of nature's music. She listened again, ignoring the impatient blaring of the convertible's horn behind her, and drove on only after the wolfsong had ended. She had more experience than Roger at locating other wolves, even under the worst of conditions, such as now, and knew just which direction to head. If any other two-leggers had heard the very distant cry, let them shut their doors and windows in their haste to ignore it. City people could always be counted on that way.

"Not even so much as a bloody trail leading from the scene," Thomas said. "Jeez. This is a nightmare."

"Most murder cases are," Hubbard said. "Now maybe you have some idea why I don't work in Homicide."

"Same here," Thomas said. "Our good luck that the most bizarre case in the world falls into *our* laps. Jeez!"

he said, slapping the steering wheel. "What about Curry? He's out there, too! What if he finds her first, and without the right bullets?"

"It's too late to update him now," Hubbard said. "We'd be spending most of our time just trying to make him believe what we were saying."

"Don't underestimate Tim," Thomas said. "He may be closer to the truth than we even know. I haven't been able to talk to him for a while, but when this first started, we were—"

"Wait!" Hubbard cried. He pointed to a car passing them in the opposite direction. "It's her! Pull her over!"

"Who?" Thomas said, craning his neck to look back. Making a U-turn at the same time took no extra effort on his part; he had performed more spectacular moves in his academy days. Hubbard pulled out the portable roof light and clamped it.

"It's Tamara, I'd swear it was," Hubbard said. Thomas gripped the steering wheel hard while the lieutenant set the siren screaming.

Tamara was nearly blinded by the lights shining from her rearview mirror. She had little doubt as to whose siren and whose flashing light were following her. She gripped the steering wheel hard, her eyes shining yellow-green and sharp teeth threatening to slice her lip—and slowed down. She switched on her turn signal and pulled over to the right, then shut off the engine. The unmarked car followed her to the curb. Its siren was switched off but not the light. She did intend to give them a chase, but not quite how they expected.

Two men left the car and approached cautiously, one more so than his partner. She could not tell through the mirror whether he had his gun out. Thomas's face came into view through the side mirror. Tamara folded her arms and pushed back against her seat. Now his face was at her window.

"Tamara," he said, "I'd be delighted if you'd step out of the car."

She stayed where she was. "Sorry, I'm not giving out autographs right now."

"NOW."

Tamara appeared unfazed, but rolled up her window and opened the door slowly. Thomas backed away to give her room.

"Turn around and hands on the hood," he said. She leaned over and complied, even to the point of letting him pat her down.

"You know, normally I wouldn't even let my manager touch me like this," she said.

"Shut up," she heard Thomas mutter from behind. "All right, turn around, but *slowly,* and keep your hands where we can see 'em."

"Let me guess," she said. "I'm out past curfew."

"You were instructed to stay in your hotel room tonight," Hubbard said, moving around the car slowly. "You admitted that you'd help Loraine any way she asked, so why, if you have such a busy day tomorrow, are you out driving around?"

She shrugged. "Just a night owl, I guess."

"I've had it with your attitude, lady," Thomas said, wagging his finger in her face. "Loraine has contacted you, hasn't she? Is that where you're going in such a hurry? Where is she?"

"Sad but true, sir," she said with a slight bow. "I only have a general idea. Yes, my chances of finding her are probably much better than yours, but who would be the one to truly help her in the end? You? Would you read her her rights or just shoot her, no doubt with brand-new silver bullets. Am I right?"

"Where is Loraine?" Thomas snarled, and stopped just short of grabbing Tamara's shirt and hauling her onto the hood of the car. He kept his hands to himself, however. Tamara watched him for a long time, and she smiled a little. A breeze whipped at Thomas's face as she . . . disappeared.

Hubbard blurted out some garbled swear word and looked all about, his gun now drawn. Thomas crouched low beside the car as if expecting gunfire, but there was no attack. No shadowy creatures slamming into his backside or anywhere else.

"There!" said Thomas, and pointed at the silhouette of a woman running from them at an amazing speed. He aimed his gun, then brought it back up. She was too far and moving too fast to risk wasting his special bullets. He had had no time to procure more than one clip; the lieutenant himself had only managed to get two bullets. Thomas was in the driver's seat before Hubbard reached his side, and he peeled out before he had shut the passenger door.

"Loraine!" Roger shouted as he ran between two ancient-looking buildings. *Why won't she howl again?* he wondered. *Unless . . . that wasn't her—*

His thoughts were interrupted as something very large, very heavy, and very strong slammed into him. He was at the top of concrete steps when the dark creature made its attack. Roger had not heard its approach. He had no time to reproach himself for carelessness, however, as he was presently tumbling over and over in a very painful descent down the steps. By some miracle he managed to keep himself mostly sideways during the tumble, and avoided smashing his head or his neck against anything harder than air. The rest of his body was not as fortunate.

Some small luck smiled upon him and provided a long step that stopped him halfway down the full length of the stairs. He landed on his back, and the remaining wind still in him was knocked away. Lighting was intermittent on the steps, but was enough to give him a glimpse of the dark, impossibly fast creature coming his way. Roger had no strength yet to flee, to search for his gun, or even to cry out. It took all of his strength simply to lift his arm, when a quiet thud at his feet signaled the arrival of an unwelcome guest. Roger looked up to see the dark-furred monster looming over him, its face silhouetted from the light behind it. He cried out as a claw shot at him, gripped him firmly by the throat, and lifted.

The creature was just taller than he, but bigger overall, and definitely much stronger. Roger held on tight to the creature's claw, but all his tugging and twisting would have pried off a steel bar before budging this beast. He dared not kick at the wolf for fear of snapping his own neck, or worse, irritating the animal until it decided to rip off his limbs one by one.

It was getting difficult to breathe or think. Roger opened his mouth wide and gasped like a landed fish, but could not pull in enough air to make a sound. The wolf was pulling him closer—the hot breath stung his eyes—and Roger shut them, his last thoughts being a silent prayer for forgiveness at having failed to save Loraine.

Roger's feet hit the ground but never quite kept their balance, and he fell backward, his head painfully hitting the concrete. The faint stars above were replaced by the towering figure of his doom.

His death did not come, however. The wolf merely stood and tilted its head from side to side, its golden eyes never moving from his face. Roger lay as still as possible, even holding his breath, fearing that a single twitch would cause the beast to attack. It began to growl, but not one that struck him as menacing. It seemed painful for the creature to make these different sounds, as if its vocal cords were unaccustomed to them.

"Rrrrraaaawwwww," it said, if it was truly a word that it had spoken. It tilted its head and moved to look at Roger from a different angle. Roger could feel his heartbeat thundering throughout his body.

"Rrrrrraaaawwwwwj—" the wolf started again, and was interrupted by a reddish-brown blur that slammed into it from behind, tumbling it down the hard, cold steps. The wolf that chased after it ran on two legs, its claws flashing in the dim light. Roger rolled to one side and watched the smaller wolf run to its much larger adversary and reach for its neck.

"Loraine," he groaned, reaching out as if offering help, then rolled the other way and back onto his feet, albeit unsteadily. He dug into his pockets for his gun, and found nothing.

Even from his distance the size difference between the two combatants was unmistakable. Loraine, in her half-wolf form, was not much larger than her human form. Her adversary had clearly been a very large man, for he loomed above her by nearly two feet. Roger stood riveted to the scene, watching them circle each other slowly. At one point the giant wolf leaned back and made a noise that could easily have been laughter, but the most evil, chilling laughter Roger had ever heard. It took all of his courage to keep his hands from his ears and turn away to search for his weapon. It didn't matter that the lead bullets would never kill; they had to be painful at the very least, and that could be all that Loraine needed to win.

The big wolf began the battle with a simple lunge. Loraine avoided it easily and darted between his legs, swinging around to kick him from behind. The big wolf grunted and stumbled to the side, more startled at her attack than harmed.

Roger darted to and fro on the way up the steps, praying for a glint of light that would reveal his gun. He was almost to the top, when he spotted the small black and silver gun reflecting the light. When he grabbed it, much of his strength returned in a rush of adrenaline. He ran down the steps, ignoring the pain coursing through his body like a river.

The big wolf lunged once more, daring her to try escaping through his legs again, but he just missed the blur that shot up and over him in a red and brown ball. So far Jan was evading his attacks, but no one could say what would win this time: speed and agility, or inhuman size and strength. The big wolf roared and swiped down from on high; Jan twisted just in time for the claw to swipe at air instead. She took no comfort in knowing that her foe could have split a car in half with that attack.

He still leaned forward a bit after his lunge, and she pushed down on his back and kneed him in the ribs. He

grunted, but did not fall, and snatched her thigh from
below. Jan yelped as the big wolf yanked her to the side,
and then up over his head. His claws dug into her legs
as he held her like some demonic wrestler before hurling
her into the darkness.

"Loraine!" Roger shouted, and fired two shots into
the big wolf's body. It cried out and touched the wounds,
but the pain only sent its anger into rage. It hunched
over and began to stalk toward Roger, whose gun shook
uncontrollably in his hands.

"Don't," he whispered, backing away one step at a
time. "Please . . . don't." He stumbled against one step
and fell back, almost dropping the gun, until the big
wolf caught up and loomed over him. The sky disappeared, replaced by the dark harbinger of his death.

Again the wolf's fingers wrapped all the way around
Roger's throat as he was hauled off his feet. Roger held
on tight to the claw with one hand, and struggled to aim
his weapon. Blood and bits of flesh shot out the back
of the creature as the gun fired. The wolf flinched but
did not let go of Roger's throat. He brought the gun up
again, and had it snatched away by the wolf, who tossed
it far away. Now Roger held on with both hands and
kicked at the animal. He was unable to get a good kick
into a vulnerable area, but the wolf dropped him and
took a painful step backward.

Its balance was uneasy. Blood poured from both ends
of the wound, darkening and matting its fur. All Roger
could do now was wait, and hope. But the wolf refused
to fall. *What is this?* Roger thought. *Silver bullets or
not, how can anything live with its heart blown out at
close range?*

He looked for Loraine or Jan, and saw something moving in the shadows.

He heard a noise from the big wolf, and started backing away slowly on the steps, afraid to make sudden movements even with the creature seeming as weak as it was. If he did not know better, he would have sworn the wolf was reaching out to him. It growled, and some blood flowed from its throat.

"Rrrraaaawwww—" it said, then coughed out most of the blood. *"Rrrraaawww-Juuuurrrr."*

"What?" he said, stopping his slow climb.

"Rraaww-Jurr," it said again, still holding out its claw. Roger kept his hands to himself, but did not try to escape when the wolf took a step toward him. *"So long . . . No speak."*

"You—said my name," Roger said. "You said 'Roger'?"

The wolf nodded. It pulled its claw away from its chest and wiped the blood onto its fur. Roger could see the impossible now: not only was the wolf still alive, the wound was healing. Quickly.

"William?" Roger said softly. The wolf whipped its gaze toward him, then growled. Roger somehow found the courage to move toward the wolf. "Will, it's you, isn't it?"

"NO MORE!" the wolf roared, almost knocking Roger backward from its volume alone. *"Will is dead,"* it said. *"I walk on four legs, not two."*

"You're on two legs now," he said. The wolf looked down as if seeing for the first time what form it had taken. Behind the wolf, Jan made her cautious way toward them. Roger tried to think of some way to signal her to stay back without alerting the wolf to her presence.

"Will," he said, taking another step forward. He brought up one hand slowly. "Of course you're not dead. I'm sorry for what I did to you. I didn't know who you were. You were attacking Loraine, and . . . I didn't mean to hurt you, Will. But now that I know . . . You're going to be okay. We'll be okay."

Behind Will, Jan advanced slowly up the steps. She stopped at a certain distance and stayed still, keeping Roger in sight.

"I want to see Will again," Roger continued. "Do you understand me? I don't want to see you stuck in between like this. I want to see Will, my brother. Please . . ." he said, now close enough to touch the wolf on the shoulder. "Let me—"

The wolf shrieked as if in pain, and Roger was sent flying by a massive blow that could have felled a small tree. Jan hesitated, an indecision that almost cost her mate's life before she leaped after him, catching him in midair and landing on the steep hill beyond the steps. She set Roger down, stroking his hair as gently as her claws would allow.

"Will," he groaned. "My brother . . . That's my brother."

"I know," she said, and leaned forward to touch his face with her muzzle, but instead yelled in pain as her nearly forgotten foe sliced at her back, spraying blood from its fingertips as they cut.

"GET AWAY!" the wolf bellowed, shoving her down the hill. Grass and dirt rubbed into the wound as she rolled to a painful halt.

You leave him be! the wolf cried into her mind. Jan's

thoughts had been growing hazy, when his mental call stung her back to consciousness. *You do not mate with me, so you do not mate with anyone! And never my brother!*

We are already . . . mated, she said, dragging herself back onto two legs. She wanted to shift to four legs, but the change would be agonizing in her condition. She needed time to heal first. *You have no claim on me. You are an outcast even amongst your own kind. You hunt without hunger. You kill without reason!*

You spurn me and take my brother instead? he said. *And leave him this way? Bring him to us! Only then will he understand. And if you do not, I will!*

Lay a single tooth or claw on him, and I will kill you, she said. *Slow, if I can!*

I challenge you to try, bitch! he cried.

Jan took a deep breath and stood as tall as her quivering legs would allow.

So I am, she said. *And of that I am proud. But you . . . You cannot even call yourself Wolf.*

What?

This is the true curse of the exiled, she said, dragging herself up the steep hill. Her strength was returning, but slowly. *To be cast out of both worlds. But you brought it upon yourself; you killed for the pleasure of it! You killed a friend of mine! A Protected One!*

She was in the way!

Does the wolf slaughter those weaker than itself? she asked. *Yes, but only for food, not for the joy of it! Why did you kill my friend?*

A two-legger, he said. *You mourn one of those?*

"Freeze!" two male, two-legger voices called from behind. Both wolves spun around to face the new threat.

Two males approached them, their small weapons aimed at them. The wolf smiled to itself; weak, stupid creatures that they were to keep using such useless weapons. Jan used the other wolf to hide her movement toward Roger, who rolled back and forth in an effort to keep himself conscious and to fight his pain.

"Both of you where we can see you!" one of the two-leggers said. Jan ignored him, but the big wolf did not. He faced them square and spread his massive arms as if daring them to fire. He kept his head low and began to move steadily toward them.

"Not another step, uh . . . wolf," one of them said, his voice dripping with fear. The wolf hoped to savor this. No doubt they were some champions of two-legger law come to save them all from the killer beasts.

"If you understand me, these are silver bullets," the two-legger said. The wolf did understand, but made a sound that reminded the humans of their own laughter. The two-leggers stood in a crossfire to the wolf and kept their guns level and steady, and yet missed the dark blur that shot between them, leaving empty air where their target had been.

"Shit!" they cried one after the other, and glanced around for the beast's new location. Just then a howl startled everyone, followed by a silhouetted figure landing just in front of Detective Thomas. A two-legged wolf smacked away his gun and sent him tumbling backward.

"Goddamn, it's the whole pack!" Thomas yelled. Hubbard moved to assist and was sent flying by the largest wolf. He fell on his back, the wolf landing flat on him, where it clamped down hard onto his shoulder. Hubbard's hands spread wide, dropping his gun. He heard the crunch of bone before feeling the pain, and was al-

most hoping for death to end it, if it were the only way
to stop this agony.

Hubbard was lifted up along with the wolf as something grabbed it from behind and pulled. The wolf let
go when they were halfway up, causing Hubbard to
smack his head against the dirt. It was soft enough to
leave him awake, but shaken, and he groped for his lost
weapon.

Tamara/Song had taken the wolf by the tail and was
regretting it. She was a singer, not a quick, agile and
graceful combatant like Loraine/Jan, and was unable to
avoid the big wolf's attacks. By the time Hubbard found
his gun, she was on her back, at the mercy of the larger
wolf's pummeling.

The big wolf arched back and howled as a white-hot
pellet entered its side, passed through both lungs, and
finally exited through its left front leg. This was a different pain than when the other pellets had passed
through. They had hurt, but had never harmed. Something was wrong. The wolf's strength was not returning,
but fading, and quickly. Something was wrong. Two-
leggers were too stupid to know how to stop his kind.
They were too slow, both in body and mind. His
wound should be healing any moment now.

The big wolf fell over, gasping for air with useless
lungs. Song dragged herself away from the dying beast,
tears of grief joining her tears of pain. She had run with
a pack herself for many years, and had seen so many
things, but had never seen one of her own die. The big
wolf's limbs shivered like blankets in the wind; its
breathing was uneven and loud but quickly growing quieter. Finally, its limbs lost their strength, and lay still all

at once. Its breathing was silent, and golden eyes stared unblinking at the stars.

"Will!" somebody called from behind Thomas. He whirled around to see a man breaking away from another one of those damned wolves and running toward him. Thomas brought up his gun.

"Freeze!" he yelled, but the man barely slowed. "I said *freeze!*"

"Roger!" the man's wolf friend cried, catching up to him and holding him in place. *"Do what he says! He'll kill you!"*

"Everyone!" Thomas yelled. "Over there! Move!" He herded Roger, Jan, and Song together as best he could with his gun. He knew that any one of the wolf-creatures could have disarmed him while his attention was divided, but all complied.

"Sir?" he called to Hubbard without looking away from the others. "Lieutenant? Are you all right?"

"Probably . . . not," Hubbard said with a cough. His good hand, clamped onto his shoulder, was very bloody. "I've been bitten."

"Mother of God," Thomas muttered to himself. He glanced at the big wolf, which had yet to move. Were they right, then? Did silver bullets work?

"It's over, detective," Tamara/Song said, pulling herself up. She was assisted by Jan, who returned to supporting Roger. Tamara looked all around the ground until she spotted a small bag, and snatched it up.

"I said *freeze,* lady!" Thomas said, his gun wavering back and forth between all three. Tamara ignored him and zipped open the bag, pulling out what appeared to be a long coat.

"Lieutenant, do you need a hospital?" Thomas asked.

"I'm sure I do," Hubbard wheezed.

Tamara dropped her bag and let the breeze unfurl her coat. She began pulling it on, and Thomas stared as her features and form began to shift. Her fur retracted into her skin; her face flattened back into the singer's features. In a few seconds, Tamara Taylor stood where the wolf once had, and she would be entirely naked but for the long coat that effectively covered everything but her legs.

"I said it's over, detective," she said. "You found your killer, and there he is." She pointed to the lifeless form of the dark wolf.

"He was my brother," Roger said. "You killed him, didn't you? Why the hell did you kill him?"

"Why? Why did he—?" Thomas said. "God, man, are you blind? That . . . *thing* almost killed Hubbard! And you say that's your brother? Jesus, are we the only ones in this town who aren't werewolves?"

"We?" Tamara said. She pointed to Hubbard, who lay quietly, his bleeding still not under control. Thomas dropped to one knee, his gun still aimed at the group.

"Yes, we," he said. He held his gun with one hand now while using the other to help press onto the wound. "He needs to get to Emergency."

"I'll call," Tamara said, tensing up for a good sprint.

"You stay where you are!" Thomas said. "All of you!"

"Let her go," the lieutenant whispered. "Peter? It's . . . hard to speak."

"Sir, you're going to be okay," Thomas said. "Just rest. I'll get someone here right away. In fact, there's a medical center practically around the corner. It's right on campus."

"You stay here," the lieutenant whispered. "Let Tamara go."

"Sir—"

"Do it."

Thomas sighed loudly. Both arms were aching now: one from holding the gun so long and the other from pressing the wound. The lieutenant was in no condition to give any orders, but it seemed important that Thomas comply.

"Go," he said quietly, then looked Tamara in the eyes. "GO!" If he had blinked, he would have missed her shooting up the hill in a pale pink blur. *Are these things slow in* any *form?* he wondered.

Jan bent down slowly to retrieve Tamara's bag. She removed clothing until she found something that would cover her sufficiently, and pulled it on while becoming Loraine once again. She and Roger now held on to each other, both from fear and exhaustion. Even Loraine wondered whether Will was truly dead, or would spring up at any moment, stronger than ever. The big wolf had not moved yet, however.

"We, . . ." she said, "that is, I was just wondering how you guys thought to get silver bullets. Unless cops always use them?"

"They don't," Thomas said, keeping his aim on her. "We figured out what's going on, that's all. You must be Loraine."

"I must be," she said. "And you are?"

"Detective Thomas of the Los Angeles Police—Fugitive Division," he said. "And may I never come across a fugitive like you again."

"I can explain—"

"Don't," he said. "Right now the lieutenant needs help, so if you can still stand, get over here."

"Okay," she said, approaching cautiously.

"I'll still use these if I have to," he said. "I have a full clip of silver in here."

"How nice," she said. She knelt beside the two policemen. Roger stayed behind near his brother's body. He crawled beside the lifeless form and dared to touch the creature's face. He thought it strange that the wolf had not changed back to his brother upon its death.

It was much easier for Loraine to press Hubbard's wound than for Thomas, and for this reason alone he allowed her to touch the lieutenant. A silhouetted figure came running down the stairs. Thomas recognized Tamara, returning from her errand.

"That didn't take long," Thomas said. "You sure you called the right number?"

"I run fast," she said. "And 911 did come to mind. How is he?"

"Alive," Thomas said. "I suppose he can count his blessings for that."

"Detective, um . . ."

"Thomas."

"Detective Thomas," Loraine said, "I think you ought to know something about . . . well, when people are bitten by werewolves."

"I don't need to hear this."

"I'm afraid you do," Tamara said, kneeling down. "Lieutenant Hubbard?" she called. Hubbard opened his eyes to a slit. "Lieutenant, there's something you should know about your injury . . ."

Twenty-two

Loraine, Tamara and Roger had carried Will's body to some nearby bushes before the lieutenant's medical assistance arrived. It had taken them awhile to convince Thomas to allow this. The evening had been strange enough without having to explain the body of a creature caught in the form of half-animal, half-man.

The other question had been where Will's body should go. For Roger, there was no question: Will belonged home in Wisconsin. There was also no question for Detective Thomas: the wolf belonged with the coroner. No one was going anywhere until it had been determined that the big wolf had been the true killer all along. It meant samples galore of blood, skin, hair, DNA and whatever else they needed.

A heated debate was brewing, with Roger and the detective the main participants, until the argument was ended by the lieutenant himself. In spite of Thomas's urgings to rest until help arrived, Hubbard convinced them to reach a compromise. The coroner could perform whatever tests he needed to determine who was the real killer, and Roger could take the body home afterward. Thomas managed to wring out another agreement: that Loraine and Tamara donate tissue samples, too. Just in case.

Deep down Thomas had hoped that the werewolf's body would stay in the city, allowing every doctor and scientist to probe into the mystery of these supernatural beings. His saner side realized that they would never allow it. The carnage at the police station would be a small altercation compared to what they might do to countless thousands of innocents to protect their secret. No, no time was too soon for these monsters to be out of his city.

He had half-expected to be killed by the remaining two werewolves, but neither one so much as threatened him. Instead, they were both as helpful as he allowed them to be, and were especially concerned for the lieutenant. Loraine and her boyfriend agreed to stay under house arrest with Tamara, who would be allowed to leave only for work, while the autopsy on Will was performed.

The report from the coroner indicated nothing of any lycanthropy. The corpse had been delivered in the morning, when the light of day had finally turned Will fully human again. At Roger's insistence, the coroner had been told nothing about the true nature of the "patient" on his table.

Lieutenant Hubbard was released from the hospital two days after his attack. Doctors were amazed at the speed of his recovery. A torn and shattered shoulder was no two-day mend, but Hubbard would give no further cooperation to their studies. It was not with a light heart that he left the hospital on foot with Thomas at his side. The men back at the station had been most generous with get-well gifts and wishes, but he requested that no other detective meet with him but Thomas.

"I hear they're pretty excited about how fast you got better," Thomas said on the way to the car. Hubbard tugged at his sleeve and nodded grimly. "Faster than a normal man, they're probably saying," Thomas added. They reached the car, but Thomas paused before unlocking the door. "Sir, about what those girls told you that night—"

"Yes, I remember," the lieutenant said. "I suppose they ought to know what they're talking about."

"Ah, jeez, lieutenant, they can't be right," Thomas said. "They can't be right about . . . what they said."

"That I'll be out running with them and howling at the moon?" Hubbard said, completely deadpan. Thomas pinched his nose and shook his head. "I suppose it could be worse," the lieutenant added.

"How?"

Hubbard did not answer, but tapped impatiently at the door until Thomas unlocked it, who then trod solemnly to the driver's side. He slumped into the driver's seat and gunned the motor as Hubbard slipped on his seat belt. Thomas pulled out slowly and navigated their way to the street.

"You know me," Hubbard said. "I'll just do whatever I have to do to deal with this."

Roger rested his hand on the large wooden crate still waiting to be loaded onto the train back home. Loraine was finishing her long hug with Tamara. The singer ended it first but paused to rub noses with Loraine and brushed it lightly with the tip of her tongue. She then wiped away a tear from Loraine's cheek.

"Hey, cub," she said. "No need for these. We'll see each other again somehow."

"Yeah," Loraine said with a sniffle. "We'll just stick our noses to the ground and track each other down."

"Well, I was thinking of telephones or letters, actually," she said. "Maybe I can talk Paul into adding a stop in Wisconsin for the tour." She hugged Loraine again, then went to Roger and did the same.

"Thanks for all your help," he whispered into her ear as they embraced. Their hug was much briefer than hers and Loraine's, but she pecked him on the cheek before they parted.

"And thanks for yours," she said. "You have no idea how much you've helped her."

"Yeah," he said, looking at the crate holding Will's body. "And she helped me find my brother again. If this really was him. I guess . . ." he said, and his lip tightened. "I guess we did him a favor, too. I guess the real Will had died a long time ago—" Roger broke down into tears for the first time since that fateful night. Loraine held him; Tamara turned away to allow them privacy, and glimpsed Detective Thomas waiting just beyond the loading area. He had brought them to the station himself, but Tamara had almost forgotten his presence.

"I'm sorry," Roger whispered.

"Oh, shut up," Loraine whispered, her own tears mixing with his. "Don't you dare be sorry for crying."

"He wouldn't even listen to me," he sobbed. "Did you hear him? It was like remembering who he was made him even angrier! Does that make sense to you? Why wouldn't he listen to me, Loraine?"

"He was listening to you," she murmured. "You know he was. But there was so much confusion and everyone shooting and screaming and—" She sighed and pressed her cheek against his. "All I've been able to think since that night is 'There but for the grace of God go I.' "

"What are you talking about?" he said. "He was wild, he couldn't control himself, he—"

"He never reconciled his two selves," Tamara said. "I'm sorry. I've interrupted."

"That's all right," Loraine said. "You could explain it better than I could."

Tamara shrugged. "I doubt it," she said. "No were-wolf deals with his or her own duality just the same as any other. It depends on the strength of each side. That's as simply as I can put it. Sometimes the wolf is stronger; sometimes the human side is. Sometimes they're equal or almost equal."

"So you're saying Will's wolf side was stronger," Roger said. "He wouldn't even let me see him as a man. He was always in that 'halfway' form."

"Actually," Tamara said, "I was going to say that both sides were equal. He never really reconciled what he was: man or animal, and . . . I hate to say it, but that inner battle must have driven him insane."

"Jesus," Roger said, looking down. He touched the crate holding his brother one last time before allowing two porters to take it away for loading. He watched them as they carted it away. "Good-bye, Will," he said. "May your battle be over now. May you dwell in peace."

"That was beautiful," Loraine whispered, leaning against him.

Tamara looked back again at Thomas, who had never taken his eyes off of any of them. "Well, I should leave you two alone now," she said. "You don't want to get stuck in this place, do you?"

"No way," Loraine said. "And to think I used to like this place. But what about you?"

"What about me?" Tamara said. "I still have my tour to finish. In spite of these . . . minor setbacks, I think it'll be a hit."

"Great," Loraine said. "But listen, if you ever need any help . . . You know, with any moves you're having trouble with or—"

"Go on, get out of here," Tamara said, her face beaming. "I promise I'll practice hard."

The two waved as they walked toward the train. Thomas watched them as they blew kisses back and forth before finally ducking inside. It had taken all his self-control to watch them leave, let alone drive them there himself. All of this had been at the lieutenant's insistence. It had taken some string pulling, but Loraine and her boyfriend, not to mention Tamara herself, were to be spared any legal entanglements from their involvement in "this matter," as Hubbard had put it euphemistically. Thomas's last bit of advice to Loraine and Roger had been more to the point: that neither one show their faces in L.A. again.

Detective Curry had the misfortune of discovering Lieutenant Hubbard at home three days later. He was lying motionless on the side of his bed, a gaping hole in his head filled with congealed blood. The death had been immediately ruled as a suicide due to two clues: a note, and the cadaveric spasm causing his hands to be clenched tightly around the means of death, namely an antique six-shot revolver containing only one bullet. Forensics learned that the bullet had been coated with silver, but made no further conjectures as to its significance save that the lieutenant had once confessed a fondness for the Lone Ranger.

The note had been very simple: "One less of my kind." Only Detective Thomas had an inkling as to what it could mean, but he was offering no clues to anyone, not even Curry.

The funeral was attended by half the force, but Thomas was not surprised that the pack of press hounds was even larger. Some of them had tried to pry comments from him on "this senseless tragedy." Thomas had opted for a "no comment" rather than explain to them the true extent of the tragedy. They weren't interested in Hubbard the man, but Hubbard the Cop Who'd Shot Himself. He was beginning to see the point of some of those wolves' comments about human beings. In a pack, people could be more brutal and bloodthirsty than any so-called wild animal.

It was a simple ceremony—one that Hubbard would definitely have approved of. Thomas had his wife Meg at his side for most of the gathering. The priest made comments such as "caring and generous" and "will be remembered with great fondness," and Thomas wondered how many really believed that. The lieutenant had been coming around, or so he thought, but "remembered with great fondness?" Ah, well. A man's funeral was no place to play devil's advocate.

The attendees broke into small groups after the ceremony. Some comforted one another, some avoided the paparazzi, and some just stood around in stunned silence. Meg had been holding Thomas by the arm during the entire ceremony, only letting go as a strange figure approached him afterward. It was a woman unfamiliar to Meg—dressed in black from head to toe, her head covered with a wide-brimmed hat sporting a veil, and black sunglasses even under that. She walked up to Thomas, who looked confused.

"Er . . . a senseless tragedy, isn't it?" he said to the woman.

She smiled. "I suppose it is," she said. "I just wish that he'd come to me first. I'd said that I'd be there for him anytime, if he needed help with the change, and I meant it."

"Tamara?" he said, pulling away from Meg. "How did you—? Or rather, *what* are you—?"

"We mourn the losses of our own as deeply as any of you," she said. "And in his case, I feel partly responsible. I've been . . . playing what happened over and over in my head and keep wondering what I could have done to help him."

"Join the club," he said. Meg touched his arm.

"Peter," she said, "I don't mean to interrupt, but . . ."

"Oh! I'm sorry, honey," he said, putting his arm around her. "Tamara, my wife Meg. Meg, this is Tamara Taylor."

"No," she said, taking Tamara's outstretched hand. "The singer?"

"Guilty as charged." She lifted her veil and winked.

"Oh, my God, Peter, you—you mean you know Tamara Taylor?" Meg said. "Why didn't you tell me?"

"Well, it's not that s—"

"Oh, Miss Taylor, I have all of your albums," she said. "Do you know that we danced to 'Let Me Not' at our wedding? I just *love* you!"

"Literally, or just my work?" Tamara said. "Sorry. A little joke."

"But—how did you know Lieutenant Hubbard?" she asked. "Were you friends?"

"We belonged to the same club," Tamara said, then sighed. "I'm here to pay my respects just like everybody else." She looked at the lieutenant's casket as it was being prepared for lowering into the ground. "It really is a 'senseless tragedy,' " she said. "He didn't have to try to face it alone."

"But face what?" Meg asked. "Honey, does anyone know why he would have done this? Did anyone ever talk to him about what was bothering him?"

"He didn't really give anyone a chance," he said. "The lieutenant was never one to confide in others."

"That's awful," Meg said. "If only he'd opened up to someone, then maybe . . ." She stopped and dabbed at her eyes with her fingers. Tamara handed her a handkerchief. "Thank you," she said, wiping her eyes properly now. "I'm sorry, honey."

"Oh, don't be silly," Thomas said. He put his arm around her. "You cry as much as you need to."

"Listen," Tamara began, "I'll leave you two together now. Mrs. Thomas . . . Detective . . . I hope you'll accept my condolences. His loss will be felt by more than you might think."

"Thank you, Miss Taylor," Meg said. "That's very kind of you. Really, I don't know why I'd be crying now, instead of during the eulogy. I-I hardly knew him. Only what Peter told me . . ."

"Yes," Tamara said, smiling. "Would you mind if I borrowed your husband a second?" Thomas looked around furtively. They were all but alone by now, the other mourners having returned to their homes, work, or wherever they needed to be.

"Well, certainly," she said. Tamara guided him a few yards away from Meg, who watched them from a respectful distance.

"I only wanted to thank you," Tamara said. "That's all. For . . . keeping quiet."

"You're welcome," he said. "But I didn't have much choice, did I?"

"Of course you had a choice," she said. "And I know it must have been a very difficult one to make. Letting Loraine go under those circumstances . . . I know I speak for her when I say how grateful she is."

"Thank the lieutenant," he grumbled. "I was just following orders."

"But the lieutenant ended his life," she said. "His orders don't bind you any longer. So . . . does this mean things will change?"

"No," Thomas said, glancing back at Meg. "No, I think in the long run it'd be much . . . safer to keep things quiet. I barely trust you as it is. God only knows what another pack coming through here could do."

"Hm," Tamara said. She was silent a moment, then: "I'm sorry that it's fear alone that's convinced you. But we have to take what we can. We don't live in very friendly or tolerant times. If it helps, in a way we're just as frightened of the consequences as you are. If our existence became public knowledge . . ." She stopped and let out a shiver. "Brrr, here I go again. Every time I think of that, I can't sleep for days. So maybe you can see now that my gratitude is genuine. Even my manager doesn't know what I am."

"Well . . ." Thomas said, shoving his hands into his pockets. He kicked at some gravel before looking her in the eyes again. "Well, let's just say we've reached an impasse. If I had my way about this . . . Never mind. But if any more mutilated bodies start showing up again—"

"They won't be because of me," she said, holding up her hand. "Humans are too gamy." She noticed his horrified expression and punched his shoulder playfully. "You dweeb, I'm just kidding!" she said. "The lieutenant has rubbed off on you too much."

"Can I go now?"

"Sure," she said, gesturing grandly toward Meg. "You didn't have to talk to me at all. Rejoin your mate, sir. May you have a long and bountiful life together."

"Thanks," he said, and turned to leave, then stopped. "But I think you owe me something," he said.

"Really?" she said, cocking an eyebrow. "What's that?"

"You never did sign a photo for my wife," he said. "She really is a fan of yours, and—"

"Consider it done," she said. "In the mail tonight."

"Thanks," he said, finally walking away, but not without casting furtive glances over his shoulder until rejoining his wife. To her surprise he grabbed her and gave her a long, hard hug, followed by a full kiss on the lips. Yes, she was surprised, but why question it? They walked away arm in arm. Thomas threw one last glance over his shoulder, and saw nothing where Tamara had once been. No sign of a car driving away, or any figures running in the distance. She was gone. He was *not* surprised.

Epilogue

Two days after Lieutenant Hubbard's funeral, the Thomases received a large manila envelope in the mail marked: "Photo—Do Not Bend." Tamara really had kept her word. Inside were two backstage passes to her opening concert in Los Angeles. Meg was so happy, she jumped up and down and kissed the tickets. Also inside was a signed photograph. And she had changed photos, or so it seemed. Rather than the silly "glam" photos she had been subjecting him to, this picture had been taken outdoors and at night. A light breeze had blown some of her hair across her face as the city lights beyond formed almost a halo about her. The inscription was in gold: "To Meg and Peter—Thank you for believing in me. Love, Luck and Lollipops, Tamara."

Thomas never did reveal Tamara's secret to his wife. There was enough trash written about her in the market tabloids as it was—all of it grossly untrue. So why be the one to ruin her dreams?

Loraine savored a deep breath of fresh air the moment she set foot back in Wisconsin. But it was not until they arrived at Joanie's llama ranch that she really tasted how sweet it was. She shut her eyes and breathed in deeply.

She could have stayed there all day, when a gentle hand startled her. Her eyes shot open to reveal the beaming face of her Aunt Joanie. They fell into each other's arms and hated to let go, but there was unpacking to be done.

Roger made certain that Will had a proper service and burial. He chose an unmarked place on a hill that was rich with greenery. Will had always loved the outdoors even before his change; Roger hoped that his brother would have been pleased with his choice.

Loraine had no taste for llama farming. Neither did the llamas have a taste for her; none would come within a hundred yards of her whenever she visited Joanie. She was and always would be a dancer at the very core of her soul. The thrill of the hunt had never compared to the thrill of the simple act of moving to the beat of her favorite music, whether it be a song from her childhood or the song of the pack. Whatever she and Roger did with their lives, she had gained something that she had never dreamed possible for herself: contentment. She could dance in the streets for loose change, open a studio or form her own troupe. All that mattered was that she had everything she needed now. Peace, a home, a mate, and the dance.